Simple Intent

LINDA SANDS

PROLOGUE
1977

HISTORIC row houses stood like silent soldiers in the lightly falling snow, brick sentinels that guarded windows with metal bars, imprisoned tiny unkempt yards with low fences and creaking gates. Some doors were covered in crinkly red paper and draped with gold ribbon. On others, fading green wreaths hung askew from plastic suction cups.

They were holding onto the holiday season. Even the overflowing garbage bags at the curb looked festive. Folks in the neighborhood didn't have much, but they took care of what they did have. In the white subdivisions they called it pride of ownership. Here it was just plain pride.

Tara told Ray she'd miss the row house when they moved. She'd planted the length of the small backyard with colorful flowers and spiky bushes and when she ran out of space, the plants followed her inside. There were herbs on windowsills, tiny green sprouts in juice glasses, and ivy in hanging baskets. There was even a flowering cactus in the bathroom. Ray thought that was strange. Strange and beautiful, like Tara.

From the first day Ray Bentley had laid eyes on Tara Stevens, he'd loved her. Not like a, she's-great-I'd-like-to-be-around-her love, but a, where-would-I-be-now-had-I-never-met-you love. A love that defines purpose. A love that says, *this* is who you were meant to be. Tara pushed Ray in a good way, calling him, "The Ray Who's Going Somewhere," and kissing him on the "somewhere," pulling him into her so hard he felt her ribs against his and the beating of her heart beneath them.

Most days that was enough to get him out of bed and down the hall to the slope-floored bathroom with its rattling pipes and cracked mirror. This morning he sat on the toilet and stared at the corner of the mirror where parts of the silver had worn away. Something grew beneath the coating, spread like a stain, threatened to overtake the whole shiny surface like a virus. Ray pulled a small notebook from the stack of dog-eared magazines, opened it to a page near the back where a pen was tucked in the fold. He wrote for a few minutes, his large, dark hands making tiny precise letters, an exercise in restraint.

"We could get you a desk. In the new place." Tara watched her husband from the doorway.

Perched on the stained ceramic toilet and balancing his notebook on his knees, he sat on the hard, cold lid that slid to the right, no matter how much you tightened it. He finished the line on the page then closed the journal and left it with the magazines.

"I don't need a desk," he said, and stepped into the hall turning her as they kissed, a silent dance of slippers and cheap carpet. "I need you."

Ray looked into Tara's eyes, finding the fleck on the right iris, a tiny, gold doubloon in a sea of green. He trailed his lips down her pale, freckled neck, paused to breathe her scent.

Tara sighed, leaned into him then reluctantly pushed him away. "Look out, Ray. I've gotta pee."

Ray squeezed up against the doorframe to allow her

protruding belly to pass.

She paused before closing the door. "Ray? I was thinking we could go look at the used cribs at the thrift store."

"Nah, I don't think so."

"Why? We're going to need a crib, and I could fix one up nice. You'll see-"

Ray held Tara's face in his hands. He kissed her, cutting off her words. "Baby, when I come back, we're gonna take a *cab* to JC Penney's and buy *everything* our baby needs."

Tara smiled. "I love you, Ray."

He told her to go back to bed and rest, that he'd be back before lunch. She closed the door and prayed again that her parents would see what she saw in Raymond Moses Bentley. He was the father of their grandchild, the man their daughter loved. They had to accept him, didn't they? What did color really matter anymore? This was the 1970s, not the 1950s.

In the kitchen, Ray drank his coffee at the sink and watched the snow falling in the street. Outside, cars were being warmed up, windows scraped and cleared. A bus rumbled by. He rinsed his cup, stacked it in the strainer and went to the hall closet, shrugged into his coat then paused with one hand on the doorknob. He walked back to the bedroom.

A thin paper shade rattled in the drafty window. Tara lay on her left side, one arm pinning the thin coverlet over her engorged breasts. Ray crossed the room in three steps, careful of the yellow rug that made him trip and the rickety nightstand from the *good* neighborhood.

He kissed her cheek and whispered, "Everything's going to change. Everything."

Outside on the stoop, Ray lifted his face to the sky. Snowflakes tickled his cheeks, melted on his lips and fell into his nostrils like tiny bits of heaven trying to cover up all the bad things on earth. He imagined Mama up there, sending him wishes on a snowflake. She'd be proud that her boy was trying to be more like her and less like Daddy. Staying clean was hard. Taking a county job that paid so little was even harder. But you do what you have to do, like Mama said. You do *whatever* you have to do, as long as you can look into that cracked mirror and feel good about yourself tomorrow.

Ray turned the corner. The street hit him. This was Philly. This was his town.

And she was waking up. The ting and scrape of snow shovels and the casual banter of storeowners comforted Ray. He dipped his head and said, "Morning" to those he passed.

Just a regular Friday in January. Not quite cold enough or snowy enough to give anyone reason to bitch—though every proud Philadelphian would anyway.

Halfway down the street on a bench under a bullet-riddled *No Parking* sign, he saw the hunched figure of Jefferson LeChance. He might have been mistaken for a load of dirty clothes someone had dumped from a duffle bag, but as Ray approached, Chancy's massive head turned and two glassy eyes opened.

He spoke slowly, his voice a growl. "I was just thinking 'bout you, Motherfucker."

Ray shook his head. "Shit, Chancy. Look at you, all messed up this early. You said you were going to wait."

Chancy looked at Ray and tried lifting the corners of his mouth in an apologetic smile, but lost it somewhere between the lips and the eyes.

"C'mon." Ray grabbed Chancy's arm, pulling him to his feet. "We got business to do."

Chancy ran his finger under his nose then pointed it at Ray. "This ain't business. This is collectin'."

Ray grimaced. "Yeah, man. We collectin', all right. All four G's and King *better* know that's what we came for."

"He knows. Shit. You *know* that motherfucker *knows* that—"

"Yeah, yeah. Let's get you something to eat." They started walking, a tall, hopeful black man followed by a shuffling gray shadow.

Sitting in a booth at the diner, Chancy felt no pain. It was good, sitting here with his friend. And then it hit him. *Aren't we supposed to be doing something this morning? Isn't there someone...?* Behind his runny, yellowed eyes, a dim lamp clicked on, blown fuse and all.

He pushed his plate away. "Done with that. Let's go."

Ray studied the ashy face and knew Chancy was back, back to the asshole he was born to be, back to the lowdown, pathetic, lying, drug-dealing motherfucker that his own mama gave away thirty-eight years ago.

We're in for it, Ray figured. We are in for it now.

They were always selling something on the corner of Tenth and Market, and judging from the view, business was bad at King's Variety Store. Grime ringed the dull chrome racks of dusty canned goods. Products well past their expiration date had been on display so long even their price tags were faded. But James King didn't mind. He didn't even notice. He was making a fine living, hiding behind stale potato chips.

Ray checked the street, pulled open the glass door for Chancy, then followed him inside. The fluorescent lights hummed and buzzed, competing with the squawk of a transistor radio propped on the checkout counter. Ray turned toward the sound and chuckled.

On a stepladder behind the counter, a voluptuous flowered bottom bounced to the beat. Maria Rosarita Conchetta looked over her shoulder. "*Hola*, boys."

She smoothed the edges of the Latino Picture Palace movie poster and stepped down from the ladder, flipping her thick, black hair over her shoulder.

"You want to see the man? I think he is expecting you, no? In his office."

Ray followed her gaze to the rear of the store then

looked back at the entrance. No customers. And from what he and his pals knew about King's Variety Store, you didn't expect any, either. Not this early, and not to buy the items on the shelves.

Maria spent most mornings doing her nails at the counter and most afternoons doing James King in the backroom. At night, she'd lock up the store and be home in time to cook her mother a nice meal then watch Jeopardy together. (It was good for her English.) Sometimes King came to her place, when he needed to pick up something he'd stashed in the spare room, or when he was picking her up to take her out and show her off. He'd lend her things for those nights, drape her in satin and stones then hold her on his lap like a doll.

"He alone?" Chancy asked.

Maria hesitated, then nodded. She turned to Ray. "How are *you* doing today?"

Her painted mouth formed each word slowly, controlling a tongue designed to click and roll. She stroked Ray's coat, raking her nails down the wool, leaving drag marks. She pressed her breasts into his arm, talking with that sexy accent, touching and stroking. Ray started to sweat.

"And how is Tara? You tell her, Maria is going to come by and give her sore feet a rub."

I got something you can rub, thought Ray.

"When my cousin Nina was pregnant, that was all she wanted. Someone to rub her feet, you know, Ray?"

"I know." Ray stood entranced as Maria pulled away. She smoothed her blouse, stretching the fabric even tighter over eraser-sized nipples.

A series of crashing noises broke the trance. A stringy-haired, acne-faced boy appeared in the center aisle, kicking aside fallen tins of tuna and cans of tomato paste. He worked his way down a stream of curses as he wrestled a cardboard box twice his size through the narrow aisle. His skin gave off an intense heat; his body reeked with the pubescent scent of desire.

"Lou, I *tell* you," sighed Maria, "Take the boxes out the back way. What are you doing?"

"I thought I heard the door."

The kid swiped oily black bangs from his forehead with the back of a dirty hand. He had the long Italian nose of his father, the large expressive eyes of his mother, and hadn't grown into either. Someday, Lou Gallo would turn heads just by walking into a room. Someday, his nose would be perfect for his face. He would be called handsome, sexy even. But today he was an awkward stumbling boy full of hormones and desires, just trying to get by.

"Yes, it was the door. You see," Maria crossed her arms and jutted out a hip. "It is Mr. LeChance and Mr. Bentley."

"Oh yeah." The young boy seemed to notice the men for the first time. "Well, I was just worried. I mean, I wanted to see if you needed any help." He wiped his hand on his pant leg. "So, do you?"

"No. I am fine. Maria is always fine. Go on now, get that box out of here."

Lou bumped and scraped his burden through the front door and out to the street, his face flushed with exertion and embarrassment.

Chancy slapped his ratty watch cap against his leg and laughed, showing a bit of fire behind his yellowed eyes. "Well, look at that! I think Louie-Boy got it bad. And you *know* what I'm talking about!"

Maria made a small sound with her tongue against her teeth and went back to her woman's magazine full of fashion and advice and helpful hints. Its page opened to "When the Big-O is just O-kay."

Ray followed Chancy to the rear of the store. He touched his coat sleeve. "All right now. Just like we said. Be cool."

Chancy twisted away. "I'm cool. I'm cool."

They climbed a single red step. Ray knocked on the steel door.

"Enter."

Stepping into the room, Ray felt it instantly. A whoosh around his heart, like the second the elevator bobbles before it stops, the moment just before the doors open and return you to solid ground. Thick, white carpet met white satin walls, which halfway up the wall became mirrors that stretched to the ceiling. Thin glass shelves displayed female figurines of wood, stone, clay, ivory and glass. Hundreds of them, all with exaggerated sagging breasts, huge bellies and wide behinds. Ray rested his fingers on a few, bent lower to see others close up.

He had never been in James King's office. Never met the man himself. Business was usually conducted at the back door. A pair of hands, an invisible face, the exchange of money. He glanced behind him. Chancy hadn't moved.

King said, "Fertility talismans."

"What's that?' Ray said.

"The figurines," King said, rolling a white vinyl chair away from the glass desk. He was tall, taller than Ray would have guessed. The light glinted off his shaved head, danced down his white polyester shirt to his sleek white trousers, all the way to the polished silver tips of his white leather boots. Everything about King was shiny—like the way a snake looks wet until you touch it, the way the pavement seems to ripple in the heat of August. His gold jewelry winked and glittered against ebony skin. The lights and the mirrors made it hard to focus on him. The room reflected itself like an ice cube turned inside out.

King paraded around the room, pointing to figurines. "The Orisha's goddess of fertility from southwestern Nigeria. The Venus figurine of the Paleolithic period." He touched another. "There is nothing so beautiful or erotic as a fertile woman." King winked at Ray, "But you know that, my brother." He slid silently behind his desk.

Chancy stepped up. "Enough of that shit. Give me my

money."

Ray watched the snake behind the desk turn his head in Chancy's direction. A chill ran down his spine. *Man, that was not cool. You gotta be cool.*

King stared at Chancy, piercing eyes from a granite face. Then King surprised Ray. He smiled. A broad gold-toothed grin. And laughed. A deep rolling infectious chuckle.

Chancy slapped him five and slipped into a sling chair facing King's desk.

Ray laughed nervously and lowered himself into the other sling chair.

Still smiling, King said, "Okay, my brother. Let's do business."

He pressed a button under his desk and sections of the wall moved. Mirrored panels slid away revealing a large safe. King turned the tumblers and opened the door. "Would you like something behind door number one?"

Tightly wrapped bricks of heroin filled the safe, with just enough room for a glass, silver-lidded bowl. King removed the container.

Ray looked at Chancy.

The brother's left leg jittered, droplets of sweat broke out on his forehead. Ray knew he'd better do something fast if they were going to get what they'd come for.

Ray stood, placing himself between the bowl and Chancy. "We didn't come here for that. Why don't you put it back, and let's talk about door number two."

King looked past Ray. "Is that what *you* want?"

Ray caught Chancy's eye. "*The money*," mouthed Ray. "*We want the money, remember?*"

Chancy leaned back in his chair. "Yeah, that's what I want. Let's see motherfucking door number two."

King returned the bowl to the safe. The mirrors moved back into place, whispering shut.

Ray tried to keep his eye on the sliding panel, as in the shell game. But he blinked, and a second later it was impossible to tell where one ended and the other started. Clever. There was something admirable about a clever man. Not this man, though. Shit. This man gave him the creeps.

King had opened another safe behind another set of mirrors. He pulled out a stack of money—fives, tens, twenties, ones, then a bunch of fifties.

Chancy pointed. "Make that four G in smaller bills."

"*Four* G?" King laughed. "You mean three, don't you, brother?"

"Don't start with that shit, man. I *know* you remember the deal with Marone."

Ray looked at Chancy. Who the hell was Marone?

"Here." Chancy tossed a folded paper bag onto the shiny desk.

King stared at the paper bag, slid his gaze up to Chancy, hardening his eyes. Then he shook his head and stuffed four grand in the bag, closed and locked the safe. He tossed the money to Chancy who caught the bag, held it in his lap and stared back at King.

Ray stood as the mirrors did their sliding trick. He offered Chancy a hand, spoke quietly in the way you soothe a sick child, calm a nervous animal. "We're done here. Let's go."

Chancy ignored Ray's hand. His muddy eyes flickered with anger and something else. He waved Ray off. "Go on. I'll be right there."

Ray nodded to King then pushed hard on the heavy steel door, glancing back at Chancy sitting with a lap full of money and his sorry ass hanging out of the back of a stupid sling chair. Ray stepped down the red carpeted stair and eased the door shut behind him.

Lou and Maria were talking at the front of the store, pointing at something outside. Ray couldn't hear what made her laugh, but he enjoyed watching the beauty of it. The way her mouth opened and her brows arched, the shake of her shoulders and breasts. Ray smiled. He started to say something, but was interrupted by the popping sound of a gunshot.

Maria screamed and ducked behind the counter. More popping. Lou hit the floor, ass in the air, his arms over his head, as Chancy came barreling through the steel door sending Ray crashing into a metal rack of soup and beans.

"*Now* we be done, Mr. King."

Ray struggled to stand. Blood ran into his eye from a gash on his forehead. Chancy, with the bag full of money tucked under his arm, waved a small black gun. He swung at Ray, clipped the side of his head. Ray went down, smacking his head on the hard tile. Just before he passed out he saw Chancy's feet moving away. The motherfucker had shined his shoes this morning.

Chancy leaned over the front counter and winked at Maria huddled in the corner. He opened the register and snatched the few bills in the drawer.

She pushed out her chin, met his eyes. Chancy smiled and said, "Love to stay, but I gotta go." He backed to the door, pulling his cap low on his forehead. Just another guy on his way somewhere, leaving footprints in snow that was already melting.

Slowly, Ray pushed himself up. Blood dripped into his left eye. His ear was on fire. He crawled toward the open office door. James King sat in his white chair, wide eyes staring. There was a perfect round hole in his perfect round, shiny head. The snake was dead.

1
BRING IT ON

NO longer the City of Brotherly Love, Philadelphia had become the City of Bitch, Moan and Sue. The more the public wanted their revenge, their justice, their due—the more wealthy attorneys became. The men at Montgomery, Deluca, Banning and Scott were no exception. They sat in calfskin chairs that smelled like well-worn currency, sipped Peruvian coffee from Limoges china and displayed framed photographs of themselves cruising to the property in Belize on the firm's yacht, the *Don't Say Anything*.

Fourteen of the top two hundred and fifty law firms in the United States made Philadelphia their home. Montgomery, Deluca, Banning and Scott was number five.

Paris Kendrick had been with the firm from the beginning, when there was just Ted Montgomery and a metal desk. But that was more years ago than she'd ever admit, and thanks to a few cosmetic surgeries, she'd never have to.

As the firm grew, law schools from all over the world sent the best and brightest to vie for intern positions. The wooing came from both ends. MDB&S spent a small fortune in symphony and theater tickets, golf outings, Atlantic City weekends, and the best box seats in three stadiums. This year's potential rainmakers hadn't been difficult to recruit, law schools were bursting at the seams in the new millennium. It seemed everyone had a dream.

Paris Kendrick had heard it all. These new attorneys said they weren't in it for the money, they said they wanted to help people that needed help. They said they wanted to make a change in the system, make a difference. She noticed they had no problem cashing their checks every payday, and thought the only difference they were making was from mainstream to Mainline, from lemon to Lexus.

Today was Day One for the interns. Today, they would learn the first rule: To see anyone, to get anything, to be anyone at Montgomery, DeLuca, Banning and Scott, you had to go through Paris.

In the lobby, Richard Early loitered by the marquee of business names. He watched the arrivals and tried to guess which floor they'd pick. So far, he'd been right sixty-two percent of the time. When a gorgeous brunette in a conservative suit entered, he figured her for floor three, Stanton Talent Agency. She had the exotic looks of a mixed parentage, the height and shoulders of an athletic father, the obvious benefits of a well-proportioned mother. He imagined her on the pages of his favorite lingerie catalog wearing red lace and leather. The young woman ran her eyes down the names on the marquee and stopped at Montgomery, Deluca, Banning and Scott. For once, Early was glad to be wrong. He followed her into the elevator.

Kenneth Reilly ran through the lobby, slid across the newly-waxed floor and jammed his hand between the closing elevator doors. "Hold it," he said, squeezing in. He glanced at the lit floor button, then at his companions.

"Looks like we're all headed to the same place." He held out his hand. "Ken Reilly. Most people call me Reilly."

Early shook his hand. "Richard Early, pleased to meet you."

The woman smiled, resigned to social niceties. "Sailor Beaumont."

Reilly shook her hand. "The pleasure's all mine."

They rode in silence, Sailor calming herself with a silent chant, Reilly bouncing in his shoes, and Early inhaling the perfumed air.

The first thing they saw when the elevator doors opened was Paris posed behind the platform reception desk. She knew that first impressions meant everything.

Reilly sidestepped out of the elevator before the doors had fully opened. "Good morning, we're the—"

"Interns," she finished. "Yes, I know. Paris Kendrick." Her perfect breasts strained beneath Coco Chanel's vision of corporate America as she extended a manicured hand to Reilly. Paris thought he'd clean up good under her tutelage. He already had that certain something. He was charming, intriguing even. If only she were younger—or he were richer. She dropped his hand, stepped down and greeted the other two, remembering Sailor Beaumont from the interviews. Even if she hadn't come to them from such a socially respected family, this beauty would be hard to forget. Unlike the dumpy man behind her.

A stocky dark-haired girl wearing a headset approached. She stepped behind the desk, plugged herself into the phone board and began routing calls. Paris introduced her with a nod of her head. "That's Missy. She can answer any of your questions if I'm indisposed. Now, if you'll follow me."

The interns followed the swaying hips of Paris Kendrick past offices with gold nameplates, rows of blue cubicles and a brightly lit break room. At Conference Room A, they filed in and selected their seats with care. This was a business where everything mattered.

As subtle as her perfume, Paris disappeared, clicking the door shut behind her.

Pure class. Montgomery, Deluca, Banning and Scott expected nothing less. Seated in soft leather chairs in climate-controlled comfort, the interns arranged themselves. Reilly unbuttoned his jacket, leaned back in his chair, and threw one leg casually over the other. Sailor sat facing the door, her signature handbag propped on the seat beside her, a worn leather satchel at her feet. Richard Early rocked in his chair, cleaning his wire-framed glasses with a handkerchief. Not long for this world of corporate lunches and client shmoozing, he'd be shipped downstairs to work at a hand-me-down desk, tread on second-grade carpet and fetch his own water from the tap. Shackled to his desk by numbers and papers and thickly bound ledgers, he would slave away in a tiny, dark cubicle and be assisted by a secretary hired for her competence not her breasts. Richard Early would become a forgotten gear in the machine.

Reilly thought it was a waste. All those years of school. For what? If you were going to be a lawyer, you should be visible. People should know who you are. Like Edward J. Deluca and Len Banning. That was what Reilly wanted. Fame. And money.

There was a knock at the door, and then it opened slowly.

A beefy man in a checked shirt and paisley tie entered dabbing his sweaty forehead with a pink handkerchief and breathing through his mouth. "Murphy, taxes. I need Early. Right now."

Sailor fought the urge to plug her nose. Murphy smelled like old sneakers and pond scum.

Early noticed. He made a face, then followed the man from a safe distance. At the door, he said, "It was nice to meet you, both."

Sailor and Reilly waved as Early shuffled out.

Sailor leaned back and crossed her long, brown legs. Reilly appreciated the view. Well-groomed, impeccably dressed, she was charm and grace, like a darker Princess

Di. She was nothing like the Irish girls from his neighborhood. She was old money, the kind of girl who'd never clip coupons or notice the price of cheese at the deli. If she wanted it, she got it.

"Do you hear music?" Sailor asked.

Ken Reilly smiled, recognizing the baritone of Henry James Scott. "Just wait," he told her.

The door opened and a stunning blonde straight from the beauty pageant circuit sauntered in. Behind her, the singing grew louder as the man burst through the door, singing and stomping and shaking hair that didn't budge. "If I was a rich man, daidle, deedle, daidle, digguh, digguh, deedle, daidle, dum..." Harry James Scott finished the song, holding the final note in perfect pitch. Miss Sweden applauded and motioned that Sailor and Reilly should, too.

"Thank you. Thank you. I am Harry James Scott. And this is Victoria." The blonde curtsied in the doorway, drawing her golden skirt behind her. Harry walked around the table then stopped behind Reilly. He boomed, "Come with me, my boy!"

Reilly jumped. His knee hit the underside of the table with a solid thud, launching a mini tsunami in the crystal water pitcher. Sailor tried not to laugh.

Reilly snatched up his things, limped after the odd couple, and then paused at the door to give Sailor the thumbs up. "Good luck."

Sailor was still staring after them when, from the back of the room, Leonard Banning cleared his throat. "Ah-hem." He loved using the hidden door to make his entrances—especially after that corny Scott performance. The startled look on the girl's face as she turned round was perfect. He set down his goblet of spring water, tucked a folder under his arm and stepped away from the sideboard.

"Miss Beaumont?"

"Yes," she said standing and extending her hand. "You must be Mr. Banning." He looked like his headshot on the website and seemed charming, in a pony-tailed Burt

Reynolds kind of way. Kind of sexy too, for an older guy.

Banning hesitated. If he took her hand she was an equal. If he let her stand there, he was a dick. He let her stand there.

Len Banning had his heyday in the sixties—thanks to sex, drugs, rock and roll—and Vietnam. Now, he mostly ran the ship for Ted Montgomery, who couldn't be bothered. He owed Ted. He owed Ted everything. So, here he was, a washed-up attorney playing tour guide to interns, hoping they'd sign on at the firm, bill two hundred hours and buy him a new Bentley, or maybe that Harley Fatboy he'd seen last week. Tiffany would love him on a Hog.

He smiled to himself then opened the folder, as Sailor sat back down. He said, "I see Mr. Reilly wasn't quite able to make up his mind. So, he'll be doing double duty, Entertainment and Criminal. Not that those two aren't already hand-in-hand." "And you?" Banning dropped the folder on the table and arranged himself in the chair across from Sailor. "Are you settled in at the condos?"

"There really wasn't much settling to do. I had baggage limitations."

"Is that so?"

"Yes, my father taught me how to pack. First, you lay out all the things you want to bring, then reduce them by half and bring more money."

It was Banning's turn to laugh. "Your father is a very wise man."

"And a very good shopper."

"Well, I'm sure you'll have no problem filling your closet this summer. Philadelphia has some of the finest shopping on the East Coast, maybe enough to convince you to make this move permanent."

Banning watched her reaction. Sometimes the summer interns were too immature, unseasoned. Not this one.

Sailor raised a brow. "Touché, Mr. Banning. But first, let's see what MDB&S can offer me." Her voice dropped into a soft, southern drawl as she tilted her head and batted her eyes. "A poor li'l ole girl from Connecticut." The act was complete. Banning had been trumped.

Sailor locked her eyes on his. "Shall we?"

Banning grinned as he slid the folder across the broad teak tabletop. Then the most amazing thing happened. Something Len Banning hadn't felt in years, not since Failson-Nough, not since he'd cracked his first law book. Banning had the feeling that whatever he said or did at that moment could matter. It could make a difference.

From some small place, it came rushing back to him, that old forgotten need to help, to heal, to change things. He started thinking that change was possible again, even if he'd already fucked up once or twice.

Helen Peterson knocked lightly then opened the door, pushing a rolling cart of white file boxes. She spoke to Banning, a question on her face. "Looking for these?' She parked the cart near him, wondered why his face was so flushed. She turned to Sailor.

"I'm Helen. Welcome to MDB&S. I hope you enjoy your summer here." She motioned to the file cart. "Looks like you'll have plenty to keep you busy."

"Are those all mine?"

Banning laughed. "Not *all* yours, or should I say ours."

Helen did a double take. Did he just say, *ours*?

Banning closed the folder they'd been looking at and pushed it aside. "You can go over that later, it's just org charts and inter-office info. But this?" He slid a white box from the file cart. "This is the good stuff."

He ran his fingers over the files then stopped and pulled an inch thick manila folder from the stack and slid it to Sailor. "Tell me what you see."

Sailor looked at Banning and wondered what he expected of her. Wondered if he actually thought she knew what the hell she was doing. She flipped through the file photos then began skimming the pages.

Helen headed for the door, but Banning motioned for

her to stay.

He looked back to Sailor. "Miss Beaumont?"

Sailor spoke without looking up. "It's clearly a case of mistaken identity. There are no credible witnesses. I can't believe she was convicted. And she's been there, what? Four years?" Sailor closed the file, slid it back to Banning. "We need to get someone to help her."

"Who? Who would you get to help?" He opened the file. "Corrine Knoeble certainly deserved something better than the incompetent, bungling counselor who screwed up the first time. Who would you get to help? Perhaps someone like you?"

Sailor balked. "Like me? Mr. Banning, I don't know anything about cases like this. I think you've got the wrong idea." She dropped her voice, ran a pattern across the tabletop with her fingers. "I might be a Beaumont, but I'm not my mother, and I have no intention of following in her footsteps."

"You couldn't," he said.

Sailor jerked her head up. "What?"

"I knew your mother," he said. "And I know you, what you *think* you're planning for your life. But look at Corrine Knoebel. Do you think this is what *she* was planning? Do you think she is so much different than you? Look, she has green eyes, like you. She is tall, like you. Do you think she loved a man once? Felt the pain of loss? Do you think she dreamed of having children, or a home in the suburbs? Do you think she deserves less than the best representation in court?"

"I'm not judging anyone, Mr. Banning. I am simply stating that I would not be the right person for the job. My father sent me here to work with Mr. Deluca. I was under the impression that was understood."

"Sometimes things change." Banning said, staring past Sailor, as if he'd heard someone call his name from far away. He blinked then looked into Sailor's eyes. "Sometimes what people think they shouldn't be doing is exactly what they should be doing."

"But." Sailor looked to Helen for help. The woman shrugged. *Shit. This was her first day. Her first morning—and look what a mess it was already.*

Banning stood up. "I think you know what I'm talking about. *That's* why you're here," he said pushing the file back to Sailor.

He followed Helen to the door. "I'll be back in fifteen minutes. See what you can learn."

In the hall, Helen said, "Very nice."

"Just doing my job."

Helen mumbled, "It's about damn time."

Reilly and Sailor sat behind their newly appointed desks in their newly appointed cubicles. Music drifted down the hall as the cleaning crew moved through five floors of wiping and vacuuming.

Sailor called through the thin wall, "I'm not kidding you, Reilly. That's what he said."

Reilly called back, "If Banning is going to work with us on these pro bono cases, I wonder if we'll get Deluca for the criminal ones?"

"Deluca won't have time for us. According to this morning's paper he has a hearing tomorrow for the Gallo case. I'm sure he'll be too busy preparing for that to play mother hen to a bunch of third years."

"Yeah, I guess you're right. Still, it would be pretty cool, wouldn't it?"

Sailor turned back to the stack of files. "No, Reilly. It would be *pretty cool* to go home and get some sleep. I wonder what he expects us to do with all of this? How much longer are you going to stay?"

"Baby, I could go all night. Just wind me up and watch me go." He jumped on his desk and did an impromptu dance on that shook the cubicle walls.

"Okay, okay," Sailor said laughing. "Sorry I asked. Get back to work, would you?"

A few offices away, Edward John Deluca, Esquire was doing some wondering of his own. What the housekeeper was planning for dinner, when he'd see Mariel again, and how to tell his mobster client that he was, without a doubt, fucked.

Deluca knew it wasn't that the guy didn't know how to run his business. He just didn't know how to keep his hands off the wrong broads. If Gallo hadn't been thinking with Little Lou One Eye that night, they wouldn't be in this predicament. If he hadn't brought Susie Cupcake to the warehouse, she never would have seen the crates. How many times had Deluca told Gallo, "Keep your business and pleasure separate." He couldn't remember. In all the years they'd known each other, this was probably the dumbest fucking thing Gallo had done, and now he needed Deluca to lift up the rug and start sweeping. Otherwise, they were all going down.

2
MARIA MADE GOOD

IT was summer on the Cape. A time of magic and dreams, when sunburns could be healed with ice-cold beer and spicy crabs, and childhood romances would prove to be the basis for all others to come.

The wind blew across the ocean, up the beach, through the saw grass and over the gardens into the open window of the breakfast nook. White embroidered curtains fluttered and danced against wooden restraints. The pages of a newspaper rustled, a small dog yapped and a coffee maker clicked then hissed on the counter. Though the gourmet kitchen was outfitted with the finest hi-tech steel appliances, the honey-glazed walls, terra cotta tiles and colorful pottery in glass-fronted cupboards made it feel warm and welcoming.

A tan, wiry man in well-worn khakis and a dirt-smeared shirt peered into the kitchen from the mudroom. "Miss Chetta? I have news about the workers."

Maria Chetta entered the room holding a spiky plant attached to a piece of driftwood. From the center of the gray-green spikes, a long red flower bloomed, the tip changed color from red to blue to yellow. She was like the flower, exotically sturdy, a bright spot appearing from nowhere. With her jingling jewelry and swishing skirt she looked like a Spanish gypsy, the kind who told your fortune in the caves of Old Madrid.

She looked at the man wringing his ball cap in his hands.

"News, Santiago? I hope it is good news."

"There is a possibility–"

"Santiago," said Maria as she set the plant on the counter, picked up a pair of garden shears, "there is *always* possibility. What I need to know is if they cannot complete the job, can you find me someone who will?"

"Of course, Miss Chetta. That would be no problem."

Maria smiled. "I knew I could count on you, Santiago. Now how is the fountain cleaning coming?"

Santiago spent the next few minutes telling Maria about the grounds of her estate, what had been done and what needed to be done. And when he returned to his work among the fountains, pools, gardens, sheds, garages and putting greens, Maria was left holding a Tillandsia Fuchsii, surrounded by silver appliances she knew nothing about.

It was all Stephan's fault. He'd been her chef for so long, and it was more his kitchen than hers. His job was supposed to have been a temporary one. He would cook when the housekeeper went on holiday. But one summer the housekeeper didn't return, and Stephan moved into Maria's kitchen.

Maria worried about him. His relationships with the men in Provincetown, his trips to West Palm; he was anything but discreet.

Somewhere in the large house, a phone rang, followed by a buzzing intercom. "Miss Chetta, you have a call. The gentleman wishes not to be announced, but asked me to say, 'He is a friend from the old neighborhood.' Shall I tell him you're not available?"

Old neighborhood? Maria cleared her throat to calm

the quaver in her voice. "I'll take the call, Sonja. Thank you."

"Very well. I'll put him through."

Maria dried her hands and picked up the phone. "This is Maria Chetta. To whom am I speaking?"

"So, it's Chetta now? And 'to whom?' Well, well. Lou said you'd re-invented yourself."

"I'm sure I don't know what you are talking about."

"Oh, Maria, sweetheart, this is not the time to play coy. But I'll tell what it is time for. It's time for that old saying to prove itself right. You know, the one: 'Whatever goes around, comes around.'"

Maria closed her eyes. Her past came rushing back at her: James King's gold teeth, Mama in the apartment with the secret closet floor, the backseat of Deluca's Cadillac, and the lie she'd told that convicted an innocent man.

"What do you want, Fast Eddie? And why are you calling me here?"

"Hey, if you don't want to discuss this on the phone, I have no problem coming up there. Fact is, I'd love to get reacquainted. We still have unfinished business, you and I, don't we?"

"I'm sure that won't be necessary. Whatever business you need to discuss with me can be handled from a distance."

"Yeah, maybe that would be best. I mean I wouldn't want anything to mess up your perfect little life, now would I? I mean you have worked so hard for your fortune."

She ignored the dig, as Fast Eddie Deluca continued. "And we wouldn't want to disappoint the Angelina partners by rocking the boat now, would we? So, this is what I need from you..."

Maria closed her eyes and listened to the voice from her past as it threatened her future. How the hell was she going to get herself out of this—again?

3

WEARING THE BROWNS
AND SINGING THE BLUES

OM Shaantih, Shaantih, Shaanti-ih."

The hard gray walls of the cell had no hold on the deep rich tone of the chant. The man's voice rose and fell, undulating and humming like the sound of someone talking into the whirring blades of a large fan. Seated cross-legged on his rag rug, Shazad's body swayed, a peaceful smile on his glistening face.

Ray watched from his metal slab bed. The 'trays' were bolted into the wall, one above the other. There was no room to sit up, and in a cell the size of a king-sized bed, no privacy, either. You hoped for the best when your cellmate was assigned. Lifers with enough cash or clout might buy themselves a single cell. Some even had cable TV and a chair. They were living luv-luv in the joint.

Ray considered himself lucky. Although others on the block thought his cellie would be more at home in the ding-wing, Ray liked Shazad's soft, clipped accent and odd turns of phrase. Shazad spun tales that allowed Ray to escape the walls. Ray never knew which stories to believe. The ones about the doe-eyed dancing girls who smelled like jasmine and served food from their fingertips. Or the three families who lived in a broken-down bus and took turns picking up cans for nickels. It didn't matter. Stories didn't have to be real. Because that was the point, wasn't it?

In return for the stories, Ray taught Shazad the basics: Don't point; don't ask why they're here; never go in the yard alone. And after twelve years together, they were as close as family. But even family moves on. When Shazad's parole came through, Ray was happy for his friend, and undeniably jealous. With a sentence of Life Without, numerous appeals shot down and parole denied, he wasn't kidding himself: this life was all he had. But Shazad was going home; he'd been given a second chance.

Ray stretched, then rolled over, retrieving a small notebook and pencil from under his pillow.

Shazad spoke without raising his head. "Good morning, Ray. Did you sleep well?"

"Like a baby." It was the old prison joke—toss and turn all night and wake up crying.

"There is no need to be missing Shazad. Shazad is with you always, like karma."

Ray's pencil stopped on the page, on the word 'miss.' *How does he do that?* "Yeah," snorted Ray. "Which karma would that be? The one that put me in here twenty-three years ago? Or the one that's going to watch my back when you're out in the world chasing the honeys?"

Shazad smiled and opened his eyes. "Oh yes, the honeys. Shazad has not forgotten about the honeys. There will be much celebration, my friend. Do you want me to send you the pictures?"

Ray whipped his pillow at Shazad's neatly-shaved head. Shazad smiled and ducked.

Ray said, "Pictures, my ass! You'd better send them in person."

"Oh yes, Ray," said Shazad. "I know you will not mind getting the bend-over search from CO Munchy to sit across the table from my honeys."

"Shazad, my man, you send me a woman, and I'll whistle Dixie while spreading my cheeks!"

"I hope that you will be using your mouth for the whistling, my friend."

Ray smiled. "Maybe I oughta just sing it."

Now that would be something. Correctional Officer Munsing, with his wandering left eye and fireplug body, bent over with his face and flashlight up against Ray's black ass, and Ray belting out, "Look away, look away..."

The joking was a way to lighten reality. Ray knew that Shazad would no more have a bunch of honeys on the outside than Ray would have a million dollars under his mattress. He also knew that Shazad was never coming back. When they said goodbye, it was supposed to be forever.

"You will keep up your yoga practice, Ray. And do not stop asking for help. It will come, Ray. Remember the dream."

"You and your dreams, man. What are you telling me?"

"It is the Universe telling me to tell you."

"Yeah, yeah. Okay, Shazad. The Universe. Right."

"Do not let your paddle float downstream. You must grab the horny bull."

"It's not horny bull, it's… Forget it. Listen, Shazad, don't worry about me. I'll be fine. And I just wanted to say thanks. For, you know, everything."

Cons came into their own in many ways. Ray had had a rough start, then learned to do his time the easy way. Before Shazad, Ray managed to side with the black Muslims and use their pull to avoid most trouble. But it wasn't easy, and they had him into shit that was strangely like the stuff he'd been avoiding on the outside. Then Shazad came. He helped Ray focus on himself, not some

Malcolm X freak named Mohammed. Ray was a righteous con, respected, respectable. He looked great on paper. But he was still here.

For the past decade he'd been staying out of trouble and expanding his mind with courses, books and tapes. He worked as a paralegal at the Law Clinic while plugging away at his case options, filing petitions, looking for opportunities. He kept on dreaming. About all there was to do behind the walls was dream, or work, or count down days, and dream some more.

CO Lytle banged on the cell door. "Bentley, get your ass up! What do you think this is, the Hilton?" He laughed too loud, like the asshole he was, then moved down the tier to harass someone else.

Ray stashed his journal then rolled off the tray and made his bed. He used the toilet, pulled on his brown jumpsuit and slipped into shoes. It took him three minutes.

Shazad rose from his seat on the plastic bin. "Are you ready, my friend?"

"Gonna be a long one today," Ray said, putting his hands on the bars.

Shazad nodded seriously. "Yes. Today is the first day of the week before my freedom."

Ray rubbed a hand over his face. It was too early. "Shazad, don't talk to me anymore, okay? Not until I've had my coffee."

CO Lytle returned to stand outside their cell. He spoke into a microphone mounted on his shoulder, and the on-duty guy in the glass bubble pushed some buttons. The door slid open and Ray and Shazad stepped onto the tier. Their neighbors downstairs, Swastika-tattooed Skinheads, were in a fighting mood this morning.

"You're going down, Shazam!" Ace yelled. "Traffic done give you the green light, you short-ass, Gandhi-loving-freak!"

"Traffic" was also known as Gerald Lane, a skinny,

whiskey-haired guy and Ace's right hand. Four months ago, the Feds came looking for information on the growing meth trade. The bait they dangled was sweet, and for some the chance of getting out was almost worth the price. After the Feds' visit with Traffic sent them away smiling, rumors started. Ace had to put him to the test. Now, Traffic had scars to prove his allegiance. The cops didn't stop coming, but Ace stopped wondering about his boy. He knew where he was at all times on the inside, and now he knew where his family was on the outside.

Born in a crack house, raised on the streets, Ace was bred for prison. At fifteen, he'd been in and out of 'juvie' six times, and learned something new each stay. By the time he was convicted as an adult, he understood one thing: in order to survive you had to surround yourself with people smarter than yourself. Fortunately for Ace, it wasn't a hard thing to do. Among the sorely outnumbered White Supremecists in Graterford, Ace was King. He had a steady stream of ladies delivering cash from a booming meth business on the outside and could buy everything except his freedom.

The men in his car were loyal. If not, they were dead. Like Shorty: his death had been ruled a suicide, and now that the barbed wire was up, it would be tough for somebody else to take the same dive from the top tier. No one crossed Ace.

Everybody had heard the story of Ace's arrest. The newspapers said neighbors heard loud music and shouting coming from the family residence. It soon escalated into property damage when a turntable, speakers and three Nat King Cole albums crashed through the front bay window and landed in the holly bushes. The cops were called first, then the fire department. When the officers arrived, Ace was standing over the charred and smoldering body of his father. The cop said, "What happened here, son?"

"He wouldn't turn off the music." Ace had leaned down and lit his cigarette off his dead father's burning shirtsleeve. "I told him to turn that black shit off."

But that was years ago. Now, Ace was on a federally subsidized path of rehabilitation that included Narcotics Anonymous meetings, anger management classes and creative outlets such as woodworking and needlepoint. Ace had his own creative outlets. Lacking kerosene, his cruelty had become Tyson-like. He bit the nose off his last enemy and shoved it up the guy's ass. Ace was definitely someone to avoid.

Ray and Shazad followed the cons down the stairs. Ray glanced over at Ace and his crew. "Don't say a word," he mumbled to Shazad. "Don't even look over there. I mean it." Shazad fell in line, head down, his feet moving forward. He was a short-timer. Six days and a wake-up.

Not many could say that. Prisons across the country were bursting at the seams. Too many coming in and not enough toeing the line to get out. Parole hearings were increasingly difficult to earn. It used to be that if a con could keep his nose clean, he'd get ten days off for every thirty served, and he had a good chance at his hearing. But thanks to more than a few parolees who went ape-shit out in the world, it was now more difficult.

For some, there was hope in the form of new testimony, information from a rolled-over snitch or exonerating evidence as a result of improved DNA testing. Others pinned their hopes on a slick attorney, one who was in it for the glory of the front page, or the movie rights.

Ray and Shazad scuffed their way to the chow hall. It always reminded Ray of high school. It wasn't where you sat, it was whom you sat with—white Peckerwoods, Italian Mobsters, assorted Black gangs and biker Nazis. The worst were the Mexican Mafia. A bunch of dark-haired kids wearing bandanas, so hardened and world-weary they approached life inside with nothing to lose. Even the Italian Nostra kept their distance from them.

Two guards stood in the wide doorway, one with a

clipboard, one with an attitude.

"Good morning, men," Charlie Scruggs smirked. "Welcome to Hell. The Hell of Scruggs."

The smaller guard laughed, checking off names and numbers on his clipboard, then shook his head and repeated, "The Hell of Scruggs. I like that, Charlie. Where'd you get that from?"

Scruggs said, "Shut the fuck up, Munsing," before something caught his eye.

Ray watched the CO approach Table Eight, hand on his stick. Most inmates would admit that the correctional officers were the worst part of lock up. A man can get used to a cell and the routine. He might even make a few friends. Some cons owed their sobriety and their life to these walls. Some of them ate and slept better in prison than in the free world. But dealing with the COs everyday—that could be worse than dealing with the cons. The officers had their own set of rules, plus bureaucratic protection. It was difficult to tell the bad guys from the hired help at most prisons. Graterford State Correctional Institute was no exception.

Built on empty farmlands in 1929, the prison was far enough away from Philadelphia to remain forgotten and unchanged for sixty years. Lazy cattle wandered the green hills surrounding the prison and slept in a spacious red barn at night. Fat free-range chickens scratched over dusty roads and fed in buggy cornfields. It would have been a normal Pennsylvania sight, except for the farm workers in drab brown jumpsuits and the armed guards on horseback.

In 1989, the maximum security facility was upgraded. Eighty million dollars went into improvements and expansion—a modern infirmary, a plush administrative building and additional cells. The prison was self-sufficient, operating its own steam, sewer and power plants. With its abundance of cheap labor, Graterford had at once become a money making machine, manufacturing garments, shoes, hosiery and providing weaving services. Most convicts earned their keep working directly for the prison, in the kitchen, the fields or the hot, noisy laundry facility. There was no unemployment behind these walls.

Ray and Shazad carried their trays to the recently vacated end of a long stained table and sat on the attached bench.

"Going to work outside today," Shazad said. "It is a beautiful day for picking up the garbage of mankind."

Shazad had pulled road duty. The six-man crews picked up litter along the public road and at the prison entrance. The opportunities were boundless for a caged man. Sun, fresh air, grass underfoot, and the off chance of a beautiful woman driving by. Not to mention the road kill cigarette butts tossed from windows of passing cars. They'd take these back to the cells, combine and re-roll them. They could be smoked, traded or sold.

Ray looked up from the book he'd pulled from his pocket. "Better watch your back, Shazad. That early morning surprise might be around."

Shazad's permanent bliss faded momentarily, replaced with confusion. "I cannot watch my own back, but I can watch the rest of my body."

"You do that." Ray checked the clock. "Shit. Catch you later, man." Ray touched knuckles with Shazad and started to leave, then leaned over the table. "Keep your eyes out for the booty. I got to know, man. On the one."

"Yes, Ray." Shazad thumped his fist against his chest. "On the one."

The term had begun as a way for a con to swear they were telling the truth, like George Washington. In a society of thieves, money was all they knew. But Shazad and Ray swore on their life. The only one they had to give.

Ray leaned out the cafeteria door, looked both ways, and then headed down the long corridor to the law clinic.

Originally designed to calm and nurture, the soft green walls were smudged and scraped. The once garden-like hue was now a non-crayola shade of pea soup. The multi-colored floor tiles were chipped and stained. On the watermarked ceiling, large round intercoms hissing static broke up the pattern of the rectangular tiles. Mounted high on the walls, pivoting black security cameras monitored every move.

Ray stopped at a barred window. Sometimes, he'd stand here late in the day, watching and listening. He hardly remembered the city noises that had so thrilled him in his youth. Now, he strained to hear the moo of a cow or the chattering of birds. He lived to see a swooping hawk or a colorful butterfly. He wouldn't leave the window until he saw or heard a free creature. Ray saw Preacher Man approach, made room for him at the window.

"It's a beautiful morning in God's world, isn't it, Ray?"

"Morning, Preacher Man."

"God loves you, Ray."

"God loves you too, Preacher Man."

Preacher Man had been here even longer than Ray. He came in tattooed and angry and fighting the system, running gangs and drinking, shooting or snorting whatever he laid his hands on. Then he spent time in the hole. Apparently, enough time to find Jesus. Preacher Man had figured his way out and now he helped others to do the same, mostly by telling stories that Ray had never heard from any church he'd been in, stories with lots of bad brothers and big-breasted women needing comfort.

Preacher Man stood quietly next to Ray, bobbing his head. He began to sing, "Jesus loves me, yes he do."

Ray listened for a minute then patted the old man on the back and walked to the law clinic. He had clients to see.

Most of the cases that came into the paraprofessional clinic dealt with pleading out inmate disciplinary charges. Crimes against a person, failure to immediately obey a CO, or failing a urine test. Sometimes it was a matter of explaining complicated words to an uneducated man. As a paralegal, Ray did most of the grunt work. When the attorneys showed up, they did the rest.

This month's most interesting case was Munroe v. Graterford. Bull Munroe headed a group of die-hard power lifters. They wanted more weights and longer hours in the tiny gym. The men needed this outlet, and Bull was going to make sure they got it.

The COs thought the small room was dangerous. Last month a man was found dead, pinned underneath an overloaded bar, his neck broken and an X drawn on his chest. But more than the safety issues of the room, the officers resented the convicts growing stronger and hated to see them draw pleasure from lifting, pressing and sweating. The prison way wasn't about health and fitness. It was about starch and poor ventilation, antiquated facilities and removal from society. It was about control.

If a con did make parole, he never really fit in on the outside. Even when a rehabilitated man was released into society, no one guaranteed his success. One thing was for certain, he was branded no matter how little time he'd served. Maybe it was the look in his eye, or a smell that followed him. Whatever it was, *that feeling* made most ex-cons seek a lifestyle in the free world that guaranteed them another stay at The Gray Bar Hotel.

Getting locked up was like coming home. Their homeboys, their dawgs, even their "old ladies" would be waiting for them with open arms.

There comes a time when a convict is a convict, guilty or innocent.

4
All in a Day's Work

MIMI BALDWIN leaned her head into the office, calling, "Mr. Deluca, sir? Mr. Montgomery is on line one. Hearing no reply, she stepped into the room. "Mr. Deluca?"

"One hundred!" Fast Eddie Deluca popped up behind his massive desk, barefoot and bare-chested. "I've still got it. One hundred *real* sit-ups, not those wimpy crunches, for God's sake! Nothing like a little exercise to get the blood flowing, right, Mimi?"

Deluca was like a rooster in a barnyard. Part rooster, part peacock. Tiny barnyard.

"Yes, that's right, sir." She turned to the door. "Montgomery's on one...when you get a chance."

"Super. Put him through. Oh, Mimi?"

She glanced over her shoulder at Deluca. He took a swig from a bottle of water and winked. "You look particularly fetching this morning."

"Thank you, sir."

Mimi pulled the door shut. "Particularly fetching, my ass," she mumbled.

Deluca punched the speakerphone button, then pulled

a fresh t-shirt from his bottom drawer. "Ted! How was Switzerland? Did Alice make you play tourist again?"

"Ha! You know I wouldn't stand for that crap, Eddie! Goddamn tourists are ruining that beautiful country. Backpackers camping out in train stations, undisciplined ass-wipes trying to *discover* themselves on cheap wine and marijuana. Listen, don't get me started. I just called to wish you luck today."

Deluca paused, one arm in a crisp Robert Talbott blue and white striped shirt. "Today? Why do I need luck today? Personally, I think I could have used some luck last weekend, when I had the face-to-face with Terry Gross. Man, I never knew NPR could be so brutal!"

"Eddie, Eddie, Eddie. You live for the media! What are you talking about? You did fine. Hell, you probably even had someone copy the broadcast for you. Now, stop changing the subject. You know I'm talking about Gallo."

Eddie finished tieing his tie, then lowered himself into his calfskin chair and began packing his briefcase. "Oh, that."

"Very funny, Eddie. Remember who you're dealing with here."

"No need to worry, Ted." Deluca glanced at his pocket calendar, saw the words *Cape Cod* and a phone number. He smiled. "Everything's under control."

"All right, then. Do me proud." With that, Theodore Wells Montgomery hung up.

Do you proud? Deluca scoffed. *That's all you got for me, Ted? I'm out of tricks here, and I'm supposed to do you proud? Wait a minute.* Deluca grinned saying, "You still got it, Fast Eddie. Yes, you do."

He shoved two folders and a tape labeled 'Gross-Deluca interview' into his briefcase and left his office tell his secretary he'd be at Nana's, and to page him in thirty minutes.

Ken Reilly felt like hell. He attempted a smile in the

mirror. It made him nauseous. He ran his hands through his hair, tried the smile again, then gave up and found a disposable razor in the shower and raked it over his cheeks.

"Hey! You okay in there?' The girl rapped on the door.

A dot of blood appeared on Reilly's chin. He grabbed a hand towel and held it to his face. It smelled like baby powder. "I'm fine. Be right out."

"I've gotta go, Sweetie."

Reilly had met her the night before in a loud, dark bar. She was still a looker this morning, but she was paler than he'd remembered and definitely too damn loud. Something he didn't plan on waking up to every day.

The girl was waiting at the apartment door in some kind of waitress uniform and holding two commuter mugs. She seemed shorter than Reilly remembered.

"Thank you." He smiled thinly, took a sip then wished he could spit it out.

She jabbered all the way down to the street, and when she admitted that last night's car had been borrowed and that they would have to take the bus, Reilly begged off. He kissed her quickly, mumbled something about calling her when he got back from Acapulco then practically ran around the corner.

He slid the cell phone from his pocket and hit the speed dial.

Sailor answered on the second ring. "Hello?"

"Help."

"Reilly? What is it? Where are you?"

"I'm stuck in Cheltenham. I need a ride. Please, Sailor. I promise I'll pay you back." Reilly took another sip of the coffee then spit it out and tossed the whole mug in the bushes.

Sailor sighed, but was secretly happy for an excuse to get out of the cramped cubicle. "Okay. Where are you?"

He gave her directions then started walking. Somewhere between the street corner and a small coffeehouse, Reilly found a little blue pill in his pocket.

He sat under the yellow awning sipping his double espresso and nibbling on a scone. Sailor saw him as she pulled up. She liked how he seemed so comfortable. He might have been a famous writer in a café in Provence. She half-expected him to light up a Gauloise and adjust his beret. But when he saw her and approached, she said, "You look like hell. Get in."

Reilly got into the car. "Good morning to you, too. Hell, huh? I was going for the sexy legal genius look."

Sailor gave him one of his mother's looks, the one that said, 'Will you please be serious for one minute?' His mom had never understood him. She took things so personally, like thinking the bogus sit-com about the overweight divorced woman working two jobs while supporting her mother and raising five kids was all about her. Reilly didn't know where she got that shit. The woman lived in Memphis, for God's sake.

Reilly was a funny guy. He knew years ago he had the gift. Teachers, nuns, or old ladies with trampled tulips: Reilly could make them all smile. He'd learned to keep them laughing to get what he wanted. It worked like a charm. As a job, it paid pretty well too, just not as well as Law.

"Don't forget, Sailor, next Saturday at Dick's, ten o'clock. I'm closing the show, so you'd better be there."

Sailor checked her rearview mirror then zipped across two lanes. "I remember, Reilly. You only plastered twelve flyers on the bulletin board."

"I guess you missed the ones in the elevator and the men's room."

"Men's room?"

"Just a little reading material."

"Yeah, I definitely missed those." She looked at him. "Don't worry, I'll be there."

"Good." He crossed his arms, reclined his seat and slept the rest of the way.

When Sailor dropped Reilly at the front of the building, she watched him walk away wondering the whole time what it was about this abrasive guy that somehow touched her. He was wrong for her. But he made her smile.

Sailor drove into the parking garage and began circling. She was about to give up and head straight for the roof when she found an empty corner on the partner's floor and pulled her dinged-up Acura in tight next to a new Mercedes SL.

She slipped her briefcase over her shoulder and hurried to the elevator while rooting around inside her purse for a mint. When the elevator doors opened she stepped forward automatically and smacked heads with the guy coming out.

"Dammit!"

"Oh!" Sailor rubbed her head.

The guy said, "Watch where you're going!"

They looked up at the same time. Sailor apologized. "I'm sorry, I wasn't paying attention. Are you okay?"

He swept his eyes over her, then smoothed his hair. "Of course." He grinned. "No problem."

Sailor entered the elevator and punched the floor button. The doors started to close and the guy stuck his briefcase in the gap.

"Sure *you're* all right?" he asked, leaning in.

"I'm fine." She waved him off. "Fine, really."

Still blocking the door, he asked, "So, are you going up?"

"Yes, actually."

"Where to?"

"Sixth floor. Second day on the job."

"Second day, huh? Well that explains it."

"Explains what?" she asked.

"Why we haven't met. All the new admin hires always go through me. Missy should have told you about the MDB&S custom."

"Custom?" Sailor asked.

"Oh yes. See, each new secretary is invited to a candlelight dinner at my place on the water to celebrate her...position."

Now that Sailor's vision had cleared, she knew exactly whom she had bumped into.

"Allow me to introduce myself." He drew himself up and extended his hand. "Edward John Deluca, at your service."

As he bowed before her, Sailor wondered why he hadn't added 'Esquire' to his introduction. *Fast Eddie*. She smiled. "Mr. Deluca, I am neither a secretary nor a dinner partner, and as far as you are concerned my *position*, is *unavailable*. Have a good day."

Toeing his briefcase out of the elevator's path, Sailor watched the doors close on a very stunned King of Repartee. Philly's homeboy: the most feared prosecutor-turned-defense-attorney, Fast Eddie Deluca.

5
Berger, Bentley, Banning
and Berger

HIRAM BERGER was off duty, tooling through the familiar neighborhood. In a few days he'd be off duty for good, and after twenty years on the force, he still wasn't sure how he felt about that. The shrink said he'd get used to the down time, but that a hobby might be good, too. Berger had had to laugh. Only hobby he ever had was drinking, and look what that got him—an ex-wife, questionable business partners and a one-way ticket to Hell.

He made a sharp left turn, which sent a leaky fast food bag sliding across the vinyl back seat. It teetered at the edge then fell to the floor, adding sausage and pancakes to the aromatic pile of debris. The radio blared; he tried to keep up with the song, inserting his own lyrics when the right ones failed him.

Berger pulled onto Stallion Lane, raised his tinted windows and turned off the engine. Parked under the big elm across from a simple green and white Cape Cod, he pulled out a worn notebook and a pen.

A blue mud-splattered minivan shared the driveway with a sleek silver Miata. The bright floral cushions on the porch rockers looked brand new, and a small purple bicycle he'd never seen before leaned against the porch railing. As a trained professional, Berger noticed these things. What he failed to notice was the mailbox where 'Berger' was now painted over with 'Johnson'. It didn't matter. To him, this would always be his home.

He jotted a few notes, thinking for a moment she would come out to the car the way she used to and tap on the window and blow him kisses, mouthing the words 'I love you'. He blinked and the image was gone, replaced by a snarling monster, one that called him a fuck-up and a loser, one that sent divorce papers to his motel room and shipped his clothes COD. The same monster that had moved out in the dark of the night, took away the baby he'd hardly held and moved in with a man who used to call him Pal.

The blinds in a room on the second floor twisted shut and Berger started the engine. "I've got my eye on you, Bitch."

He pulled away from the curb, angling toward a racing squirrel then smiled at the satisfying pop. Berger drove his killing machine too fast across town, gliding through stop signs, straddling the dotted line.

He rolled up the cracked concrete driveway of a tiny 1950s ranch, revved his engine before killing it, then snatched up the pharmacy bag and coffee cup from the console and slammed the door of the Impala.

Berger heard the toss and slap of rolled papers hitting pavement, as the paperboy made his way down the street. The kid did a shitty job. Most times the thing landed nearer to the mailbox than the front door. Berger walked to the end of the driveway, poured the remaining dregs of convenience store coffee on his neighbor's roses and waited for the little twerp.

The boy approached on a bike that seemed too small, tossing papers left and right. Walkman blaring: he didn't stand a chance when Berger stepped out armed with a full trashcan.

"Hey! Watch it. You almost dented my trash can." Berger laughed.

"Asshole!" The boy brushed himself off, gathered his papers and flipped Berger the finger as he rode away.

Berger said, "Damn kids. No respect."

It took a key, a foot and a shoulder to force the stubborn front door open and when it closed behind him, his tough guy demeanor dissolved. Standing there, among all the things she'd left behind, he could hear her: "If you don't do something, you're gonna end up just like them. Just like those losers."

She was right. He dropped his keys on the coffee table and sank into the worn corduroy couch, rubbing his finger where the ring used to be.

"I'm one of the good guys," he whispered, opening the pharmacy bag. "I'm one of the good guys," he repeated, swallowing the pills. "I am one of the good guys!" he shouted then began to cry.

Hours later, as the sun strained through the vinyl-backed curtains, Berger woke. In the bathroom he stripped, adding his clothes to the pile of laundry on the floor, then stood in the shower for a very long time.

Detective Hiram Berger scrubbed his bloated body with a sliver of soap and made a mental list of all the things he needed to do today.

Ray Bentley dropped an armload of folders on the table in the Graterford SCI Law Library. He sorted the stacks and was just about to sit down when he heard the scuffling start.

"Ooof! Fucker!"

A disagreement that may have stopped at a few unkind

words, or maybe even a shove on the outside, could escalate into a full-blown fight, or even homicide, behind prison walls. Ray hesitated for a minute, not wanting to get involved, but when they smashed into the books and broke two shelves, he got up.

"Hey! That's enough!"

The two men scuffled on the floor, arms and legs akimbo, hands slapping, mouths going.

"Watch it!"

"You dumb fuck!"

"That's mine!" The bigger guy on top rolled onto the squirming smaller guy.

Ray yelled again, and when they didn't stop, he smacked the big guy in the head with a book.

"Take it outside! This is not the time or place!"

They actually looked sorry as Ray picked up the books and papers. They fell off each other, and the smaller one started to giggle. The big guy looked at him, then drew back his fist and smashed his little buddy's teeth in, saying, "That was my book, Squirrel. Next time you *ask* before you touch it."

Ray dialed an extension he knew all too well, and in a few minutes a guard, a janitor and a nurse arrived.

It was a typical morning at Graterford, until a skinny black guy with a head like a bobble doll showed up.

DeShawn "Stash" Neely sat across the table from Ray and said, "This new fish told me, if the cop beats you when you was signing that bullshit paper he wrote up, then you can get a new trial. That right? I mean, how do I get my justice, dawg?"

Ray wondered who the new fish was and why he was giving legal advice. "There are laws against coercing a confession, Stash. But proving it is another thing. You need witnesses who'll talk, other cases against the same cop, and I gotta warn you, the CO's won't like you going after one of their own. Even if you get through all that, it'll take time. A long time."

"Time I got, and as far as the CO's, I be ass out anyway. It's justice I want, lawdawg. I want him to go down! Dicks never should have left me alone with him! They all knew what that motherfucker was gonna do. Shit! Berger done fucked me up, couldn't piss for a goddamn week, and my mind, it still don't work right. Gotta take all these meds now. Shee-it."

Berger? Ray looked up from his pad, pencil in mid-air. "Detective Hiram Berger? Of the Twenty-First?"

"There another one?"

Ray shook his head.

"Better not be, cuz one of those motherfucker's enough, know what I mean?"

Ray knew what he meant.

Stash said, "Fuckin' Berger beat me half-stupid with the phone book. The business section. When I finally came to, I was in lockup and going down hard."

He looked in Ray's eyes, "That was eleven years ago. I been all up and down the state, supposed to be for my own good. That's bullshit! Had me doing diesel therapy, that's all." He leaned in. "When I came to Graterford last year, they hemmed me up in PC, then some bum rap landed me in the J-cat wing. They finally figured I wasn't supposed to be there, so they put me back in the mainline. Now, from what this fish said, I think maybe I got something comin'." He spread his arms and leaned back. "So, here I am, whatever you need, dawg, you just ask Stash. I can get you tailors, the real smokes, bro." He looked around. "Or you want some more books?"

Ray stared at Stash Neely and saw more than books and cigarettes. He saw a loophole—one to approach cautiously.

Ray said, "Look Stash, I don't know you *or* your people. But if I get involved in this, shit's gonna roll, you understand? I'm telling you now, you better be straight up with me."

Stash bobbed his head and smiled, revealing one gold

tooth that seemed out of place alongside its yellow neighbors. "It ain't no thing. Stash be a righteous con, lawdawg."

Ray picked up his pencil. "All right, start from the beginning and go nice and slow. Don't leave anything out."

At Montgomery, Deluca, Banning and Scott, plans for the interns were underway. Len Banning pulled files from a box labeled 'Pro Bono'. He remembered his early years, homeless advocacy, prisoners' civil rights. The poor, the crazy and the forgotten. Now he was too busy nursing martinis on the nineteenth hole and totaling his Swiss accounts to care much about the indigent. But the work was good PR for the firm and hell, it was state-mandated. He finished separating the folders into three stacks, then adjusted his cufflinks and pressed the intercom.

"Helen, what time's the meeting?"

"You're in A at eleven, Mr. Banning. I took the liberty of ordering from La Famiglia. They'll be here at one."

"Very good. One more thing?"

"Sir?"

"Have you heard from Tiffany?"

"No, Mr. Banning. Would you like me to call Spa Royale?"

"No. I'm sure she just forgot to call. I'll catch up with her at home. Thanks, Helen."

"Anytime."

Banning leaned back in his chair, ran his hands over his face. *Tiffany, Tiffany, what the hell are you doing this time? Better yet, who?*

They had been married in Bermuda on the beach at sunset. That was her idea. God, the younger generation could be so cliché. Len Banning had begun a pattern of running away from the hard things, and now he was stuck with the easy thing—a beautiful young wife with a wandering ass and a six thousand dollar chest. He missed his kids. He missed going home to a real house, with furniture you could really sit on. He hated to admit it, but money wasn't everything.

Banning stood behind his desk, picked up the glamorous photo of Tiffany Number Three, all mink and lipstick. He kissed the glass, then dropped it in the wastebasket. He pulled the elastic from his ponytail and shook out his famous curls.

Down the hall in Conference Room A, the credenza overflowed with bagels, Danish pastry, coffee, juice and tall bottles of Evian. Helen entered pushing a cart of files.

Reilly and Sailor sat at one end of the long table, sipping coffee. They were weary, yet trying hard not to let it show. This was the life they wanted; hard work was part of the drill. Put in six or seven years, kick some serious butt and make partner. With a nice-sized starting salary and loads of comps, they could pay off school loans, buy their dream cars and vacations abroad. Sleep was highly overrated.

"Morning, morning." Banning entered the room, hair flowing around his shoulders, eyes sparkling. He set his briefcase on the floor, pulled out a chair and sat down as if he were one of them.

Helen looked up from sorting supplies and saw Banning's boyish grin and un-tethered hair. On her way out she paused to whisper in his ear, "Welcome back."

"Thank you, Helen," Banning said, as the door clicked shut.

He scooted in his chair then pulled a pen from his pocket. "Okay, gang. Let's get to work." He passed out the case files. It was shaping up to be a wonderful morning.

Ray Bentley was having a fine morning himself. Yes sir, the weather report was looking good at Graterford. Intermittent showers of hope mixed with a slight chance of luck. Having just read the file of his new pal, DeShawn Lincoln Neely, he felt he might have a chance re-opening the case of Raymond Moses Bentley.

Now all Ray had to do was arrange a call to his long absent outside counsel. He'd need more than luck and hope, so he headed back to his cell to stock up on stamps and cigarettes.

In the suburbs, Berger put the finishing touches on his newly waxed car. He waved to the mail carrier then heaved three boxes of Goodwill donations into his trunk. Running back inside for his checkbook and sunglasses, he decided to rearrange the bedroom furniture.

The house smelled of lemon and pine. The furniture gleamed. Vacuum tracks were visible on the carpet. The sound of the dishwasher competed with the rumbling of the washing machine. Bags of trash stood on the back porch waiting for the next pick-up day. Shiny white counter tops in the organized kitchen displayed a dog-shaped cookie jar, a photograph of a smiling woman cuddling a white terrier and an overflowing tray of prescription drug bottles: Ativan, Noroton, Librium, Tegretol, Depakote, Lithium, all with the lids ajar, all half-empty.

6
The Women

PARIS KENDRICK entered Spa Royale and signed in at the reception desk. The name above hers had been red-lined, but Paris could still read, "Tiffany Banning." She smiled under her hat and dark glasses. Of course this was where she'd come. This was where everyone came.

Paris walked through the marble entry to one of several waiting areas. This one was a Chinese theme, deep red walls, black lanterns and rice paper screens, low tables and silk meditation cushions. The perfect balance of chi made you sigh as you entered. Paris helped herself to a cup of green tea and turned off her cell phone.

A few moments later, a perfect twenty-year-old brunette in a starched lab coat appeared beside the rice paper screen.

"Miss K.?"

Paris followed the girl to the room at the end of the hall. There would be no massage today, no vichy shower sea kelp scrub. Today, Dr. Simone would inject Botox into Paris Kendrick's forehead, collagen around her lips and eyes, and transfer fat into her cheeks. It was a dance against time, a ploy some women used to remind them of the glory of youth. Paris wasn't stupid. She knew she would never see thirty again, no matter what she did to her skin. But she was a vain woman, and working on her outward appearance was so much less painful than an hour on the analyst's couch.

She imagined if she looked young and carefree, life would reciprocate. She missed that feeling of endless possibility, perpetual hope. She needed to believe something good was on the horizon.

Gina stopped wiping the counter top and leaned into Deluca's face. "What are you saying Eddie? You know this has nothing to do with my kid." She looked at him harder. "Jesus. Don't tell me. Lou's got something on you, too?"

"Gina, I swear I wouldn't ask if I knew any other way. I'm telling you, he's going down. Unless—"

"Jesus, Eddie. Unless what? Unless I lie?"

"I know, I know. It sounds like a lie, but Gina, come on. It's not like it hasn't happened before, right? Lou *has* spent the night. He *has* been drunk. These are all things that have happened, aren't they?"

"Well, sure, but..."

"Listen to me, Gina. If he does the time, what will happen to you? What about Holly? Please. Do it for me. For old times sake."

Gina snorted. "Old times, huh, Eddie? Yeah, I remember those old times." Her voice was low and angry. "Turning tricks in the street, sleeping in the back of unlocked cars. Those were the *good* old days. Shit."

"Gina. I need you."

She stood there with her arms crossed, eyes on the floor, in her sensible waitress shoes and yellow pom-pom socks. Finally she tipped her chin to the ceiling and exhaled loudly.

"Only for you, Eddie. Not for him." She looked Deluca in the eye. "Only for you."

Deluca hopped off the stool, leaned over the counter and kissed her. "Thank you. I'll need you in the office later. Call Mimi, okay?"

Gina nodded.

Deluca peeled a fifty from his money roll and slid it under the coffee cup just as his pager went off. He turned, halfway to the exit, shot back a wide grin and winked.

Gina had to smile. She watched him leave, then turned away shaking her head. "Fucking Eddie. You do it to me every time."

"What's that, Boss?' The cook stood next to Gina, rubbing at a stain on his apron.

"Nothing, Chuck. Just talking to myself. So, what's the soup today?"

Sonja checked the greenhouse, study and exercise room. Maybe Miss Chetta was enjoying one of her foreign films in the media room. She passed the kitchen where the chef stood at the marble workstation, his whisk tapping the sides of a deep copper bowl.

"Stephan, have you seen Miss Chetta?"

"Not since breakfast. She said something about going into town." He dipped a spoon into the creamy mixture and held it out to Sonja. "Here, tell me what you think."

The soft warm cream melted on her tongue. Honey and cinnamon mingled with a tart spike of something. She swallowed, licked her lips, then guessed, "Anise?"

"Very good. You're learning, Sweetie. But, do you like it?"

Sonja blushed. Sweetie. "Of course. Of course I love it, Stephan. I love all your desserts." She tugged her long jacket over her ample hips and watched him dip another strawberry into the bowl. The fruit rested on his full lower lip as his tongue darted out to lick the dollop of cream on the tip. Sonja sighed.

Stephan popped the fruit into his mouth and turned back to the stove. 'She might be in her dressing room,

Sweetie. Did you try there?"

"Um. No, I'll just head over there, I mean *up* there now." Sonja began backing out of the room. "Is there anything you need? That is, if Miss Chetta is going into town, is there anything you need her to pick up?"

He called over his shoulder, "Just one order of tall, dark, and handsome."

Sonja laughed. "Yeah, me too."

In the closet of her dressing room, Maria Chetta knelt in front of a large wall safe. She added a cassette tape and two envelopes to a bulging leather satchel then closed the safe door and pulled the evening gowns back into place.

Sonja knocked. "Miss Chetta? I have some papers for you to sign."

Maria left the leather bag in the closet and walked to the door. "Come in." She sat in the chair at her antique vanity as Sonja passed her the papers. "Is that it then?"

"Yes, Ma'am. I'll get these out right away." Sonja turned to leave. "Oh, one more thing. Will there be anyone joining you for dinner?"

"No. Not tonight. Just tell Stephan to serve something light, and not until seven."

"Seven?"

"Yes, I'm going into town. I may be delayed."

Sonja stood at the door, a question on her face.

"Was there anything else, Sonja?"

"No, Miss Chetta."

Maria heard Sonja's receding footsteps, waited a moment then retrieved the satchel.

Paris dimmed the lights and adjusted the volume on the CD player. Music filled the room mingling with jasmine incense. She checked her reflection. Hair perfectly tousled, makeup artfully natural, lips plump, zebra-print panties barely visible under the open wrap. Smiling and humming to Ravel's Bolero, she sashayed on feathered mules into the living room then arranged herself on the divan.

A bottle of Veuve Cliquot Ponsardin peeked from the sterling ice bucket. Two crystal flutes waited to be filled as a key turned in the lock and the penthouse door opened.

"In here, darling." Paris Kendrick twisted the diamond band on her finger, adjusted her robe and turned to welcome Ted Montgomery.

Maria exited the bank adjusting her sunglasses. She glanced up and down the street. Boys with green and purple hair on skateboards to the north. A scattering of obvious tourists complete with maps and walking sandals to the south. Just another summer day at the cape. She hurried across the street to the parking lot, the empty leather satchel hanging loosely at her side.

Sailor cradled the phone as she finished applying the top coat of nail polish. "No Dad, I don't sound tired. I sound like I'm working hard and learning. Now stop worrying and tell me about dinner at the Smith-Houghtons." Sailor wished she could be there with him, wondered what he'd think of his little girl in her grungy sweats with her home manicure. He'd always provided the best for her and expected the best in return. Dr. Beaumont was tough but fair, and Sailor respected and loved him. He'd been both father and mother the last ten years, and Sailor wanted nothing more than to please him, to make him proud of her.

"Your mother is watching you, Sailor."

"Dad. I wish you wouldn't say that."

"I know. You don't want to talk about it. I'm just saying that she's with you in spirit. Philadelphia is your town too."

"Okay, Dad." Sailor glanced over at the family photo on the end table. A smiling, nappy-haired girl holding a Pooh bear stood between a tanned, blond couple in tennis whites. "I'll call you soon." Sailor hung up, and then sunk back into the couch, blowing lightly on her drying nails.

7
Who's doing whom?

REILLY was on. The whites of his green eyes weren't too red today, his clothes were neatly pressed, shoes shined, tie knotted perfectly. He wore cologne that hinted of scarf-draped women in exotic lands. In the secretarial bullpen, six young ladies leaned over the cubicle walls, all breasts and teeth. Five others stalled en route to urgent meetings.

Reilly said, "A guy phones a law office, says, 'I wanna speak to my lawyer.' The receptionist tells him, 'I'm sorry but he died last week.' Next day he phones again, asks the same question. The receptionist says, 'I told you yesterday, he died last week.' Next day, the guy calls *again* and asks to speak to his lawyer. By this time the receptionist is getting annoyed and says, 'I keep telling you that your lawyer died last week. Why do you keep calling?' The guy says, 'Because I just *love* hearing it.'"

As the ladies laughed and repeated the punch line, Reilly searched the room.

Behind him, she said, "Looking for someone?"

Reilly smiled, turning around. "Good morning."

Victoria wore glasses today, giving the impression of a

studious Playboy centerfold. "Good morning to you, funny man. Don't forget, you've got to run down that depo before the meeting with Harry."

"Don't worry Sweden. I'll be right behind you and let me say, it's not a bad place to be."

"Hey, Reilly." Missy broke in, touching Reilly's arm. "Do you have it?"

Reilly reached in his pocket and pulled out a small square of paper. He passed it to Missy, his eyes still on Sweden.

Missy snatched it. "You're the best!" She took off to the break room, waving the paper. "I've got Reilly's top ten!"

Sweden raised her brow. "They all love you, don't they?"

Reilly said, "I don't know. Do they?"

Sweden shrugged, then pushed up her glasses and walked away, feeling Reilly's eyes on her back.

Across town in Paris Kendrick's penthouse, Ted Montgomery felt obligated to ask, "How long will Arnold be gone this time?'

Paris rolled onto her side, propping her newly tightened face on her chemically treated hand. "The usual. Three weeks. He'll be back just in time for the Van Gogh opening. Are you taking Alice?"

"Oh hell, probably. She hired a house manager last month, and already this broad has us committing to every damn invitation that comes along. Alice says we need to be seen at more charity and social events. Some crap about the firm's importance to the community, and our commitment to mankind." Ted tugged gently on the silk sheet covering Paris, drawing it down across her surgically enhanced forty-something breasts, past her lipo-suctioned abdomen, all the way down to her carotene-lotioned pseudo-tanned thighs of steel.

"Umm-hmm. Now that's what *I* call mankind."

Paris giggled as Ted buried his face in her breasts.

Deluca primped at the mirror, speaking into his headset. "Mariel, I swear, I'll be there. You know how it is with these high profile cases, if they call at the last minute, I have to go. Why don't you meet me at Le Bec Fin? The press will be there and you can show off your new stones." He walked to the couch and lay back on the cushions. "So, baby? What are you wearing, now?"

"Chuck! I'm out of here!" Gina slipped into her sandals, while pulling bobby pins out of her loose bun.

"Okay, Boss." Chuck poked his head through the order window. "Anything else you need done before the lunch rush?"

"No, I think we're good. Susie should be here in ten minutes. Table eight's already paid. He can sit there as long as he wants." Gina shook out her hair and smoothed the front of her dress. "How do I look?"

"You look great. You got a date or something?"

"Hi's coming around. He's taking me to the zoo."

"Tell that guy, Chuck said to watch his manners. He's in the company of a lady. And besides, if he pulls any crap on you, I'll be happy to bust his fuckin' nose again."

"Aw, Chuck. What would I do without you?' Gina blew him a kiss from the door, bells jingling behind her as it slapped shut.

The air was heavy and warm. A slight breeze from the south served only to stir up the downtown smells— Chinese food from Huy Fong's, pitch tar from the roofing job at Starbucks, bus exhaust, bad cigars. Gina kicked a few cigarette butts over the curb, checked the street traffic and began to pace. She had always been a pacer. It helped her think. That and a long hot shower.

Her Grandmother used to say, "Gina Lee, if we had an eight-foot shower and a ninety-gallon water heater, you could solve all the world's problems." God, she missed her

Nana.

"Excuse me, Miss?"

Reilly held an old street atlas and a piece of paper with an address. "Could you tell me where the One Hour Dry Cleaner is? It's supposed to be Fifth and—"

"Yeah, they moved last month. Ernie lost his lease; he's over by the bookstore now." Gina pointed, "Go two blocks down and turn right at McNally's."

Reilly saw her do something with her arm, but he was really watching her face. She had the most amazing lips. "Uh, thanks. I appreciate it." He stood there, staring.

She smiled, so he asked, "Can I buy you a cup of coffee? I mean, to thank you for your help."

Still smiling, she cocked her head.

"I'm Reilly." He extended his hand. "Kenneth Reilly."

"How do you do." She grasped his hand firmly. "Mr. Reilly, I'm Gina. That's my place." Her eyes motioned to the diner.

His followed to the neon sign flickering, "Nana's."

She said, "I'm all coffee-ed out for the moment, but thank you for the offer. Could I have my hand back now?"

"Oh, sorry." Reilly released his grip. "Maybe some other time, then?"

"Some other time, then."

A shiny Impala pulled up to the curb, rattling to a stop with Sinatra singing, "Luck be a Lady Tonight." A well-groomed Hiram Berger leaned over the roof of the car. He held a long-stemmed rose in his teeth. Gina laughed. She waved to Reilly as they pulled away.

He watched for a long time, until the Impala was lost in a sea of cars headed to the highway.

Banning signed the last page of a thick document then hit the intercom. "Helen, see if Deluca's around. I need to borrow Jeremy."

Helen picked up the phone wishing she could borrow Jeremy, too.

DeLuca's henchman, Jeremy Strom, was revered at MDB&S. He was the stuff tall tales were made of—six-four, two-ninety, with thighs like tree trunks, biceps like bowling balls, and an oak barrel chest—he was an anatomical masterpiece. And when God made Jeremy, he didn't stop at his body. He gave him large cornflower blue eyes, high Nordic cheekbones, and a perfect smile. Like the hero on the cover of a romance novel, Jeremy Strom was beautiful.

"So, you're really going to do it?' Helen asked from the doorway.

"I'm really going to do it. I *should* have done this years ago. Tell me again, Helen, how did I get here?' Banning looked around his plush office.

She smiled. "You cared, Mr. Banning. You got here because you cared what happened to the guy without the means for proper representation. You got here because everyone knew you deserved it. You got here because you were good and you were honest, and everyone knows that what you give is what you get."

"Yeah." Banning stood. "That's right. That's it exactly, Helen. What you give is what you get. The universal truth of man's existence. The ultimate karmic experience. So what happened? Here I am becoming the system, succumbing to all I had rallied against for so long, contaminating my mind with the pollutants of a material world."

He walked over to the window then looked back at Helen. "This isn't just a mid-life crisis, is it?"

She shook her head. "Afraid not."

He stared out the window then walked back to his desk and picked up the divorce papers.

Harry James Scott had been holding his own at the meeting for almost an hour. When Reilly burst through the door, all sweaty and apologetic, Harry was ready to kick him off the case. But in seconds, Reilly had the rap stars laughing. Harry sat down.

Keeping the press away from this story was going to be very difficult. Philadelphia loved their bad boy rappers when they brought money and fame to the city but tended to slap them publicly when they brought shame and disgrace. Seems Mikey-Mike and his sidekick were more than just close friends—and someone had the video tape. This could seriously hamper CD sales. Reilly found a great deal of humor in the predicament, especially when he heard the part about the cleaning woman and the king snake. "Speaking of sex—"

"Yo mans! What you talking about? We was doing some rolfing, see? It wasn't no sex, homes." Mikey-Mike adjusted his formidable girth over his diamond-studded belt.

"Yeah, man. It's like this European thing for your proper 'linement of the physical body, see?' Mini-Mike added.

"Oh yeah, right. Hey did you hear about those lawyers, Tom and Joe? They're talking one day and Joe says, 'Last night I took the new intern out. We had dinner then I took her home and we *had sex*. Man, I'm glad we did cause she is *a lot* better than my wife.'"

The rappers laughed and punched each other in the arm.

Reilly continued, "The next day Tom says to Joe, 'You know what? Last night *I* took the new intern out. We had dinner then we went to my house and *we* had sex. I disagree with you, man. *Your wife* is a lot better.'"

Mini-Mike burst out laughing.

Mikey-Mike joined him. "You are one funny motherfucker, white-boy. You got any good black jokes, some I can tell my friends? Hey, Money? What do you think?"

Maurice "Money" Jones turned around, phones on each ear. He said, "Let me call you right back," into one of them, then clicked off both calls with his thumbs. "Good thinking, Mikey. Let the public see you as the funny guy you are. That might be just the thing... considering the circumstances."

He tipped his chin to Reilly. "Call my office, we'll work out the details." He looked at Harry. "Back to what you were saying, I agree. Get a dollar amount on that videotape and get it back. Whatever it takes."

Money turned to Mikey-Mike and Mini-Mike, who were holding hands underneath the table. "C'mon, boys. I'm going to find you some lady friends."

In the break room, Deluca read Reilly's list posted above the water dispenser. "Top Ten Things to Never Say in a Law Office." Number ten: Can I see your briefs?

"He's good, isn't he?" Sailor said.

Deluca turned to the voice. How had he missed this babe? And she was coming on to him. Oh, yeah.

He took a step back. She stepped into the space, extending her hand. "Sailor Jane Beaumont. Although I believe we have already met, Mr. Deluca."

"Really?' He racked his brain. Come on Eddie, you're losing it. "So, where does the name 'Sailor' come from?"

"My Dad. He loves the sea. It's very symbolic, don't you think?"

Symbolic? "Oh, absolutely. It's also very wet."

Sailor was trying to decide whether to slap him or laugh in his face, when he snapped his fingers and said, "Oh, right—the elevator. You're the intern." He grinned. "So, do you want to have dinner sometime?"

Ray waited his turn for the phone. He played by their rules. He'd seen his advisor, slipped the CO a few bills, and even traded some real cigarettes to Mama "Frederico" Bell to buy ten minutes. As an added measure, Ray promised to write Plump Daddy's parole board a letter in exchange for protection. He was straight-up. He was next.

Outgoing calls from the prison were always collect and

charged an enormous rate. The surcharge would put a damper on a *rich* man's income. No wonder their mamas told them, "Don't you call me from prison, boy!" They had to pay the rent.

The cons watched whom they called and what they said. With a restricted list for each inmate, the guards listened in and could cut you off at anytime. Ray had only five numbers on his list. Two were for his attorney. He tried the first. After a series of rings, the tone was replaced by a computerized voice stating the number had been changed, and for a mere ninety cents he would be automatically connected to the new number. Ray stayed on the line. When the call went through, he had to wait for the collect call acceptance, and finally got a human voice. She sounded real pretty, too.

Reilly walked the Mikes and Money to the elevator and said good-bye with a complicated hand slap, snap-clap combination that impressed Missy. She watched from her seat behind the reception desk thinking, it's going to quiet around here when he goes back to school.

Reilly caught the look and smiled. He was about to say something clever, something like, Hey there beautiful, where have you been all my life? Or something poetic like, the sunbeam on the north shore whispers your name. Or something smart... when the phone rang and Missy answered it saying, "Montgomery, DeLuca, Banning and Scott. How may I direct your call?"

"What did you say? Where's Denise? I'm looking for Mr. Herring. He's my attorney."

"I am sorry, sir. Mr. Herring is indisposed. Would you like to speak with Mr. Banning?"

"Mr. Banning? Who the hell is that? No, I need to speak to Mr. Herring—about my case. *He's* my attorney."

"Sir, Mr. Herring is unavailable to speak to anyone."

"What? Is he in a meeting? You tell him Ray Bentley's on the phone. That son of bitch hasn't come to see me in three months!"

"Sir," Missy lowered her voice, "Mr. Herring won't be coming to see anyone. He is deceased. Montgomery, DeLuca, Banning and Scott took over the offices of Herring and Son. All the casework's been transferred here. I can connect you to Mr. Banning's office. He's in charge of Herring's cases."

"Deceased?" Ray said.

This might have been funny if Ray wasn't calling from Graterford Prison. This might have been humorous if Ray Bentley wasn't serving a life sentence for a crime he didn't commit. Ray rolled his eyes to the ceiling and sighed. "He's dead? My attorney died and no one said a goddamn thing? What about Denise? Is she there?"

"No, she's gone, too."

"What? She died, too?"

"No sir. I believe Miss Brody is alive and well."

Ray pulled the phone from his ear. He was tempted to smash it back onto the hook and call it a day. *Motherfuckers!*

Mama Bell looked at her watch, and folded her huge arms over her broad flat chest. Ray exhaled loudly, brought the phone back to his ear.

Missy said, "Sir? Sir? Shall I transfer you now?"

"Yeah, sure. Transfer me."

Reilly heard the whole thing. He watched Missy send the call to Helen at Banning's office and checked his watch. It was late. They might talk to the guy, but they wouldn't request the files, not until Monday. If then… The law moved at a sloth's pace.

Reilly said, "Poor guy. His attorney died and no one told him?"

"Worse than that, the guy's calling from prison."

Reilly's curiosity peaked, "What did you say his name was?"

Missy smiled. "I didn't."

"Come on, Missy." Reilly flashed her a grin and

reached for her hand.

Missy looked at his hand on hers. She smiled back and leaned forward whispering, "Ray Bentley." When the phone rang she tipped her head toward the elevator and told him, "The Herring files are in the basement. Good luck."

8
Some Beginnings
Start In The Middle

FROM the safety of the glass bubble, the COs controlled everything in the tiers—cell doors, telephones, lights, electricity, gas, water, even TV channels. During training exercises, they were taught to use the bubble as headquarters in the event of a prison outbreak. There had been a few all-out riots and some hairy times at Graterford in the past decade, and even though they were paid well, the deputies weren't heroes. When they were on the tiers they left their weapons locked up, the only armed officer was the sharp shooter in the perch.

Most nights were quiet in Ray's block. These were the lifers. They knew the drill. Do your time the easy way.

Deputy Munsing leaned back in the rolling chair, his feet braced on the generator panel. "Now this is my kind of girl, likes to hunt and fish, says she don't mind baiting her own hook."

"What the fuck you reading, Munch?' Scruggs moved the camera joystick, checking out the upper tier.

Munchy rolled across the smooth floor, dropped the magazine on the desktop. "There you go, buddy. Think you can find Mrs. Scruggs in there?"

Scruggs glanced at the magazine cover, "*Backdoor Babes*? Jesus Christ, Munch. Where the fuck do you buy trash like that? What was that one you had last week? *My Neighbor's Nuthole*? Why don't you get out in the real world, find yourself a real woman?"

"Them are real women!"

"Yeah, right." Scruggs flipped open the magazine, pointed to a thick brunette in a red teddy. "Look at her, Munch. She's probably forty-five, married to an English teacher and living fat in the suburbs of Chicago."

"She ain't that fat."

"She ain't a twenty-two year old virgin who enjoys holding hands and watching college football, either. I mean, did you ever really look at these pictures, Munch?' He turned the page. "Like this girl—"

"Yeah, she's real pretty."

"Don't look at her. Look around her. The picture frames on the mantle are turned around. What's she hiding? The fireplace looks fake, or has never been used. See the hospital stamp on her blanket? The only way she would have that is if someone had been sent home wrapped in it. And who do you think took this picture? Her pimp? Or her boyfr—"

"Okay, okay. Geez, you gotta be a cop all the time? I was just looking at her fuckin' tits. Shit." Munchy stood, tucked his shirt tighter into his cinched-up pants. "I'm gonna do the count. Be back in fifteen."

Scruggs dropped the magazine into the trashcan when Munchy left the bubble. He twisted open his thermos of Mocha Delight and ran a camera check on the prison's exterior.

On the way up the stairs, Munchy muttered, "Find yourself a *real* woman. Get out in the *real* world. Fuckin' Scruggs." He glanced in the small windows of the cells, counted heads on makeshift pillows, flailing arms, thrashing legs or lumps under sheets. The metal clipboard was cool to his touch, the paper logbook soft and worn. As he approached the last cell on the upper tier, Munchy paused and looked around. Scruggs sipped from a plastic thermos lid in the bubble below. Rifleman stood in the crow's nest. Nothing moved in either direction. But, something was off. He listened, heard a few deep sighs, a meaty cough and some snoring. Everything sounded normal for midnight in Graterford, but something was wrong. The hairs went up on James P. Munsing's arms.

He stepped up to the nearest cell door and checked his sheet; Bentley and Ahzir. Their beds were empty, sheets neatly folded down. The cons sat cross-legged in the dark on the hard cold floor.

"What the fuck?' Munchy was about to rap on the door and tell those assholes to get on their trays, when he was struck by the absolute stillness. Had he been an enlightened man, he might have been able to truly feel the moment, to be as uninhibited as the two souls who had left the bodies of Ray and Shazad. Instead, Munchy registered fear. He felt overwhelmed. His breath grew loud. He heard nothing but the awful sounds of himself—rushing blood, pumping heart, and panting breath. Munchy took three steps backward until he bumped the railing with his ass, then bolted for the stairs.

"What is it?" Rifleman's voice broke the silence, crackling through the two-way.

Munchy spoke into the mic on his left shoulder, "Uh, nothing. I gotta take a dump."

"10-4."

Scruggs broke in, laughing. "Didn't your Mama tell you not to wait till the last minute, Munch?"

Munchy didn't reply. He was halfway to the bathroom and wasn't planning on coming out anytime soon.

Neither the locked door or thick cement block walls, nor

the armed guards or yards of barbed wire could contain their souls. Ray flew over buildings and landed lightly in trees. He felt the breeze on his back and smelled freshly mown grass. He smiled. A voice called to him and he floated down from the tree and stood with his long arms wide open. He saw no one. The voice grew louder. Still there was no one. Ray looked down. In a small bed at his feet, Tara lay curled on her side, a baby in her arms. He bent to touch her and a teardrop coursed down his cheek, splattered the bed and washed them away. Ray blinked. He was back in the cell, his bones cold and stiff.

Shazad sat next to him swaying, his lips moving as he whispered, "Munchy, Munchy. Do you feel me?"

Ray went to the sink, splashed water on his face and swallowed hard. He heard Shazad rise.

"Something is wrong, my friend?"

Ray said, "I saw Tara and the baby. Just like last time."

"It is what you want it to be. You see what you need to see."

"I don't need to see that. That's like a heroin dream or something. That's not real."

"How do you know?"

"What?"

"How do you know that it is not real? You said yourself Ray, you never knew what became of the baby, after..."

"After what? After Tara died?' Ray looked at his friend. "Is that what you were going to say, Shazad? Go on. Tell me what I don't know. I don't know what happened, except what her mother told me. Some stupid-ass letter telling me this is what's right for the baby. A second chance, a new beginning... Tara needed me, and where was I? I was here." Ray looked around, tears in his eyes. "I was here. I should've been with her. That motherfucker Gallo. If I'd been there, she'd be okay." Ray broke down sobbing.

Shazad held him. "I know, my friend, and Tara knows too. She has forgiven you, Ray. You need to forgive yourself. Listen to your heart; it will guide you."

Fast Eddie was on his way to losing his first case out of the courtroom. "Mariel, come on sweetheart, I didn't mean anything by it. It was just innocent flirtation... No. But that was months ago, you said you'd forgiven me... You can't take it back. Dammit, Mariel, you're acting like a child!" Deluca's phone lit up. "Listen, I have to go, Mariel. We'll talk about this later."

He clicked over to the other line, snapped, "Deluca. What is it?"

"Mr. Deluca, it's Sailor Beaumont. I had a message to call you."

"Ah, yes." He leaned back in his chair. "I need you to assist me on a few loose ends. Montgomery thought it would be appropriate."

"Appropriate? How's that?"

"Do you know the Witherspoons?"

"Richard and Lee?"

"Yes."

"They're friends of the family. I've known them for years."

"Good."

"Why? What's—"

"Did you see this morning's paper?"

"No, not yet."

"Let's just say, this is one socialite party I wish I hadn't missed. Be in my office in fifteen minutes." Deluca hung up.

Sailor rummaged through her backpack for the morning edition. She flipped the pages until she found what she was looking for. There was her father's friend on the front page of the Inquirer's Living section, wedged between two tall, large-breasted blondes. His hair was mussed, eyelids drooped, and there was something dark stuck between his front teeth. Richard Witherspoon III had seen better days. Worse yet, was the disgusted expression on his faithful wife in the background. The copy read, *Philadelphia Philanthropist or Philanderer?*

She had one thought, *phuck.* Sailor hung up the phone and began to read.

Two noisy gulls down by the water's edge fought over a piece of crab-infested kelp. Maria adjusted the beach towel under her head and scootched down into the sun-warmed blanket. She checked her watch then scanned the deserted strip of beach, saw the small human dot grow larger as he walked toward her, a straw bag in one hand and a picnic hamper in the other. Perfectly balanced. What had she ever done to deserve a guy like this? Maria smiled and waved. She couldn't see his face yet but knew he'd be grinning.

Her cell phone chirped once, twice. Maria pulled it from her handbag and checked the incoming number—unlisted.

"This is Maria."

"Nice day for the beach, eh, *Maria*?"

"Excuse me? Who is this?"

"Aw, I'm hurt. You don't remember me? What? Did you forget your own husband?"

She got it then and wondered why she was suddenly so popular with the Philly crowd. "That's *ex*-husband, Lou. And no, I didn't forget you." Thinking, how could I possibly forget you and saying instead, "Look, I'm busy. What do you want?"

"I need you to go to a party for me in Philadelphia and deliver a message."

Maria laughed. "Right. Now why the hell would I do that?"

"You want me to remind you, Sweetheart?"

When there was no reply he said, "I didn't think so." And went on, "Our friend, Detective Berger is finally retiring, and the city's putting on a shin dig at The Ritz. I can't be anywhere near town this weekend. So you're going go in my place. I'll put the invitation and the details in your mailbox."

"Wait a minute."

"Hey, buy Berger a nice present, would you?"

"Jesus, Lou. I can't."

"Yes, you can. And Maria?"

"What?"

"Tell your friend he looks good in blue."

"What?"

Maria stood up, phone to her ear and scanned the beach. Across the grassy dunes, on a crest of land by the access road, she glimpsed a large black SUV and two bulky figures. One man waved.

On the phone Gallo said, "Boo."

Maria watched the men climb into the vehicle and speed away. *Shit. He's here.*

9
Get Ready, Get Set

GINA tossed the cordless phone onto the bed then stepped into the steaming bath. Glass jars filled with colored powders lined the windowsill over the large tub. She selected the third jar from the right, sprinkling the purple dust as she sang softly, "Oh, when the shark bites, with his teeth dear..."

Scents of lavender, lemongrass and chamomile filled the room. Gina replaced the jar and sank into the water. A newspaper lay open on the floor near the toilet: Deluca's beaming face next to the hardened mug of her ex-husband Lou Gallo. The story continued from the front page under the headline, "Deluca Does It Again." Eddie was good. For a few minutes up there in the box, he even had Gina believing she'd been with Lou that night, that he hadn't been anywhere near the docks or the man with the crushed skull.

What a week. Between the courthouse, questions and reporters, all Gina wanted was a little peace and quiet. And for five blissful minutes, the only sound she heard was the drip of the faucet and the hum of the air-conditioner—

until the phone rang. Torn between duty and curiosity, she raised herself halfway from the warm water, then dropped back into the tub and let the machine pick up.

"Hey Babe. It's Hi. Guess I must have missed you. I called the diner. Susie said you were taking the day off. Bet you're getting all dolled up for the big party tonight, huh? I'll pick you up at seven, okay?' After a pause long enough to make Gina think he'd hung up, he added, "You know who loves you."

Gina closed her lips and disappeared under the lavender froth.

Reilly was in the bathroom again.

Sailor called down the hall, paper menu in hand, "How about pizza for lunch? Do you like pepperoni? Or they have Hawaiian…"

Reilly answered through the closed door. "Anything's fine with me." He hadn't really eaten in a day or two and wasn't hungry, but knowing what she wanted to hear he said, "Get whatever you want, Sailor."

"You sure?"

It sounded like she was just outside the door. Reilly said, "Yeah, sure," and wondered what she was waiting for. When he heard her on the phone in the kitchen, he snorted the last line.

In the living room, he ran a finger under his nose, pinched the nostrils and did a quick inhale. He wondered if he smelled okay and almost left the room to slick some deodorant under his pits then looked around the room and figured who the fuck cares. Newspapers and books overflowed from the easy chair onto the carpet. The thickest books were stuffed so full of notes and scraps of paper that their bindings had given way. Reilly hadn't seen the surface of the coffee table since he'd moved in, but was sure it was somewhere under the coffee cups, legal pads, files, pencils, highlighters and books. Against the wall, t-shirts and more trash littered the tops of poorly stacked, white file boxes.

Reilly plopped himself on the couch and flipped the page of his legal pad. He pretended to be interested in his notes as he watched Sailor in his kitchen. She tapped the pencil eraser into her chin, smiled into the phone. Reilly wanted to kiss her. Then he remembered who he was and where she came from. He looked away.

Sailor hung up the phone, saying, "Should be here in thirty minutes."

Reilly tugged a flat wallet from his back pocket, flipped it open. "How much is it?"

"Don't worry about it. I already paid him."

"You didn't have to do that." He pretended to flip through bills in his wallet. They were receipts, yellow, white, blue. "I got money."

"I know. You can pay next time, okay?' She smiled.

Next time. "Sure," he said and slipped his wallet back under him, back to the worn spot in his jeans.

"Do you have any beer?"

"In the fridge, bottom shelf."

Reilly admired the view of Sailor reaching into the refrigerator. As she approached him with her hands behind her back, he thought the view wasn't so bad from the front, either.

She said, "Which hand?"

He smiled, getting into it, thinking she was coming on to him. "The right. It's always the right."

Sailor revealed a box of garbage bags in her right hand, two beers in her left. "Sorry." She tossed the box to Reilly.

"What?"

"Go on." Sailor motioned to the messy room with a nod of her head then glanced at the beer. "It'll be here when you're done."

Reilly mumbled something about a slave driving clean freak and shot Sailor a mock evil look as he pushed himself off the couch. He almost bitched about having to clean up, when she sunk down into his recently vacated spot on the couch and crossed her long tan legs, tipped her head back and raised the beer to her lips. There was something about her throat, how it was so fully exposed, or the way her hair fell away from her face. Maybe it was the way he could almost follow the path of the beer from mouth to throat with each swallow, see the liquid moving down and down. *Jesus*. Reilly was suddenly very warm. Maybe cleaning up wasn't such a bad idea.

Sailor balanced the beer on her knee and licked her lips. She said, "Don't say I never gave you anything."

"Thanks, pal." Reilly pulled a bag from the box and shook it open. "So what were you saying about 'actus reus' and 'mens rea'?'

Sailor rubbed her bottom lip with her thumb. "The 'actus reus' is the guilty act and the 'mens rea' is the evil intent. But it depends on the state of mind, the depth of the intent, so to speak, that determines the degree of guilt."

"Which is how you get murder in the first degree."

"Premeditated."

"Or voluntary manslaughter."

"Or involuntary manslaughter."

Reilly said, "So, the harshness of the punishment depends on the degree of the intent."

Sailor nodded.

"Dude, that sucks."

"*Dude*, that's the law."

And it was. There were people who said trust the system and justice will prevail. But they were the ones who would never be put to the test. They lived safe and warm in their glass houses on the hill, setting their alarm systems every night and crawling into bed after a Seconal and scotch. They were the same people who misunderstood poverty and unemployment, the same ones who treated child prostitutes as criminals instead of victims. They used generic phrases like, "They must not want it enough," "You just don't wake up one day and that's your life," and

"Anyone can get a job."

They tossed things back into the world that didn't make sense, ignoring the fact that it had taken money, connections and beauty to get them what they had. Not everyone was so lucky.

Reilly finished clearing the trash and stacked the bags at the door. He watched Sailor run that same thumb over her plump lip and wondered what she was thinking about and if he'd ever get the balls up to ask her out—on a real date.

He said something so she'd look at him. "Have you talked to Banning lately?"

"Not since Friday. Why?"

"I heard there might be a new case, something more...challenging."

"Challenging?" Sailor scoffed. "What could be more challenging than representing bums who pee in storefronts, or women who think the asshole that's been beating on them for five years will suddenly stop when a piece of paper is filed? Don't forget, we're the interns, lowest on the totem pole. They won't be giving us any *challenging* cases."

Reilly reached for his beer and sat on the couch next to Sailor. "I know, I know what they say. Pay your dues, prove yourself and all that, but Missy said—oh maybe I shouldn't tell you." He took a long pull on the beer.

"What did Missy say?" Sailor asked.

Reilly belched into his hand. "Just that some guy called from prison. Poor son of a bitch didn't know his lawyer kicked the bucket. It's kind of funny, actually."

Sailor shot him a look.

"Yeah. Well anyway, it's one of the Herring cases that Banning's assigning. He didn't say anything to you about it? I mean, you did spend the day with him, and all."

"We were working together, if that's what you mean."

Reilly said, "I know, I just thought." He didn't know what he thought. But from the way Sailor was looking at him, Reilly could figure out what she thought. That he was acting like a real jerk.

Sailor shook her head. "Maybe he's waiting for our meeting on Monday. Damn, I'm already working four. How many do you have?"

"Six."

"Six? How the hell did you get six?"

Reilly shrugged, "Double duty, remember?"

Sailor looked at Reilly, noticed his red eyes. No wonder the guy's beat. He must be putting in twelve hours a day at MDB&S, and with the studies and the gig at The Comedy Club, he'd hardly have time to eat, much less sleep.

But if that's what it took, she'd do the same. There were only so many slots to fill. Sometimes she felt guilty, knowing Dad had pulled a few strings to get her here. But she'd had the grades, and this was where she wanted to be—because of Mom. She wondered if Reilly's family was supportive, then she stopped herself. That was his business. And besides, they were only here for the summer and they were here to work, not build a long-lasting friendship or anything else.

"What is it?" Reilly said.

Sailor looked away. "I was just thinking, it would be great if we knew more about the case, maybe had some background." She flipped to a fresh page in the legal pad. "Do you remember the guy's name?"

Reilly hopped up. "Oh, you are gonna love me for this. Wait here."

He disappeared down the hall. Sailor heard something crash, some cursing and then Reilly was back, holding a thick, worn file over his heaving chest. He stood there with his flushed cheeks and saucer-sized pupils, adorable in a friend-of-your-little-brother way. But there was something else. Something brewing just below the surface, something that touched her and it wasn't just that he could make her laugh.

He said, "I got it."

"What?"

"The case. Commonwealth of Pennsylvania v. Raymond Moses Bentley."

"How did you get the case out of the office? Never mind, I don't want to know."

Reilly grinned. He sat down and opened the file. "That's Ray."

Sailor took a long look at the skinny black man with the swollen eye, bruised cheekbone and overgrown Afro. His shirt was torn and there was dried blood under his nose, but he held his head high and in his one good eye, she could see determination. "What the hell happened to him?"

"He confessed."

"Well, there's that, but I was talking about the hair, and that shirt!"

"Sailor. He's been in prison since 1977."

"Oh." She started flipping pages, then stopped and looked sideways at Reilly. He was too quiet. "There's something more, isn't there?"

Reilly smiled. Sailor liked him like this. Confident. Quiet. Still.

"Oh yeah, there's more." Reilly jumped up, began pacing and reciting the facts of the case. Names, dates, convictions and appeals. It had all the makings of a landmark case: coerced confession, prosecutorial misconduct, drugs, mafia, bad cops, bad laws and now a big, bad prison.

Sailor couldn't believe it. She shook her head saying softly, "It's Banning's next Failson-Nough."

"It's better than that. It's *our* Failson-Nough. We could be famous."

Sailor leaned over Ray's picture and said, "We could make history." Then softer, "What did they do to you?"

Reilly tapped the attorney's name on the file. "I never liked Deluca, you know?"

"What do you mean?" Sailor asked.

"I don't know, it was just a feeling, like he was always

trying too hard, or hiding something."

"He's had it rough."

"Rough?"

"Easy, there. I just meant, with him losing his family and all. It was a tragedy. Such a gifted man, cut down in his prime."

Reilly snorted. "Cut down in his prime? Jesus. Listen to you. The guy's only human. And a lousy human at that!

"Hey. Be nice."

"Tell that to Ray." Reilly finished his beer, set the empty next to Ray's open file and looked at Sailor. "Wake up, Sleeping Beauty. Deluca was the prosecutor in Ray Bentley's case, and look at all the stuff he missed. Don't try to tell me he was gifted. More like he was the gift. Bought and paid for in full."

"What are you saying?"

"What, Sailor, can't you believe there are bad people on the right side of the law, too?'

Reilly went to the file boxes, slipped out a folder and said, "Listen to this. 'Commonwealth v. Hix, July 1981. Detective Hiram Berger, investigator. Edward John Deluca, defense counsel.'"

Sailor started to say something, but Reilly hushed her with a hand as he skimmed the page.

"Hix, arrested on a murder/robbery charge in 1975, charges are dropped for lack of evidence then he's re-arrested and taken to trial in 1981 where *Deluca,* as defense attorney, goes on record about a known drug dealer, *James King.*"

Sailor had to say something now. "Hold on. The same Detective Berger that beat the confession out of Ray?"

"The same Deluca who said there were no drugs in King's Variety store, even put that woman, Maria on the stand to say so."

"Maria Conchetta? Let me see that." Sailor reached for the file, began flipping through the pages. "This is huge, Reilly. You realize that, don't you? Where's Hix now?"

"Died 1998, in Alabama."

"Well there goes that depo." She picked up her pad. "You've got everyone in here but—"

"The mayor?" offered Reilly.

"Yeah, really," Sailor said.

Reilly held up his hand, ticking off his fingers, "We've got Gallo working for King."

"Dead," Sailor said.

"We've got LeChance buying drugs from King."

"Dead and dead."

"And," Reilly continued, "Ray Bentley mentions Moreno."

"Great, add one convict and a Mob Kingpin."

"Don't forget our pal Deluca and the cop, Berger."

"Alive and kicking."

Reilly drummed his fingers on a leg, "Maybe I *should* go."

"What? Go where?" Sailor asked.

Reilly smiled. "To a party."

"What are you talking about? One minute we're discussing a case, now you want to go to a party? Are you serious, Reilly?"

"Dead serious. This is for the case."

"What does a party have to do with Ray Bentley?"

"It's Detective Berger's retirement party. And MDB&S is helping to foot the bill. Apparently Hiram Berger did a few favors for the big guns in the past, and this is their way of showing appreciation for one of Philly's finest. Everyone who's anyone will be at The Ritz tonight."

"And we'll just walk right in?" Sailor scoffed.

"Well, sort of."

Sailor looked cautious. "Sort of, Reilly?"

"All you have to do is call Deluca and have him invite you."

"Call Deluca? Me. Uh, no." Sailor fell back onto the couch cushions, shaking her head.

Reilly leaned in. "Just tell him you have to talk to him.

He's sweet on you and he'll want you to go with him. I know for a fact he got dumped today, and the last thing Fast Eddie wants is his picture in tomorrow's social pages without a beautiful girl on his arm. So, here." Reilly pulled a tiny silver phone from his pocket and tossed it to Sailor.

She caught the phone.

Reilly grinned, knowing he had her. "Worse case scenario, counselor?"

Sailor gave him her best *why-I-oughta* look, then punched in the number to the MDB&S message service.

A few clicks later she was connected to Deluca's cellular.

"Deluca? Sailor Beaumont. I have some information on the Witherspoon case. I could send it to Mimi, but I think you're going to want to see this yourself."

Deluca pulled his eyes from the jiggling breasts of the manicurist, tried to concentrate on what Sailor was saying. He'd been wondering what the rest of the girl's tattoo looked like and wasn't happy about the interruption. But he switched hands and let the girl buff and file as he spoke into the phone. "Why don't you bring it with you tonight."

"Tonight?"

"There's an MDB&S function. Didn't you get the memo?" he quipped. They didn't call him Fast Eddie for nothing.

"I guess I missed that."

"That's okay. It's at the Ritz at eight. I'll have a car pick you up."

"No," she said, " I mean, why don't we meet you there? Mr. Reilly and I, that is."

Deluca scoffed. "Sure, Reilly's welcome to tag along. And Sailor?"

"Yes?"

"You might want to help him dress."

Sailor closed the cell phone, tossed it to Reilly. "We're in."

Reilly whooped, raising his palms to the ceiling. "Party.

Party. We goin' to a party."

Sailor watched him dance around. He was undeniably cute and with that body... She looked away, gathered her things. "Yeah, Ry. We going, all right. Listen." She glanced at her watch. "We've got less than four hours and I've got to do some shopping."

"Me, too."

"Please, don't say Wal-Mart."

"Hell, no. Radio Shack."

"*Radio* Shack? I don't want to know. Do I?"

Reilly smiled, held a finger to his lips, shaking his head.

Sailor hesitated at the door, not wanting to leave. It was so quiet in her apartment, so empty. She looked back at Reilly standing at the stereo, CD in hand. "Wear a suit, Reilly. And a clean shirt. I'll pick you up at seven-thirty."

"Works for me." Reilly turned up the volume as she left, then danced to his bedroom, making another pit stop in the bathroom.

10
Life is One Big Party

A man in a black suit and small cap stood near the open door of the Lincoln Town car parked on the tarmac. Maria looked through the plane's tiny window. She could see Philadelphia's high rises in the distance and wished Mama was still alive to see her baby coming home in a private plane on the arm of a doctor. She would love him.

Doc finished signing paperwork with the pilot. "Great flight, James. See you tomorrow." He waved off any assistance, grabbed two bags from the underbelly of the plane and tossed them in the trunk of the waiting car.

Traffic was worse than Maria remembered. Unhappy memories came rushing back with every mile. There was no ocean to gaze into, no gardening to demand her attention, no distractions, except the one sitting next to her. She raised the driver's partition and distracted herself all the way to the hotel.

The penthouse suite was fairytale perfect, lace and satin, glass and silver. Maria sipped the complimentary Chardonnay and took her time getting dressed while Doc napped on the large bed. She watched him sleep, glad she hadn't come alone. She allowed herself to believe, if only for a minute, that everything would be okay. Maybe she would go to the party, deliver the message and that would be the end of it. Maybe she could go back to Cape Cod and start her new life with Doc, putting her past behind her once and for all. Maybe she wouldn't have the dreams here—the ones where she stood on a street corner talking to strangers and calling them by name. The dreams that ended like nightmares, with shouting, guns and blood.

"You're beautiful."

Maria turned around. Doc stared at her from the bed. How long had he been awake?

She went to the bed and kissed him then asked, "Could you?" She turned her back so that he could pull up the long zipper on the satin gown. The deep navy dress complimented the sapphire earrings perfectly and a large opal brooch winked from her cleavage.

Doc whistled. "I'll be the envy of every man at that party."

Maria's smile disappeared. "Well, let's not make them wait any longer then."

It was hot and humid in Philly. Hair stuck to the pimply foreheads of the valet runners. Their starched white shirts bunched up under snug red vests and escaped waistbands of black Dockers. Ties hung loosened and askew. Their mandatory black sneakers served them well as they sprinted from parking garages three and five blocks away. They drove Bentleys and Porsches, Mercedes and Lexus SUVs. They fought over Ferraris and made themselves scarce when a minivan was next in line. The tips were good, the hours great. But it was the driving they loved.

Maria and Doc arrived in a white stretch limousine. Cameras flashed, reporters scribbled as security men spoke into shoulder mics. The party was in full swing.

Sailor drove while Reilly went over the plan. Her purse was now a fully automatic camera and Reilly was wired with a mini-recorder. Sailor declined the hardware, claiming she had her own secret weapon. One look at her dress, and Reilly had to agree. They pulled up to the stoplight.

Reilly fumbled with wires attached to a gold angel-shaped pin. "Why do I feel like I'm in a bad Scooby-Doo episode?"

Sailor giggled. "Here. Let me help you." She tucked the wires inside his shirt, straightened the lapel pin and tightened his tie before the light changed.

Constructed in 1908 as a bank, the neoclassical building that now housed the Ritz-Carlton had been modeled after the Pantheon. Sitting at the right hand of City Hall, the world class hotel with its adjoining thirty story tower was an impressive sight, even to Sailor who'd seen the ruins of the real thing.

As they approached the huge columns at the entrance, they heard strains of music. A little Jimmy Buffet escaped with each pull of the heavy glass doors. The doorman tipped his hat and motioned with a white-gloved hand to enter. Reilly hung back. A small group of men stood just inside the rotunda at the nearest column, their eyes on the arrivals. Whether they were waiting for someone or hoping for someone was unclear. It was obvious only that they were alone and uncomfortable. A similar group of well-dressed women gathered on the opposite side of the entrance. It was like dance night at Catholic school.

Fast Eddie Deluca noticed Sailor, excused himself from his conversation with an older couple and approached. "There you are. I was beginning to wonder if you'd changed your mind." He held out his arm. "Shall we?"

Sailor looked for Reilly, who smiled and waved, then ran a hand through his hair and adjusted his lapel pin.

Deluca spoke into Sailor's ear, steering her by the elbow toward the rotunda bar outside the ballroom. "You clean up good, Beaumont." She felt his eyes on her. "You got something for me?"

"Excuse me?' Sailor jerked her head back, twisting to face him. Deluca's blue eyes twinkled, half a smile on his full lips.

Sailor understood what women saw in him. His custom-tailored suit fit his body like a glove. Cufflinks on his sleeve gleamed as only real gold and diamonds do. The streaks of gray at his temples gave him just the right amount of authority and the year-round tan hinted of a life of leisure. He was a walking advertisement for success. And he smelled good, too. Sailor drew her eyes back up to his face, reminding herself she was here for information, and nothing else.

"Well?' Deluca seemed amused. "Witherspoon?"

"Oh," she said. "Yes, of course. I had the most interesting conversation with my father about Mr. Witherspoon and his condition."

Deluca raised his brow.

"Oh yes," Sailor nodded. "Mr. Witherspoon should have known better than to mix over-the-counter allergy tabs with his heart medication."

Deluca grinned, then motioned to a strolling waiter. He selected two flutes of champagne from the waiter's tray and handed one to Sailor.

"Beautiful. I knew you were the right girl for the job." He toasted her. "To success!"

"To success."

Sailor drank, toying with the long pendant that swung between her breasts, pleased to see Deluca's eyes follow. It was like taking candy from a baby.

In the Grand Ballroom, Reilly found the hors d'ouevre table and would have pulled up a chair if he hadn't heard the guy next to him say, "Berger looks the same, don't he?"

"Yeah," the other guy said. "Still looks a like an asshole." They laughed.

Reilly followed their gaze to a table near the stage. A loud group of cops clinked mugs with a guy in a Hawaiian shirt. Berger. Reilly watched him move off, thinking he looked familiar, but it was too far away to get a good look. The guys went back to drinking and punching each other on the arm, while at their table three buxom, bored redheads waited.

Reilly saw his in. He bought a pitcher of beer from the bar and headed over to the table. "Refill, boys?"

The cops looked at him, then the full pitcher and shrugged.

Across the room, Sailor watched Reilly. The guy worked fast. He had the redheads smiling and the cops drinking. A few feet to her right, Deluca had been pulled into a conversation with an up-and-comer in the hotel business. She pretended to be interested in the architecture and decor of the room, as she worked the hidden purse camera. Detective Berger was easy to find, with everybody buying him shots and toasting him. Sailor took pictures of anyone he talked to.

She saw Reilly snaking through the crowd with two empty beer pitchers held overhead. He saw Sailor and headed her way.

"How's it going?"

Sailor tipped her head in Deluca's direction, "It's going."

"I know what you mean. I swear, if I have to keep up with these dicks for another hour, I'll be too shit-faced to remember to turn on my recorder when they finally do say something important. I don't know how many more blowjob-in-the-patrol-car stories I can listen to and frankly, I'm running out of cop jokes."

"Just do your best. Drop some names, see what kind of reaction you get."

"Yeah." Reilly glanced at Deluca, then back at Sailor. "And, I'll try to keep my eye on you, so I can, you know."

"What? Rescue me?" she said.

"I'd love to," Reilly said.

Sailor laughed, surprised that she wanted him to do just

that. She met Reilly's eyes and almost said, "Let's get out of here." She imagined them running out of the ballroom holding hands like in a sappy musical, her glass slippers tapping across the marble floor. But Reilly wasn't anyone's Prince Charming, so she said, "Shouldn't you be getting back with those?"

And maybe it came out a little rougher than she'd hoped. Reilly looked down at the pitchers he'd forgotten he was holding and when he looked up, Sailor darted her eyes away, as if she was searching for someone in the crowd.

Reilly followed her gaze. "Who's that?"

"Who?"

"The blonde in the blue dress," he said. "The one talking to the band leader."

"Isn't that-"

"Gina," he said.

"Yeah," Sailor said. "Wait. Reilly, do you know her?"

"We've met."

"You've met?" she asked.

"Yeah. She helped me with some directions."

"Reilly, that's Berger's *girlfriend*. Gina Chamblee? Deluca had her on the stand last week, remember? She was Lou Gallo's alibi."

"No," Reilly said. "That can't be right. I heard Gallo was with his ex-wife. Hold on a second."

"Hold on a second? Reilly? Where are you going?"

It didn't matter what she said, because Sailor was talking to his back as Reilly snatched champagne and glasses from an empty table in exchange for the pitchers. He pushed and excused himself through the crowd to get to Gina.

"Pardon me," he said to her sequined back, his breath warm on her neck. "Would you know where I can find the best breakfast in town?"

Gina spun around. "Mr. Reilly?" She laughed. "Are you lost again?"

Reilly smiled. "'If I am lost, let me search no more. 'Tis here I find all that I need or wish for.'" He handed her a glass. "Don't ask me who said that. If I could remember the rest, I'd give them credit."

"It's lovely. You're a man of surprises."

They touched glasses. Reilly said, "To my inspiration."

Gina took a sip, smiling. "So tell me, what are you doing here?"

Reilly looked around. "Isn't this the Alfonso wedding? I was hoping to kiss the bride."

Gina laughed. "Sorry, no brides here. You'll have to find someone else to plant that kiss on."

"I don't think that will be difficult."

"You sound pretty sure of yourself," she said finishing her drink, then handing him the empty glass. "As a matter of fact, you're beginning to sound like Fast Eddie."

Before Reilly could respond, the song ended and the band moved off stage, to be replaced by a silver-haired gentleman at the microphone. The man cleared his throat, then raised his glass. The words were carefully chosen, his voice strong with the Irish lilt that was his calling card. "To my dear friend, Hiram. May you never forget what is worth remembering—aye—or remember what is best forgotten. Happy Retirement, my lad."

Cheers of "Happy Retirement!" resounded through the ballroom.

Reilly whispered in Gina's ear. "Is that who I think it is?"

"The one and only. His honor, E. Patrick Shanahan."

Oh, this just gets better and better," Reilly muttered.

"Sorry? I couldn't hear you."

"I said, I think I'd like a little bread and butter. Would you excuse me?"

"Sure. Looks like I'm needed, anyway." She tilted her head toward the table of tough guys. They were attempting to lift Berger and pass him through the crowd.

Reilly made his way back to Sailor. A redwood of a

man blocked his path. Reilly reached up to tap the man's shoulder. "Excuse me."

The giant turned around. "Yes?"

"Sorry, I just wanted to get through."

Sailor heard Reilly.

The large man stepped aside, his arm knocking a waitress who went sprawling, dropping her tray of crabmeat canapés and staining the white dress of a guest.

Sailor pulled Reilly closer. "Kenneth Reilly, this is Jeremy Strom."

The men shook hands. Reilly winced.

"I was just telling Jeremy how you left me standing here all alone."

"Me? Where's your escort?"

Sailor shrugged, finished another glass of champagne.

Strom answered for her. "Mister Deluca was called away, and that's okay by me, pal, I never would have had the distinct pleasure of meeting this fine gal, if you two hadn't abandoned her the way you did."

Reilly couldn't take his eyes off the huge man before him. He was as big as a linebacker, as handsome as a movie star, but had a voice that sounded like Sylvester the cat. Reilly didn't know whether to laugh at him or cheer for average guys with normal voices everywhere. "How do you know Detective Berger?"

"I work for Deluca. Used to be in the old days, Berger was the kind of guy you kept close. Know what I mean?" Jeremy tried to wink, ended up blinking both large cornflower eyes.

Reilly nodded knowingly. The band began to play a loud dance tune, fortunately rendering all conversation impossible. Reilly mimed sipping a beer then waved goodbye. Sailor replied by scratching her cheek with her middle finger.

Reilly made his way to the bar. Waiting for his beer, he searched the crowd. His eye landed on Gina, the youngest one at a table of white-haired women. As she leaned forward to speak to one of the women, her dress fell away from her chest.

"Nice, eh?" The man on his left elbowed him, hard.

"Excuse me?' Reilly turned to the voice.

Hiram Berger squinted his bloodshot beady eyes, tried to still his body's sway by leaning into the mahogany bar.

"I said, nice. As in, her tits are nice. Don't you think?"

"I wouldn't know." Reilly ran his eyes over the room. "I was just looking for my friend."

"I saw you talking to her, earlier." Berger took a long pull on his beer. "Haven't I seen you around?"

"I don't think so."

"Yeah well, I'm getting older, the memory is going. Probably why they retire us at this age. Nobody wants a cop with a bad memory, right?' Berger at his own joke, spilling beer on his pants.

Reilly forced a smile. Berger made him uncomfortable. There was something creepy about him. Like a caged hyena, he seemed harmless enough, until the raw meat hit the concrete.

Maria watched Berger give some good-looking kid a hard time at the bar. *Still a jackass, aren't you, Detective? Nice choice for your party. The loud Hawaiian shirt, tuxedo pants and sneakers. Look at you: fat, balding and now a has-been, too.* She smiled.

"What are you thinking about, darling? Do you feel okay?" Doc asked.

"I'm fine. I was thinking how happy you make me." Maria lifted Doc's hand to her cheek, kissed his palm. What the hell was she doing here? It was loud and busy and smoky, and the waiter had probably lost her note to Berger.

She should have said no, and accepted the consequences, should have made Lou and Deluca do their own dirty work. She was tired. Too tired. She wanted to go home, but when a woman in a rainbow dress approached she realized she was cornered. It had been years, but Maria would have known her anywhere. Mrs. E. Patrick Shanahan, Kate.

Doc stood with Maria to greet the woman. The ladies exchanged air kisses, then Maria introduced Doc and there was another round of kisses.

Kate Shanahan smelled the way women with money smell. Rich. Her beaded dress bulged over an obvious girdle and she struggled to speak over an unruly maribou wrap that circled her neck. A few errant feathers stuck to her bright red lipstick, giving His Honor's wife the appearance of a well-fed fox.

"Kate, you're just in time," Maria said. "I need to find the ladies room, and Doc is dying to dance. Aren't you, darling?"

"Only if Kate will have me."

"You'll be lucky to get him back." Kate tugged Doc through the crowd to the dance floor, feathers flying.

Doc mouthed, *Help me,* making Maria laugh.

She waited until the crowd swallowed them, then took her purse and glass and slipped out of the ballroom. The note she'd given the waiter asked Berger to meet her in the cigar bar's humidor. She hoped he wouldn't be late.

11

Extenuating Circumstances

AND that was when I knew I was going to be a lawyer," finished Deluca.

Sailor furrowed her brow. "But, that was just a television show. How could you base your whole life on a television show?"

"Hey, I was seven. What the hell did I know? So, tell me something about you? How did you get to be so beautiful?' Deluca popped the cork on another bottle of Dom Perignon.

It had been his idea to come here, with a little coaxing from Sailor and the dress. And here they were in a million dollar condo sipping hundred-dollar champagne and pretending neither one of them knew what they were really doing. Sailor watched Deluca as he refilled her glass, wondered how long it was going to take for the capsule to work. She must have slipped it in Deluca's second glass, and weren't they on their fourth? Reilly assured her he'd never know what hit him.

Deluca sat beside her on his suede couch, an arm draped casually over the back. He said, "I bet your Mom's a real knockout, isn't she?"

My Mom? God, I can't believe I'm doing this. "Oh, Eddie. Let's not talk about me anymore. Let's talk about you." She watched Deluca struggle with his bow tie. *Jesus, he's pathetic.* "Here."

Sailor set her glass on the table and pulled herself into his lap. "Let me." She slowly untied the knot and began unbuttoning his shirt. She could hear his breath quickening, feel his pulse in his neck. It wasn't what she was here for she reminded herself. But, damn he really did smell nice.

Sipping his Dom, Deluca regaled his female companion with tales from his youth. Boarding school in England, his years at Harvard Law, the trip around the world. Sailor nodded at all the right times, but her mind wandered. She needed to keep him talking, but she was also dying to snoop. Here she was, an arm's length from a home office crammed with files and papers and probably a state of the art computer system.

Sailor had to agree with Reilly. There was more to the Bentley case. And that more had something to do with Deluca. On the way to the party, Reilly had filled her in on Deluca's past. It seemed her "ideal" attorney figure had a few skeletons in his closet. According to Reilly, in the seventies when most people were concerned about war and peace, Deluca's focus never left the city. He made cleaning up the streets his priority. As one of Philly's Assistant District Attorneys, Deluca had a hand in everything, legal and not, and he worked it. Cops respected him. Judges ruled for him. The public loved him. Deluca was on his way up. He seemed to have it all.

Then something happened. In a matter of months, Deluca took a nose dive. He lost three consecutive cases, all mob-related. There were rumors of jury tampering. Then, a co-worker filed sexual harassment charges and photographs of Deluca in compromising situations with women named Candy and Starr started appearing in the paper. His marriage fell apart and his high-school-sweetheart-wife filed for divorce. It was public and messy and expensive, forcing him to sell his family house and sell out his inheritance. Fast Eddie was living a quicksand life. Some said his father's sudden death was the final straw.

But somebody did Deluca a favor. Montgomery and Scott offered him a job on the other side of the courtroom and he began again—defending the same people he had worked for years to put away. Publicly, it was said to be a political move, but behind closed doors, folks said he sold out. Some thought the mob owned him, others couldn't care less. They were just happy to not have to work with him anymore. He could be a real pain in the ass. And now Sailor, in the pleasure of his company, had to agree.

"May I?" she pointed to the stereo system.

"Be my guest." Deluca kicked off his shoes and leaned back on the couch, hands behind his head.

Pulling out all the stops, Sailor arched her back and sashayed over to the entertainment wall. She flipped her hair back, bent over a stack of CD's, ass to the ceiling. Deluca watched appreciatively from the couch, eyes at half-mast. She loaded the music in the carousel, adjusted the volume. Soft strains of an alto sax filled the room. She dimmed the lights, posing by the wall of glass facing the marina. Soft moonlight cast her in silhouette. The effect was not lost on her audience.

"Oh yeah."

The sax wailed, Sailor began to dance a sexy strip tease, slowly first, drawing her hands over her hips and thighs then back up again into her hair, then faster, gyrating her hips, throwing her head back and exposing her throat. Her high, firm breasts were barely contained by the low-cut gown. She turned away from Deluca, reached behind her neck, loosened the halter-top knot and let the top fall. Bare to the navel, she turned around and approached the couch, her long pendant swaying from breast to breast.

"Eddie," Sailor said watching Deluca. He was almost

out, fighting to stay awake. "You like what you see, don't you?"

Deluca smiled, then slumped into himself. Sailor waited a few seconds then stretched him out on the couch, pulling up his legs. She leaned over, skimming her breasts over his chest and kissed his cheek, smiled at his goofy grin and the rather impressive tent in his trousers.

"Maybe another time, *Fast* Eddie."

Retying her dress, Sailor headed for Deluca's office.

Maria walked into Vault tavern, looking out of place among the burly men. Maybe this hadn't been such a good idea. She made her way past the crowded bar and the smoking room to the walk-in humidor. The door opened easily, a whoosh of regulated air. It was still, quiet and smelled of more than tobacco. There was a hint of men's cologne, bourbon and cedar. She closed her eyes and saw Puerto Rico—stony streets and dirty alleys, yelling mamas, a man with a belt. She blinked, had to remind herself she was in The Ritz-Carlton in Philadelphia, and no longer a naive young girl.

Berger pushed on the door too hard, smacking it into a rack of Havana imports.

"Fuck. Smells like my old man in here!" He was drunk, swaying. He looked around, stopped on Maria.

"Congratulations on your retirement, Detective."

"Well thank you, sugar. Now come over here and give an old cop some love."

He grabbed at his crotch, missed the first time. "Whaddya say?'

Berger stepped closer to Maria, squinting. "I know you." He tried to snap his fingers. "Little Maria Conchetta. I'll be damned."

Maria muttered, "Yes, you will."

"Well, well, aren't you all grown up." He ran his eyes over her. "Did fine for yourself, didn't you, Maria? Got yourself another Sugar Daddy? What's he into? Gambling?

Money laundering? Not drugs. No, no, no."

Berger waggled his finger in Maria's general direction, fumbled a fat cigar off the shelf and stuck it in the corner of his mouth. "Well, pleased as I am to see you, you'd better get out of here. I'm meeting someone, and you don't want to be anywhere around when he gets here."

"Lou isn't coming, Detective."

"What do you mean, he isn't coming?"

"He sent me." Maria crossed the small space. She reached up and tugged the cigar from his mouth. Spit shined on the back end. She held it gingerly. "Listen. You're working for Gallo now. Meet him at Pier 12. Tomorrow night at ten. Look for a Chinese crate marked C445. You know the drill. Pier 12, C445, 10 p.m. Can you remember that, Detective?' He nodded, still staring at her. She pushed the cigar back between his slack lips and left.

Berger stared after her, didn't notice the waitress in the doorway until she said, "Need anything, Mister?"

He blinked. "Yeah."

The waitress stepped halfway in, holding the heavy door with her hip.

Berger took the soggy cigar from his mouth and laid it in the nearest box. *Arturo Fuente Grand Reserve*, $11.75.

The girl grimaced. Berger belched loudly, blowing beer-scented air to the ceiling. As he looked up, his body made circles of its own, defying the stillness of the environmentally perfect room. The girl looked over her shoulder at the bar and wished she hadn't stopped here. She had a napkin full of orders already.

"Let me use your pen." Berger grabbed a pack of matches from her tray and motioned for her pen. She hesitated, then handed it over. Berger scribbled something on the matchbook, shoved it into his pocket and dropped the pen on the girl's tray. He stumbled out of the humidor and made his way to the exit, one hand on the wall, the other on his stomach.

The waitress called after him. "You okay, Mister?"

Berger kept going. Double doors were propped open with two silver ash cans at the end of the hallway. Berger focused on the space between the cans. Air. Door. Outside. Air. Door. Outside. He stepped into the Philly night and fell onto his knees between the perfectly trimmed hedges. He puked up three pitchers of beer, four shots of tequila and seventy-five bucks worth of spicy Maryland crab.

A few minutes later, a janitor pushed a gray cleaning cart up the path toward the open doors. He saw Berger's feet before he heard the guy heaving in the bushes.

"Must have been some party, man. Some party." He snapped his headphones over his ears, cranked the volume and sang, "Welcome to the jungle."

12
The Morning After
and Then Some

REILLY smelled coffee. He rolled out of the tangled sheets of his bed, wondering when the girl had left. He followed the scent to the kitchen where the coffeemaker gurgled out the last cup. Thick brown heaven filled the carafe. Reilly grabbed a dirty mug from the dishwasher, rinsed it out then dried it on his boxers and poured a steaming mug. He took a sip, closed his eyes and sighed.

"It's not too strong, is it?"

Reilly jumped. Coffee sloshed over the lip of the mug onto his bare foot, hot, then warm between his toes.

"Too strong? Not for me." He took another sip. "I like it like this."

"Me too."

The girl was in the living room on her hands and knees. Her wet hair made a dark mark on the back of her shirt. She reached under the coffee table for a single black stocking and snapped it toward Reilly. He grinned, raising his mug in a mock toast. She tucked the stocking into her purse and slipped on her shoes. Reilly watched her button the pink satin blouse over her large breasts. She had to suck in to tuck the shirt into her black leather mini-skirt.

She said, "I'd better go. It's my turn to take Grandma to church."

She approached the breakfast bar gathering up her bushy hair and twisting it into a loose bun. She jabbed a pencil into the mess, securing it. Reilly watched her, admired the way her breasts fell back into place when she dropped her arms.

"Can I have some?" She asked, pointing to the coffeepot.

Reilly poured the coffee, trying to remember her name.

The girl chugged the hot coffee: "God, I love a good, hot..." she passed her eyes over Reilly's bare chest "...strong..." she licked her lips "...cup of coffee."

She rubbed her abdomen, walked around the counter to Reilly. "Is it true you can burn your stomach lining if you drink hot coffee too fast?"

She took Reilly's mug out of his hand, set it down and moved his hand to her stomach. "My roommate's always saying, 'Slow down, Shelly.' Is she right?"

Reilly moved his hand lower. "I wouldn't know, Shelly. I'm studying law, not medicine. But I don't think you'd burn your stomach." He pulled her close, his hand on the small of her back. "Maybe right here." He reached out, skimmed two fingers from the base of her chin down her throat. She tipped her head back in response. Reilly paused, his fingertips in the valley between her collarbones. She pressed into him and they kissed. Warm coffee tongues and bruised lips, nerves still raw from the night of excess.

Shelly broke the embrace, moaning softly. Her cheeks were flushed. "Don't start something you can't finish."

"Who says I can't finish?"

Shelly laughed, slapping his arm playfully. "I have to go."

"Are you sure? I can be very fast."

She laughed. "I wouldn't advertise that."

She opened her phone, asked for a taxi service, reading his address off a stack of mail on the counter. She finished her coffee and headed to the door, calling over her shoulder, "I left my number on your desk and my email, just in case."

Reilly followed her to the door, kissed her good-bye, murmuring something more than his usual false promises, then watched her strut down the hall to the elevator, wishing the whole time that Sailor would poke her head out of her apartment.

He went back to his kitchen, to his coffee and remembered last night's dream. He and Sailor had been walking on a garden path. Sailor wore a white dress. Reilly held a red flower the size of a dinner plate. Dark green vines curled around thick tree trunks and yellow, orange and purple flowers bloomed at every turn. The path kept circling, but they never passed the same sight twice. Every few feet, Reilly looked down and saw that he had lost something. A shoe, a sock, then his pants and shirt. He felt the breeze on his bare body. Sailor walked next to him. She was talking as if nothing was happening. She was so beautiful. A halo of white butterflies encircled her head. He reached out to touch her face. She became Gina. He leaned forward and kissed Gina's lips. They changed and he was kissing Ray, their teeth smashing, his mouth too big. When Reilly opened his eyes in the garden, no one was there. He dropped the red flower and ran, naked and cold, into a tangle of briars.

An hour later, Reilly knocked on Sailor's door.

"Just a second," Sailor called, wincing. She rolled off the couch, holding one hand to the side of her head as if the contents would dribble out of her ear. She checked the peephole then unlatched the door and let Reilly inside.

"Don't look at me. I look like shit. And for God's sake,

don't make me laugh." She shuffled back to the couch and lay down, watching him from hooded eyes.

Even hung-over, she was beautiful. Reilly couldn't bring himself to give her a hard time. "Maybe I can help." He held up a small blue package labeled, "Morning Relief", a bottle of acetaminophen and tea bags. "Reilly's remedy."

He went to the kitchen. It was clean and organized with healthy green plants everywhere. He put the kettle on and filled two water glasses, pouring the powder from the blue package into one.

"Oh, my head." Sailor moaned from the other room. "I thought good champagne wasn't supposed to give you a hangover."

"Here." Reilly returned with the water, shook out three pills into Sailor's hand then looked at her and added a fourth to the pile. "So, what happened to you last night? I lost track of you after the loony tunes dude."

Sailor shot him a look. She liked Jeremy, hadn't seen a body like that since her dad took her to Greece. Jeremy was different. He actually looked into her *eyes* when he spoke to her. She drank the powder water, knew Reilly was waiting.

"I got Deluca to take me back to his place. The mickey in the drink took a little longer than you said."

Reilly raised his brow, Sailor pretended not to notice. "Oh, and I've got the film from the camera. I was going to take it to the one-hour photo, as soon as I stop seeing double."

"I can take it."

"Thanks, Ry." She smiled. "That would be great."

The kettle whistled and Reilly called from the kitchen, "So, what's Deluca's place like?"

Sailor described the high-tech electronics and sound system, the modern furniture, the view of the marina. She told him almost everything that happened. He brought the tea and noticed Sailor had switched to just stating the facts. Where the files were. How the computer was set up.

She gestured to a stack of wrinkled papers on the coffee table. "I found those jammed into his shredder."

Reilly picked them up, shuffled through them then shook his head. "Am I supposed to know what this means?"

"I wish you did, Reilly." Sailor yawned. "I wish you did."

Reilly watched her fall asleep. The tea did its job. He wanted to kiss Sailor's forehead, smooth her hair back and feel her breath on his cheek, but instead he draped the chenille throw over her and twisted the blinds shut. He grabbed the roll of film and cleared away the cups and glasses. He paused to smell the miniature roses she'd planted in a casserole dish.

At the door, Reilly looked back at the sleeping figure on the couch and whispered, "So maybe Fast Eddie isn't so fast after all."

High in the air over New York, Doc and Maria made love in the tiny cabin of the private jet. Afterward, getting dressed proved more difficult than getting undressed, but they worked well together, silently bending down, zipping up and sorting shoes. It was a choreographed play of politeness and grace. Grown-up love was so much neater than the hurried spasms of youth. Not less complicated, just a lot more reserved.

"We'll be home soon," Doc said. "Do you have plans for the rest of the weekend?"

"Plans? No. I had Sonja clear the calendar. The Cape will have to do without me for a few days." She smiled. "Besides, I wasn't sure if the weather would hold. I know how you hate to fly in the rain."

"That would have been nice."

"What's that?"

"Me and you, stranded in a hotel room in Philadelphia for the whole weekend." Doc smiled and drew Maria into his arms. He bent to her ear. "I love you."

Maria answered him with a kiss, trying to tell him she wasn't the same girl she'd been, that she was sorry for keeping secrets and that she finally deserved him. Unspoken words passed from her head to her mouth to her lips to his, like an urgent Morse code, dots and dashes of lip and tongue.

Deluca woke up on his couch. *What the fuck?* He felt around. His shirt was undone, his pants were in place, zipped and buttoned. His head hurt. He remembered escaping the party with Sailor. Then what? The rest of the night was unclear. The stereo was on, tuned. There were champagne glasses, one with a lipstick smeared rim, and an empty bottle in the ice bucket. If she was good enough for the Dom, why isn't she here? And why am I on the couch? "You're losing it, Eddie." He hated losing.

After two hours of housework and a chat with her daughter Holly, Gina placed the call she'd been avoiding all day.

"Hello?"

Gina thought she had a wrong number and almost hung up. The voice sounded like Aunt Jeannie, not Hiram Berger.

"How are you feeling today, Detective?"

"Oh, shit. Don't talk so loud. Do me a favor, G. Come over here and shoot me. Please?"

Gina stifled a laugh. She had given up hard liquor years ago. "Poor baby. Do you need anything?"

"Yeah, a new head, smaller and lighter. Oh, God. I don't feel so good."

Gina heard the phone drop, then running footsteps and retching. She winced and gingerly hung up.

She'd always dreamed of the perfect man, someone to share her life with. A man who was well-read, yet not snobby; well-liked but not narcissistic; good-looking, but not too vain. Hiram Berger was none of those things, and

Gina wondered—not for the first time—why she was still with him.

Sailor wondered if she should call first or just show up. She didn't want to interrupt if he had company, but she wanted to show him what she'd been doing all afternoon. She picked up the phone and hit redial.

"Hello?" Reilly said.

"How's my hero?"

"How's the helpless victim?"

Sailor laughed. "Better."

"I got the pictures."

"Really?"

"And Chinese."

"Kung Pao?"

"Absolutely."

"When?"

He said, "How about now?"

"On my way!"

With a bottle of Pinot Grigio under one arm and a bag from Jade Garden, Reilly was at Sailor's door in less than three minutes.

They ate while Reilly messed with the photo disk. He enlarged and cropped, then printed out pictures of Berger and his party pals. Sailor pinned them to the dining room wall next to a magnetic dry-erase board. She'd written: *Bentley, King and LeChance* on one side and *Berger, Deluca and Gallo* on the other. There were more names underneath with strings on magnets connecting them.

Reilly pointed to Maria's photo. "Who's the fashion plate? She looks a little out of place."

"That's Maria Chetta."

Reilly shrugged. The name meant nothing to him.

"She's pretty big East Coast money according to Jeremy."

"Jeremy?"

"Yeah. I asked him about as many people as I could,

until he started getting suspicious. Then today, I ran the names through an internet search." She pointed to the white board. "That's what I got. Chetta's heavy into local politics and charities in Massachusetts. She owns an import business called Angelina. The lady in the rainbow sausage dress is Kate Shanahan."

"The wife of The Honorable E. Patrick 'Pay-me-and-I'll-throw-it-out' Shanahan."

"Reilly!" Sailor laughed.

"And who's he?"

Sailor shrugged, squinting across the table at the picture of Doc. "I don't know. But he's nice arm candy."

"Arm candy? I think I'm offended."

Sailor chuckled. "You'll get over it." She leaned in, digging her chopsticks into Reilly's take-out container. She looked at him. For a second, Reilly thought she was going to kiss him, until she said, "Is that the tofu delight?"

"Uh, yeah." He let her have the container and watched her eat, wondering where she put it all. She didn't seem to have an ounce of fat on her, at least not in the wrong places.

Sailor gestured to the empty spaces under some of the photos. "Maybe we'll be able to fill in some of those blanks after tomorrow."

"Tomorrow?"

"Reilly, don't tell me you forgot Graterford? The prison? Banning?"

"That's tomorrow?"

Sailor nodded. "Banning said Ray Bentley's one of the ten we'll see. It's going to be a very interesting day."

Interesting wasn't the word Reilly would have used. "I guess I must have forgotten to check my 'Today I go to Prison Calendar'."

Sailor laughed. "Oh. One more thing." She pulled a computer disk in a green sleeve from her pocket.

Reilly looked at it. "And, this is?"

"Let's just say it wasn't a *terrible* night with Fast Eddie, and I am *so* glad he didn't upgrade to Windows ME."

Reilly smiled. He slipped the CD from the packaging and spun it on the table. "What's on it?"

"Not sure. It's like the papers from the shredder: initials, dates, abbreviations. There's more, but the encryption will be harder to break."

The disk clattered to the surface, wobbled then stopped. Sailor looked through a stack of papers, chose one and slid it to Reilly.

"This is the print-out."

He glanced at the sheet, "What do you think it is?"

"I don't know. It could be case files or a client list. What I can't figure out is why Deluca would have it *encrypted* on his home computer?"

"Here's a better question. How does Deluca afford a million dollar condo *and* oceanfront property in Seaside on a MDB&S salary? And why doesn't Deluca have to call ahead for a table at Delmonico's?"

"Delmonico's?' Isn't that Moreno's old place? Where Jimmy The Greek was gunned down?'

"The same." Reilly laughed. "Listen to you. Gunned down. I'm afraid to tell you what Shelly said."

"Who's Shelly?"

Reilly waved his hand like he was shooing a fly. "Just a girl from the party. Turns out she's from my old neighborhood."

He hesitated, then said, "It wasn't so different when I was growing up, kids hanging out on street corners. You hear stories. See things. I knew what bars to avoid, who owned what corner, that Friday was pay-up day. The Irish and the Italians had their own turf, and you were supposed to stick to your side of town. I knew about Lou Gallo and his crew. A bunch of low-lifes. My brother Sean lost an ear to one of Gallo's boys in a poolroom brawl."

Reilly leaned back in his chair. "My Uncle Mick had an import-export business. a warehouse on the docks. Always had cash in his pockets, drove a new Caddy every year.

Never seemed odd to me as a kid. Hell, I never knew what they imported or exported, never thought to ask. Didn't hurt that he was Black Irish. He could blend with the Italians. Anyway, when Mick went to prison, his business ended up in Moreno's hands."

"Moreno? Not *the...* "

Reilly nodded.

Sailor grimaced. "Is it true? About the head?"

"Oh, yeah." Reilly said. "Gallo killed him."

"Gallo?"

Reilly shook his head, looked right at Sailor. "*Gallo* cut off Moreno's head and delivered it in a pillowcase to his *mother.*"

"But Gallo had an alibi. And didn't they indict John…"

Reilly shook his head. "According to Shelly and her cop pals, Gallo's alibi was shit. The other guy went down as a favor to the family."

Sailor watched Reilly sip his wine, then set the glass down gently, speaking softer now. "Cops didn't care. Moreno had been getting harder and harder to handle. Nobody mourned the loss. And besides, the boys said Gallo paid better."

"What else did you get from these guys?"

"More than you want to know." Reilly tugged on the pocket of his cargo pants and withdrew a mini recorder. "Maybe you should hear for yourself." Reilly pressed play.

The man's voice was easy enough to hear over the music and the background sounds, like he was used to making himself heard in such situations and liked the sound of his voice.

"You wanna hear a story about the Mikey Hiram Berger? Well, bet you never heard this one. Hey, Joe, pass the pitcher. Let me see, it was '76 or '77. Me and Berger got assigned to the Twenty-Sixth. We had foot patrol. Fuckin' sucked. My dogs would ache for hours after—used to have to soak 'em in Epsom salts every night. Anyways, we was up in this high-class neighborhood, just checking it out, when we hear this banging noise. We look around and see this guy standing in a window. Naked as the day he was born. Hair all wild and shit. He's standing there smacking his palm against the glass, smacking hard enough to bust it. We figure we ought to check it out before he spooks the old lady across the street or scares some kid, you know? So, I go to the front door. Gonna ring the bell, right? But Berger? No. He goes over to the window and stands right in front of this guy. Me? I don't know what this wacko is on, so I'm staying as far away as possible with one hand on my stick. Then I look over and here's Berger, playing charades with the fuckin' guy. Pushing his hands through his hair and tugging on his shirt. He even pretends to step into a pair of pants. Sure as shit, the wacko does the same thing. He stops the banging, pushes his hair down, puts on a shirt and steps into a pair of sweats. Then Berger points and the guy answers the door, invites us in without a word. Calm as a pussycat."

On the tape, a woman's voice asked, "Then what happened?"

The detective continued, "I'm getting to that part. The wacko was on some bad speed or some shit. Said he hadn't slept in a week. Sure as hell hadn't had a shower either. Jesus! It stunk in there. Berger told the guy to take a shower, then we'd talk. Well, I figure here was where we see what he's holding, you know? High-class neighborhood and all that. Berger gives me the nod, and I head to the garage and he goes to the kitchen. I come back with the blow and some cash, and I see Berger tying up a trash bag and heating up soup.

A deep voice interrupted. "What the fuck?"

"Yeah, Berger's playing fucking nurse maid to this wacko. But you know what? That guy comes downstairs all cleaned up and grateful that Berger makes a connection. That wack-job was Berger's top informant for ten years. Without him, we never would've got Moreno in '82. But that's a whole other fucking story. Right boys?"

Reilly clicked off the recorder.

Sailor stared at him. "Holy shit. Is there more like that?'

Reilly yawned behind his hand. "You want to hear more?' He slid the recorder to her. "I'll be right back."

Sailor listened to more wild tales, cops one-upping each other, trying to impress the women. She wrote down the names she heard: Four Eyes, Junior, White Shoes, Fat Ollie and Tony Cigars.

When Reilly returned from the bathroom, his eyes were brighter, his pupils enlarged. "So, sounds like you had a pretty interesting night. What about that guy Strom? What did he tell you?"

Sailor kept writing. "That my eyes are like pools of stars."

Reilly looked at her and wondered how she could fall for crap like that.

"I think he's sweet."

"Sweet?" Reilly went off on an Italian accented comedic riff about donuts and tira misu and the wonderful things a man could do with a jelly filled donut when lonely.

Sailor laughed. "Stop," she said. "You're killing me." She threw her napkin at him and they both laughed— harder than they should have, for longer than was necessary. They laughed because they had stepped in some deep shit, and the truly funny stuff was going to be far away for a long time.

Berger threw the can opener. "Motherfucking piece of shit!" It bounced off the wall, leaving a black mark and a four-inch dent then skittered across the vinyl tile. "Come on, you cocksucker! I just want a fucking bowl of soup." He pressed down hard, punctured the tin and twisted the rusty handle. Three tries and two cuts later, the can opened.

He hadn't eaten all day and wasn't sure he could keep this down. But the shakes had finally stopped and he had things to do. Berger looked at the clock. Eight-thirty.

While the chicken soup warmed in the microwave, he grabbed a bottle of water and swallowed four different pills. He ate the soup standing up at the counter, with a few beers to wash it down.

By the time he was halfway to the docks, Berger felt better. The drugs were kicking in and the dry heaves had passed. He still felt like he had fur on his tongue and a helmet on his head, but he'd meet Gallo and tell him one more time to go fuck himself. Then he'd drive straight home and sleep like the dead.

13
Never on a Monday

SHAZAD had been awake for hours, listening to the sound of Ray sleeping. Out with the bad, in with the good. Out with the bad, in with the good. And after a while, Shazad climbed down from his tray and unrolled his rug on the cool cement floor.

He was sitting there when Ray woke. Without opening his eyes, Shazad said, "The papers and magazines are for Snap and Crackle. All of the books go to Pop." Shazad pointed and Ray followed the finger to the yellow bin stamped with the letters, S.C.I. Graterford. When Ray didn't reply, Shazad opened his eyes and looked at his cellmate. "You are sure you will be all right?"

"I'll be fine. Just get your stuff together. They'll be here any minute."

Shazad rolled his worn rug. "I have no use for these things." He offered it to Ray. "Remember, Ray, they do not own you. Your body is only here for them to count."

The cell door clanged open. Deputy Scruggs stood outside. "Said all your good-byes, Shazam?"

Shazad ignored the dig and slipped into his prison

shoes for the last time.

"Come on, they're ready for you in discharge."

Ray touched knuckles with Shazad, "On the one, my man."

"On the one, my friend."

Before the door slammed shut, Shazad called back, "Everything will be fine, Ray. You will see."

Deluca paced in his office, tapping a rhythm on the coins in his pocket. He checked his Rolex. Two minutes. He walked to the adjoining bathroom, stood in front of the mirror and raised his hand then dropped it. There was nothing left to adjust.

The intercom on his desk beeped, then Mimi said, "Mr. Deluca, Miss Beaumont is here."

Deluca called, "Send her in, Mimi. And see if she'd like coffee or something."

"Yes, sir."

Mimi looked up at Sailor. "Would you like some coffee?"

"No. I'm fine. Thank you."

"He'll see you now."

Mimi watched the girl close the heavy mahogany door behind her. She hoped Fast Eddie knew what he was doing. Sailor was an intern, but this wasn't the White House. What the hell was Deluca doing here at seven a.m. on a Monday morning with a beautiful young girl behind closed doors? And why was he wearing his favorite Hugo Boss jacket?

Deluca's nervousness disappeared the moment he saw her. Something about her presence was soothing. He slipped behind his desk and gave her his best money making smile. "Good morning, Miss Beaumont."

Sailor sat down across from him and crossed her legs. If this had been the forties she would have tugged up her gloves and asked for light. She was that classy. "It's back to Miss Beaumont, is it? Eddie, call me Sailor."

"Sailor." Seeming pleased with the feel of it, he said it again. "Sailor, perhaps you're wondering why I called you here." He kept his eyes on her, still trying to figure out what she had done to him the other night. Or what he might have done to her.

"It has come to my attention that with your connections and social background, you might do well with more high profile cases. I have suggested to Ted that I intern you here, myself. That would be in addition to your responsibilities with Len, unless that would be too much."

"Not at all." Sailor smiled. She toyed with her pendant necklace, uncrossing her long legs then wrapping them in the other direction. Eddie felt an urge to leap over the desk and throw himself at her feet. He thought for one second that he'd give her anything she asked for and in return he'd be able to touch her and be humbled by her. He felt that just being near her made him a better man. Then he blinked and shook his head. What the fuck?

Sailor spoke, breaking the trance. "So, you'd want me to start tomorrow, then?"

Deluca nodded. He watched her leave, even heard the door close behind her, but could have sworn that he was miles away, lying naked on a warm sandy beach.

Len Banning backed his Jag out of the garage, humming along to the Top 40 Station. He hardly ever sang anymore. The house was too empty, the stereo system too damn confusing and the shower had crappy acoustics. But all that was going to change. He had the realtor out right now nailing down properties that had "Len Banning" written all over them. One was a Craftsman-style house on three acres with a barn and workshop. Len smiled. I'm going to get three big dogs. Hell, maybe even a cat.

At the firm, he parked in his assigned spot then headed for his office. They had to leave for the prison soon or they'd miss the morning visitation cut-off.

As Sailor waited for Reilly, she glanced around his cubicle. No photos, no plants. Just a few black-and-white comics tacked to the upholstered walls—a confused penguin, angry office workers and a fat cat. "Ready?" she said.

"Ready as I'll ever be. You're sure they said no phones, no palm devices?' Reilly emptied his pockets into his briefcase.

"Nothing mechanical." Sailor said, adjusting her collar. "Unless you have special permission to videotape a deposition. Just paper and pen."

"Hope I can write fast enough."

"Hope we can read your writing."

They met Banning in the foyer. He was finishing a call on his cell phone and writing a message at the reception desk under the watchful eye of Paris. He jerked a thumb over his shoulder indicating the file boxes. Reilly nodded, handed his briefcase to Sailor and carried the boxes onto the elevator. Banning followed, still on the phone. He punched the garage level and they rode down.

"I don't care, Theo. I want to sell. All offers will be considered. Yes, all offers." Banning glanced at the interns, then said, "Listen, just call me later," and hung up as the elevator opened.

"Here we are." Banning motioned to a gleaming ebony and chrome Jaguar XJ12 and popped the trunk.

"Oh, she's beautiful." Sailor walked the length of the car, grazed her hand over the hood ornament.

"You'll never find another Jaguar, (he pronounced it, jag-u-are), like this. She's custom-built."

Reilly ignored them. It's a fucking car, people. Hello? He loaded the boxes in the trunk, removed Ray's file from his briefcase and added it to one of the boxes.

Sailor ran her thumb over her lip, looked like she was about to ask something then bent down, peering under the vehicle. She stood, grinning. "Pininfarina?"

Banning was surprised. "Yes. But how did you..."

Sailor walked the length of the car. Two summers dating Benny the mechanic had taught her something after all. She said, "It's genius. Borrowing from the lines of the Series II with the larger rectangular air intake beneath the front bumper, but look at this sleek body. Larger windows, great profile, and the curves are gorgeous. She's a real beauty."

The men thought the same thing about the woman in front of them.

Sailor grabbed the passenger door handle and looked at Banning. "We're still talking fuel-injected v12, OHC, aren't we?"

"Absolutely. All the way to Graterford."

Reilly slid into the backseat and opened the morning paper. What did it matter what was under the hood? It was about how you looked behind the wheel. And for this attorney, that meant sports car. Sleek, shiny and convertible. He didn't care what was under the hood. It could be hamsters on a wheel or rabid squirrels on a treadmill, as long as he had a full tank of gas and a beautiful girl in the passenger seat.

Hiram Berger wore a sweat suit and sneakers with absolutely no intention of exercise. He held the refrigerator door in one hand, the phone in the other, cord stretching across the kitchen. He tried to keep his voice level. "Yes sir. I understand. It's just that—No, Mr. Frappolli. I still want the security job. Next week would be fine. Thank you, Sir."

Berger closed the door of the empty fridge and hung up the phone. The long cord twisted around itself like a night crawler on a hook. *Fucking Gallo. I had plans. Me and Gina, we had plans. Why do you have to come around and pull my strings?* He glanced at the employee handbook on the counter. *Safeguards, Inc. Because Security is Never Convenient.*

"You got that right pal," Berger said, twisting the plastic pill sorter to Monday then dumping half the contents in his hand. Frappolli and the night job would wait. He still had his job at the school. Money would be all right for a while.

He headed for the garage, swallowing pills along the way. Berger had plans. As he backed the big Impala out of the garage and down the driveway, he thought of Gallo and his little wops at the dock. They were on his mind while he made stops at the hardware store and army surplus warehouse. He thought of them while he grabbed a bite to eat at the diner. He thought about them all the way to the library.

Reilly didn't say much the entire ride. It looked like they had taken a detour into suburbia, like someone had wrongly posted the ugly brown sign, SCI Graterford in the middle of a sleepy little town, until he noticed the uniformed guard on horseback. He wore a wide-brimmed hat and held a shotgun across his lap, reins in one hand. A few feet away, men in prison jumpsuits picked up trash. They dragged bright plastic bags behind them and looked up as the Jag slowed then turned onto the prison road. Sailor and Reilly stared out the open windows.

A large black man ina red headwrap called, "Hey bay-bee. Wanna ride in my car?"

The other cons joined in the catcalls.

"Ooo, mama. You go girl."

"See what I tell you, man. It takes a Jag to get a bitch like that."

Sailor raised her tinted window as they continued up the road passing lush green fields with buildings and barns in the distance. The road crested and the first tower appeared. Reilly swallowed hard.

Banning drove through the employee parking lot with its wide, newly painted spaces, then bumped off the pavement onto the visitor's dirt and gravel lot. Trash littered the ground and the cars were parked haphazardly as if a tornado had dropped them.

Banning pulled in between a beat-up Chevy and a deep purple, fully accessorized Z-28. He said, "Just another way to remind the con who he is, and who he isn't. The theory is: Further isolation from society and removal of privileges teaches the inmate to stop taking things for granted and to realize all actions come with consequences—good and bad."

"Sounds like law school," Reilly muttered. He looked at the Z. "Hey, what's my Mom doing here?"

Sailor laughed. "Cut it out, Ry." She turned to Banning. "Is it always this crowded?"

"Only on a Monday," Banning said. "The beginning of the week holds much promise."

He popped the trunk and handed a file box to Reilly and took one himself. Sailor rolled a cart with additional files. They made their way through the lot, kicking up a dusty trail. To the left of the prison entrance was a beautifully landscaped brick building with curtains in the windows and flowerpots on the steps: The administration building.

They passed under the main gate tower. Reilly looked up at the armed officer on duty. He could have sworn the man mouthed "Good-bye."

The first check-in was at the main gate. A tough CO in a plexi-glass bubble motioned them forward. Banning, Sailor and Reilly walked through a scanner, then waited for another Corrections Officer to look through the file boxes. The officer's keys jingled on a long chain at his side and his weapon jabbed at his waist—a personal war waged against his own girth. He moved a wand sensor over the boxes then passed them around to Reilly. No one had said a word since the parking lot.

At each checkpoint, they were searched, scanned, tested. They passed through three rooms with three heavy metal gates, each one clanking shut behind them with a finality Sailor thought impossible, and still no one said a word as they arrived in the waiting area.

A series of desks formed a wall to the right. All the faces behind the desks wore the same expression of disgust and boredom. Lit by their outdated computers, employees strained to cradle oversized phone receivers while typing, writing and pushing buttons. This was their job, their prison.

Banning handed a sheath of papers to the sergeant behind the desk.

"ID," the guy said.

Banning, Reilly and Sailor slid their licenses across the laminated surface and waited for the man's inspection. The sergeant had a face like a day-old scone on the markdown rack, his eyes like tiny raisins peering out from the lumpy surface. He motioned to the machine mounted on the countertop. "Take a number."

Banning pulled a number then led them to a row of wooden pews to wait.

Sailor tried to sit without touching anything, tried to imagine who had sat here before her. Tried to be nonchalant and cool like Reilly, but shit, she was in prison. Behind the desks where they'd come in, uniformed bodies bobbed behind desks, going about their business. Of course it was just a job to them, something they did every day—surrounded by barbed wire and concrete walls. They did their filing and typing twenty-eight feet from convicted murderers. Sailor started to freak. This was the real deal. The girls back at Miss Porter's School in Farmington would never believe it.

At the end of the pew, a skinny black woman in a clear shower cap nursed a sickly baby. The woman's leg jittered, shaking her slack breast and the baby. She stared straight ahead and occasionally pushed her lower lip out with her tongue. Two toddlers who might belong to her played nearby. They banged their plastic cars on the token machine and stuck their fingers into the change return slot, screeching each time the metal flap slapped down. Young girls who should have been in school learning history and algebra, instead primped in small mirrors, adding layers of eye shadow, liner and lipstick.

Banning slid the file boxes along the pew, sat between Reilly and Sailor and ran his long fingers over the folders, checking names. He pulled three, then closed the box and pushed it to Reilly. "You should be set. There are notes in each file, and a brief synopsis. You've done this before, right?"

Reilly nodded. "A few times. Just not in there." He pointed to the metal door bind the steel gate.

Banning shrugged. "The law's the same. You'll do fine." He counted the files in the second box then looked at Sailor.

"We'll take these."

Reilly looked inside his box twice. "Mr. Banning? Where's the Bentley file?"

"Bentley? Why?"

Torn between telling the truth about bringing the file home and admitting that he really wanted to work the case, he said, "Well, I was working on it this weekend." Before Banning could say anything, he added, "Actually, Sailor and I did some research and we think-"

Banning interrupted. "How did you come to be working on the case this *weekend*, Mr. Reilly?"

"It's complicated. I know. But, there's something. I mean there *might* be something." He swept his eyes sideways toward Sailor.

Banning noticed. "We've got a long wait. Might be a good time to fill me in."

There was one thing all of Banning's ex-wives agreed on. He was a good listener. Reilly told Banning as much as they knew based on the file and Ray's recent phone call. Sailor filled in the blank spots, leaving out the retirement party and the war room wall in her apartment. She watched Banning's expression as Reilly stated the facts of the case, saw his smirk when Deluca's name was mentioned.

Banning said, "I remember following the original case in the papers—what little there was. I wouldn't doubt the connections went deep, even back then. It sounds like you two have invested a great deal of time on this." He looked at Sailor, then at Reilly. "These allegations are not to be taken lightly. We can't afford any mistakes." He flipped through the file, paused on Ray's picture. "Do we have any idea what we're up against with Ray? Is he cooperative? Educated?"

Reilly smiled. "He works in the law library as a paralegal. He's clean. A model con."

Banning raised a brow, then scratched a note on his pad. "I'll run lead on Bentley, but this is your case." He looked up at the interns, kids really. God he hoped this was the right thing to do. What would Montgomery think? Fuck Montgomery. Banning said, "All right then." And slid out of the pew to talk to the sergeant.

"Excuse me, I just wanted to make an adjustment in the order and let you know we only need two rooms, not three."

The thick man behind the desk raised his head slowly. The raisin eyes turned toward Banning. His meaty jowls jiggled with each word. "You ain't getting even one room. You can use the visiting room like everyone else. What you think? You special?' Spittle gathered at the corners of his fat lips. "Mr. Big City Lawyer? Go sit down, till I call you."

Banning returned to the pews muttering, "Asshole."

They waited, watching visitors go through a final search before being allowed to pass inside. There was another wave of the sensor wand looking for drugs and weapons, then an invisible hand stamp.

Sailor began to feel like a prisoner herself. Without personal property or privileges, she sat under the scrutiny of ensconced guards who would call her by number not name. She wondered if that was one of the reasons why they made you wait.

For everything the visitors had to go through, the

prisoners on the other side of the metal door were subjected to even more. Some cons chose phone calls over visits to avoid the waiting, the inhumanity of body cavity searches.

That stuff had never bothered Ray. He followed the warden's requirements, even decided to stay in his cell all morning so he'd be easy to find when the attorneys arrived.

Ray memorized exactly what he wanted to say to the attorneys. By the time he was standing at the visiting room door, he held the six papers that had been counted by each guard at each checkpoint. Ray knew he had to return to his cell with those same six papers—or he'd get three days in the hole. And even though the cell without Shazad was as quiet as the hole, he still liked his walking around time, and his bed—so he'd hang onto the papers. He sat in the front row and watched the door.

Banning entered first with Reilly and Sailor in tow. He gave his name to the CO, who checked his clipboard, then indicated which one was Ray. Sailor recognized him, even without the Afro.

Ray stood. "I'm Ray Bentley. Thanks for coming."

They exchanged names and shook hands. Ray held Sailor's a little longer.

"Can I get you something, Mr. Bentley?" she asked. "A soda or snack?"

Ray smiled. She was easily the most beautiful woman he'd seen in fifteen years, but she was still a child, and the way the cons were looking at her brought out the protector in him. He saw the tokens in her hand. "Call me Ray, and yeah, a Coke would be good. But let him get it." Ray pointed to Reilly.

Sailor said, "That's okay, I can go."

"No. Let *him* get it."

Reilly held out his hand for the tokens.

Ray was surprised, hadn't realized you could be so

young and be a lawyer. Things must be good on the outside. He'd asked around about Len Banning. Word was he'd keep it real.

Banning said, "I have a few questions about the previous handling of your case, then we'll get into the new information, regarding..." He flipped a few pages. "Stash Neely."

Ray nodded.

Banning said, "Let's start with this." Sailor passed him a copy of the signed confession stating Raymond Bentley and Jefferson LeChance had planned and committed the murder of James King. He showed it to Ray.

"That's bullshit. I never should have signed it. But I was a dumb scared kid who didn't know better. I told them that. At the trial."

"But we're asking now, Ray." Reilly leaned in, connected. "Tell us what happened."

Ray sighed as he looked around. In a low voice, he said, "It was Berger. He had this way, you know? The "Yellow Page Dick," they used to call him. He beat me for hours. No food, nothing to drink. He threatened me. He had me so confused. I would have signed anything to make it stop."

Banning said, "He threatened you?"

"Yeah." Ray stared off, playing the movie back in his head. "He told me that he'd go after my wife, Tara, if I didn't sign it. Shit, I figured I could fix it later—that I'd get my chance. And when the truth came out, it would all be okay, you know?' Ray looked from Banning to Reilly to Sailor.

Sailor looked down at her papers, unable to meet his eyes.

Banning said, "Let's go back. Why would Berger threaten you? And why bring your wife into this? Was she involved with the robbery?"

"No, Tara had nothing to do with any of that." Ray shook his head. "Berger was on the take, him and his partner. That was how King stayed in business all those years. Shit, everyone knew he was dealing out of that place. He paid off the cops, kept a few lawyers on the string. He even had a judge in his back pocket. Week before this whole thing went down, Chancy was talking about some big score. Things were all fucked up." He flipped his eyes to Reilly. "That's one of the reasons I wanted out. That, and the baby."

"Baby?" Sailor asked.

"Tara was pregnant. She only had a few weeks to go." His voice softened, "But she's dead, and nobody knows nothing about the baby. Her family moved away, and I don't have anyone on the outside."

Sailor reached out as if to touch his hand, but pulled back and picked up her pen instead.

"Anyway," Ray wiped his eyes with the backs of his hands. "The way Berger did me? He did the same to Stash. That's what I wanted to talk to you about."

Ray handed Banning four of the papers he'd brought. There were concise notes on coerced confessions, relevant case notations, and outlined steps of approach.

Banning flipped back through his pad. "Where's Stash now?"

"In the hole. He'll be out in a few days. You can see him then."

Sailor coughed. "In the hole? You mean solitary confinement?"

"Yeah."

One of the COs looked their way and Ray slipped into prison lingo, as if speaking gruffly made the crime more acceptable, almost normal. "He went down bad. Some beaners clicked him in the yard. Good thing Stash was ready. He sliced up one of them pretty good." He tipped his soda can draining the last few drops. "Lucky son of a bitch."

Banning wrote as he spoke. "Ray, we're going to need access to Neely's file."

Ray passed the rest of the papers to Banning. "Like that?"

Banning began to smile before he'd finished the first page. He glanced at Reilly. Stash Neely's coerced confession at the hands of Berger gave credence to Ray's case.

Sailor nudged Reilly and whispered, "Don't forget Deluca."

Ray said, " Deluca? You mean Fast Eddie? From what I hear, he's still goose-chasin' that wreckin' crew."

Sailor said, "What?"

Reilly understood the hip-hop reference. He said, "Our boy keeps some rough comps."

Ray nodded. "First Moreno, now Gallo."

"That was never proven," said Banning.

Sailor was lost. "What goose? What was never proven?"

Banning waved her off, saying, "Let's stick to your case, Ray. The reason Sailor brings up Deluca, is for a push at prosecutorial misconduct. Did you know Jamal Hix?"

"There was a Jamal who hung with Lou back then. I don't know if his name was Hix. Why?"

Reilly said, "Commonwealth v. Hix was one of the first cases Deluca took on as a defense attorney. In *your* case, Deluca went on record stating there were *no* drugs in King's Variety Store. He hid the fact that James King had been arrested for selling drugs on the premises in 1975, *and* we have reason to believe he instructed Maria Rosarita Conchetta to lie on the stand."

Ray shrugged. "I *know* all that."

"But," Reilly continued, "when Deluca defended Hix in '81 on charges from a 1975 street shooting, the counsel's primary defense was to establish the extensive drug dealing that Hix and his partners were involved in."

Ray shook his head. "Two-faced motherfucker."

Reilly continued. "During cross-examination, Deluca brought out the following points: Hix was a drug dealer;

Hix worked for James King; King kept drugs at the variety store. And, everyone in the neighborhood knew the store was a just a front."

Sailor said, "Deluca was with the DA's office in '75, when this case was supposed to go up. So by the time your case came around in 1977, he should have known what was happening at Taylor's."

"Should have *known*? Shit! Fast Eddie was one of King's *investors*."

"Investors?" Sailor said. "So, he knew about the drugs?"

Ray laughed, "Knew about them? The man was buying there. Sent his boy to do his deals. Yeah, Eddie was always slick like that. Wanted to play in the mud, but didn't want to get his pants dirty."

Deluca, doing drugs? Sailor couldn't see it. The guy was too much of a control freak. But acquiring the drugs for someone else, or moving them? That she'd buy. Fast Eddie was slick like *that*. But, something was missing.

Then she heard Banning ask, "Where's this Maria now?

They split up and the rest of day passed uneventfully. Each of the subsequent cases was handled quickly and efficiently with hardly a blink between assault and divorce. The inmates seemed less interested in talking about their case and more interested in scoping out the new sights in the visitation room. Most of the women seemed to have missed the paragraph in the visitor's manual about proper apparel. They wore lace bras and tiny panties under boxy trench coats. Promises were made for a flash of the coat, a shift of fabric. In the back of the room, some inmates stood back-to-back forming a circle around one of their own and his old lady. The couple fucked standing up while the cons glanced over their shoulders murmuring words of appreciation. The COs pretended not to notice.

Reilly finished earlier than Banning and Sailor. He collected the car keys and hauled his file box out to the parking lot.

In the backseat of the Jag, Reilly checked his cell phone. One message.

"Hi Reilly, it's Gina. I was just cleaning out my purse and found your card. I must say I'm rather impressed with your sleight of hand. Remind me to keep an eye on my wallet next time I'm around you."

Reilly smiled.

"Anyway, I was hoping you'd come by the diner this week. You still owe me that cup of coffee. Call me, or better yet, stop by Nana's. Bye."

Before she disconnected the call, Reilly heard a doorbell ring. He played the message back twice, would have played it a third time if Sailor and Banning hadn't showed up.

Banning slid behind the wheel. "Come on, I'm buying lunch."

He drove the Jag out of the dusty lot. Vivaldi streamed from the speakers, cool air flowed from a whispering system. Part of Sailor wanted to take off her pumps and pantyhose, curl up on the seat next to Reilly and sleep all the way back to the city. A greater part of her wanted to make notes while the day was fresh in her mind, her head full of ideas, her heart bursting with hope. She rubbed her neck, glanced at Banning, then at Reilly with his phone to his ear.

"Ry?"

"Yeah?"

"I think we need to tell Banning about The Ritz."

Banning looked at Sailor, then in the rear-view mirror at Reilly.

Reilly yawned. "Sure, Sailor. Why don't you start, with your escort."

14
Just Where You Need To Be

BANNING dropped the interns at the MDB&S building and drove to meet the realtor, thinking this was the perfect time to move. There's nothing like spending the day in prison to make a man think of acreage, lots and lots of space. Hell, the way his day was going, he ought to be thinking about another move. He'd always appreciated the view from Fast Eddie's corner office.

In the elevator, Sailor watched Reilly rub his eyes then yawn behind his hand. She wondered how he was going to make it another five hours. She said, "What have you got for the rest of the day?"

"Oh, let's see. There's work. More work. Or, maybe I'll just do a shit load of work."

"Okay, grumpy. I was just asking." She'd never seen Reilly like this. He was always so *up*. So *on*.

Reilly felt Sailor's eyes on him. He forced a smile and an apology. "Sorry." He affected a bad German accent and said, "Prison does strange things to a man."

Sailor laughed. "Hey, did you see the trench coat mamas?"

Reilly looked serious, and again with the accent, "Ah. *Prisoners* do strange things to a woman."

They were still laughing when the elevator opened onto MDB&S. As they passed the reception desk, Paris waved two pink message slips to Sailor. One was from Deluca. He wanted to see her.

Reilly dropped the files in Banning's office, told a few jokes to Helen who laughed politely, though she had no idea what a banana hammock was. Halfway to the cubicles, he felt the drain. He was coming down, hard. Reilly turned the corner, almost ran into Victoria.

"Hey!"

"Hey, Sweden."

"Don't forget. Harry wants to see you before the meeting."

"Yeah, no problem."

"You okay?"

"Sure. Just need to get my second wind."

She was about to say something about the bags under his eyes when Missy came around the corner. Reilly tipped his head in her direction.

Victoria said, "Okay, then," and walked away. She looked back, saw Reilly and Missy whispering, saw him pass her something. Missy smiled and giggled. Victoria pursed her lips and kept walking. That was his business, not hers.

Missy waited until Reilly left, then opened the paper and read: Top Ten Reasons to Avoid Hotdogs. She laughed.

Instead of waiting for the elevator, Reilly went straight for the stairwell and took the stairs two at a time. By the time he reached the lobby he was dripping sweat.

On the street he headed south, removed his tie and turned east. Soon the sounds of chattering shoppers, executives on cell phones and purring imported cars were replaced by blaring TVs, shouting men and crying babies. Every block the buildings seemed to sag more, their stoops piled with trash bags and boxes.

Reilly stopped at the corner shop, a dilapidated clapboard building with blackened windows. He looked left, right, then entered AAA Pawn and Collectibles.

"No problem, Eddie. I'll be fine. We've got the supporting affidavits, and I can write the motion and file it in the morning. Sailor pointed to the clock. "Don't want to keep the client waiting, now do we?' She helped Deluca into his jacket then shooed him out the door. A moment later she opened the door a crack and peeked out. Mimi's desk was empty, her computer screen black. It must be after five.

Sailor closed the door and kicked off her heels then danced over to Fast Eddie's sprawling desk and plunked down in the massive leather chair. Right where she needed to be.

By the time Len Banning returned to MDB&S, there were only a handful of cars in the parking garage. A pale blue Mercedes convertible was in his assigned stall. It was parked too close to the pole and hanging too far out. Meaning only one thing. Tiffany.

He pulled in next to it and glanced at the crystal beads hanging from the rearview mirror, then counted seven shopping bags in the back seat. Just what he needed.

After the realtor lost the bid on the Craftsman and broke the news that there was a bidding war on the other property, Banning was in no mood for his soon to be ex-wife.

The elevator doors opened to an empty lobby. Most of the partners left before the traffic got bad. The administrative staff was usually next, then the associates. Banning had been staying late since the marriage went sour. He felt more at home here than at the white castle Tiffany had created. He enjoyed rehashing the day's events with Helen and was disappointed when he turned the corner and saw her empty chair. Preparing himself for the worst, Banning opened his office door.

Tiffany reclined in the leather chair with her feet on his desk, giggling into her diamond-studded cell phone. She heard Banning enter and whispered something to her caller then snapped the tiny phone shut and sat up. "Honey, I'm home." She flashed him a smile, shiny collagen-enhanced lips and capped teeth.

"Tiff. I don't know what you think you're doing here. You signed the papers last week, remember?'

He hung his jacket on the peg behind the door, loosened his tie and went into his private bathroom. Tiffany followed. She posed in the doorway and watched him splash water on his face, then handed him a towel. She traced lazy circles around her breast.

"Lenny?' she said, moving her circling hand lower. "Honey? I'm not wearing any panties."

"Jesus, Tiff. I just got back from the prison."

She sighed, dropped her arm and let him pass.

Banning brushed by. "What do you want, anyway? Where's 'What's His Face?' Does he know you're here?"

"He's in Vegas. Without me." She began to cry. "I think he's seeing somebody. Oh, Len!"

She flopped onto the leather couch, hair falling over her face. Banning watched the drama unfold from a safe distance. Pure Tiffany. He grabbed a box of tissues from his credenza and sat beside her on the couch. He put his arm around her shoulders and patted lightly, offering the tissues.

Tiffany took one and snuffled into it then leaned into Banning's chest, hiccupping softly. "I think I made a big mistake."

Banning lifted her chin and wiped tears from her cheeks.

"You'll be fine, Tiff. You always win, remember?"

It was something she used to say during every disagreement in their first year of marriage. He'd learned to accept that she needed to get her way and he was happy to give it to her—at least where furniture, clothes and vacations were concerned.

"Maybe you just need to decide *what* you want to win."

"Oh, Len. You know just the right thing to say." She kissed him, her salty trembling lips on his own surprised ones.

Banning gently broke off the kiss and stood with his back to her. He shook his leg and adjusted his pants. He didn't want her to see how she affected him. She'd hurt him enough already.

"Tiff, I have a lot on my mind. This case is pretty big."

"Is it worth a lot of money?" Tiffany reached into her top, adjusted her bra strap.

"No, Tiffany. It's a pro-bono case."

Seeing her face, he began to explain, then broke off. "Look. I really have to get to work. I—"

"It's okay, Lenny. I'd better get home and see if, well…I'd just better get going." She pushed herself upright and tugged her skirt into place, then retrieved her purse from the desk.

Banning watched her sashay to the door. He smiled thinly when she blew tiny kisses from pink fingertips. Sitting at his desk, he saw the doodles on his calendar, the un-capped pen, the half-open door, and reminded himself to never marry another woman like Tiffany.

Helen returned, glad Tiffany had given up, though she could still smell her cologne. Helen reached to pull Banning's door shut when she heard something. She poked her head into the office.

"Mr. Banning! What are you doing here?"

"This is my office, Helen. Where else would I be working?"

"It's been a long day. I thought you would have gone home by now."

"I know, it's crazy, isn't it?" he said. "But I'm not even tired and I've got all this to keep me busy." He pointed to the files from the prison. "This is just where I need to be."

Helen smiled. "How can I help?"

Reilly looked at his bare wrist, then at the clock on the wall. He tugged his sleeve down, covering the tan line of the missing Cartier. I'll get it back next payday, before I see my folks, he promised himself. His right leg bounced under the desktop, his fingers flew across the keyboard. Two more paragraphs and his brief would be finished. He could go home. He could get high. He could have some fun.

As the printer spit out his brief, he slipped his phone out of his pocket and called the first number on the top of his list. He spoke for a few minutes more, then hung up and checked the next cubicle to see if Sailor had appeared. Her chair was empty.

Reilly dropped the brief on Victoria's desk on the way to the elevator.

At his apartment, Reilly headed straight for the bedroom. He rummaged around on the floor and found what he was looking for. Sandwiched between yesterday's socks and last week's comics was a small mirror. He dumped a white chunk of cocaine from a tiny baggy and crushed it with the side of a razor blade. He chopped the smaller pieces with the blade and when the powder was fine enough, he made lines, drawing the blade across the mirror.

Reilly surveyed his work, then sat back. When his mouth began to water, he rolled a ten-dollar bill into a straw, stuck the end in his nose and snorted all four lines. Eyes watering, nostrils burning, he tipped his head back and snuffled. He cleaned the mirror with his pinky, then rubbed it over his gums. He stashed two more baggies of coke in his underwear drawer and checked the clock. Just enough time for a quick shower before his date.

The study was stuffy and warm. Antique furnishings and a rare collection of books set the stage for the room design.

No one knew posh like the current resident, Salvatore DelliCompagni, the Philadelphia Inquirer's silent partner and all-around money mogul. A true Italian, he had most of his home furnished in Tuscan style, giving up only three spaces to modernity: a theater room that seated twenty-five comfortably, a fully equipped gym and a sleek restaurant-style kitchen.

Deluca sipped his glass of Port, drew on the Cuban cigar.

"What do you think, Eddie? Do you want in?"

Deluca turned to the gentleman on his right, then looked back at the old man behind the desk. "Throw in a box of these." He held up his cigar. "And you've got a deal."

The old man smiled. The black-haired gentleman shook his hand then poured another round of the rare Sportoletti-Villa Fidelia port. Deluca sunk into the cordovan leather and listened to tales of dangerous safaris with man-eating lions, beautiful European courtesans and wives that never asked questions. He was pleased and comforted in the presence of these great and influential men. Comforted by the knowledge that they accepted him into the fold and pleased that right now, they needed him. He sipped his port, admired the foxhunt oil over the fireplace and wondered where he could get a pair of those boots.

Finished with Deluca's motion, Sailor went back to her cubicle. She squirmed uncomfortably on the cheap task chair, her ass spoiled by partner luxury. Scraping around in her purse, she found a stale Tootsie roll and two breath mints; dinner and dessert.

She popped a mint into her mouth then scooped up the crumpled papers by her chair and spun to face the wastebasket. She leaned back and took aim like a professional basketball player, then let it fly.

"She shoots, she scores! The crowd goes wild!"

Sailor did a little victory dance in her chair, tapping her nylon-covered toes and shaking her breasts, her hands pumping to the ceiling. She finished off with a wild spin of the chair and when it stopped moving she opened her eyes.

Jeremy Strom stood outside her cubicle, looking delicious and grinning ear-to-ear.

Oh shit. "Jeremy, I-well, how are you?"

She rolled her chair back and reached up to fluff her hair. She felt around under the desk with her toes trying to connect with her shoes.

Jeremy said, "I was hoping I'd find you here. I know I said Tuesday, but something came up. How about, today instead?" He produced a large brown bag from behind his back.

"Let me check my schedule." Sailor mimed turning calendar pages. "Well. Look at that. I happen to be free."

Jeremy borrowed a chair from another cubicle while Sailor cleared her desk and arranged the spread: two Reubens on rye, a turkey club supreme, Hawaiian chips, pickles, cookies, and real egg creams.

They sat knee-to-knee in the cramped space. Jeremy's tree-trunk thighs hid the small desk chair. He was so close that Sailor could feel the warmth radiating from his sun-tanned skin. She snuck another peek at this beautiful man, his white t-shirt stretched across his huge chest, binding at the sleeves over bulging biceps. She wondered how anything ever fit loosely on a body like that? He wore Italian sandals and beat-up denim shorts—which had the beginnings of holes in all the right places. Golden hair on his legs and arms glistened in a sea of bronze.

He said, "This is nice."

Sailor smiled. "Yeah it is."

Jeremy twisted open the drinks, handed her half a sandwich on a napkin. In other places, at other times, Strong's ham-like hands maimed and killed. But here with her, they served with grace and tenderness. She wondered if Jeremy would still like her when she started asking questions about Deluca.

Maria Chetta sat in her kitchen with a cup of tea. She told herself that waiting for her chef to return wasn't odd, nor was the fact that she was concerned for his welfare. Stephan would find it endearing. They would laugh about this when he came in. He'd tease her for months that she mothered him. And maybe she did. But he should have been back hours ago. If he'd run into friends or had car trouble, he would have called. Maria wouldn't have been this worried before Lou Gallo reappeared in her life. But once he was in the picture, everything changed.

15
Cause and Effect

IT'S a matter of supply and demand. You supply whatever I demand."

The walking billboard for Gold's gym laughed. "That's good, Tone, supply and demand."

The man behind the desk didn't look so hot. After a couple of slaps, his toupee had gone west, hanging off his head at a queer angle. His shirt buttons littered his desk, and his pants had acquired a mysterious stain in the crotch area.

If Vince Gable had known he was having company this morning, he would have been prepared. He would have locked the door to the tin house on the docks.

With the Union talking strike and Immigration hanging around, he'd been camped in the trailer for three days. And now this.

"Look, Mister Cigars. I told you, I was going right out there. I just had to make some calls, grab a coffee. These guys never get here on time, they have their own plans. You really didn't need to bother yourself with this. See?' He tapped a sheet of paper on his desk. "I got the numbers and the locations right here. I'm pretty sure you'll be pleased, not like the last time."

"Jesus! Shut him up, will ya?' Tony Cigars rubbed his jaw and twisted his head around until his neck cracked.

Billboard moved in. "What you want me to do, Tone?"

"Just shut him the fuck up!"

The guy behind the desk blinked his watery Pekinese eyes, shrinking back into his chair. The toupee completed its slide revealing a red swollen ear and a ring of hair like a Trappist monk.

"I told you, Vince." Tony reached for his lighter. "You know the trip. Out to the yard and back, then put the dogs up." He paused to light a half-chewed cigar, "And turn off the video monitors. There's no one else here, nothing for you to do but whack off. What the fuck you been doing all morning? I got three pissed-off guys out there running a truck and wasting gas. Now you're cutting into my delivery time. You want me to call in your marker, Vince? That it?"

"No. No, I told you, it wasn't my fault."

Billboard took another step. Vince raised his pale, nail-bitten hands. "Please Mr. Cigars. Don't let him hit me again. Here." He held the paper over his head like it was raining. "The gate's open, just pull that plug over there."

"Plug? What plug? This plug, Vince?' Tony Cigars reached down and yanked the cord of a large black plug. The trailer shook, monitors went dark.

"Good one, Tone."

The two men stepped down from the trailer, headed across the terminal yard toward a stack of containers and a forklift. The rumble of the idling tractor-trailer became a whine as the big vehicle shifted gears and pulled into view.

Vince Gable adjusted his hair then looked out the window. "Fucking guys. What am I going to tell Marie? This shirt was a gift from her sister. I swear to God," he said as he raised his right hand to the ceiling, "I will never bet on the ponies again."

Reilly had been dreaming the Sailor dream. She leaned into him saying, "There's something I need to tell you." But then he woke up. It took him a second to realize he wasn't in that garden. And he wasn't with Sailor. He was naked in someone else's bed. He traced his finger down a beautiful curved spine, cupped the warm buttocks in his hands. Gina shivered, then rolled over to face him, whispering, "Morning."

Parked in his car across the street, Hiram Berger sipped cold coffee from a Styrofoam cup. There was just enough left to wash down the greasy egg sandwich. He yawned and scooted down in the seat, folded his arms and tipped his head back for a quick nap. He'd been sitting out here since midnight and hadn't seen a thing. Maybe he'd misread her. Maybe it had only sounded like she was making up the whole thing about girl's night out. But he'd driven over anyway, and now it was six a.m., and time was beginning to wear on him.

The screen door slammed. Berger jerked awake. Shit. A cab idled at the curb. The man Gina kissed goodbye was young and handsome and somehow familiar, like the guy you see on a game show and swear you've seen him in the produce section of Genuardi's. Berger watched her wave from the porch, holding her red robe closed. The robe he'd given her last Christmas. Then he remembered where he'd seen the guy. His retirement party. Fuckin' Gallo. Can't take no for an answer, so now he's got his boy shtupping my lady. We'll just see about that.

Hiram Berger's sleep-deprived, pill-addled brain, wrapped itself around an idea. Gina was his and he would not lose her. She was just mad at him, like before. He'd buy her something nice, show her how he'd changed. He'd win her back. Whatever it took. Berger followed the cab downtown to a fancy condo complex. He took a container of pills from the glove box and watched the guy enter the building. Berger swallowed the pills. He could give Gina whatever she wanted, didn't she know that? He pulled into traffic without looking, a screech of brakes behind him.

The self-storage facility was located at the rear of a run-down industrial park. Faded names of fly-by-night businesses appeared as shadows on the park's signboard. Berger passed empty warehouses and forgotten offices partially hidden by unkempt landscaping. He pulled up to the entry gate and entered the code. Moments later he parked in front of J19 and turned off the Impala's engine.

The resident manager, Bob Murphy, caught a glimpse of Berger as he drove to his unit. He trained one of the mobile cameras mounted to Building J on the new arrival and checked the time. He watched his customer work the keypad then pull up the overhead door.

Eight minutes later, Berger was back on the screen. He stormed from the unit, pulling the door down behind him so abruptly it hit bottom and bounced back up again. There was no sound on the monitor, but Bob could tell the guy was pissed from the way the car sped off.

"Oh shit." Bob winced. The pissed-off dude was headed his way.

Berger crashed through the front door, stood there in the lobby, yelling to the walls, "I need to see the manager, and I need to see him now!"

Bob zoomed in with the ceiling-mounted camera. It didn't look like the guy was packing. Still, Bob really didn't want to deal with a looney. He pulled the file for J19, keyed the intercom.

"What seems to be the matter, Sir?"

"What seems to be the matter? I've been ripped off! That's what seems to be the matter. Now I want to see the manager, and I want to see him now."

Bob decided being the manager wasn't a good thing today, so he said, "He's not here right now. Come back after two."

"Listen asshole, I need to know who's been in my space, and when, and I know *you* can do that!" Berger stepped up to the camera, making his point with what looked like a very large hand.

"Okay, okay. Hang on, man." Bob flipped through the log for unit J19. The computerized tracking system enabled facility operators to track activity inside each unit. It showed dates and times of each unit's entry and departure, and from the looks of it, J19 was a pretty lonely place.

Bob keyed the intercom, "Sir, I don't see any recent activity." He flipped a page. "Just the one visit last week, and today."

Berger stared slack-faced into the camera. "What?"

Bob spoke up, "Other than today's visit, and ten p.m. Sunday, there hasn't been any activity at your unit in over three months."

Berger was still staring into the camera when he said, "That motherfucker." Then he wrenched the door open and stomped to his car, muttering the whole way.

Bob watched the Impala speed away and hoped that whoever J19 was headed for would be well warned the dude was coming.

Banning hung up the phone, made a note in the file, then buzzed Helen.

"Yes?"

"Could you check with Paris, and see if she still has any contacts over at the courthouse?"

"Sure. What do you need?"

"I need Judge Shanahan's schedule. I want to talk to him about the Bentley case. He's our best chance."

"Okay. Let me track her down."

Helen was already on the other line, paging Paris Kendrick when Banning clicked off. She hoped there was still someone over at Shanahan's that Paris could sleep with.

Who else knew about the money in the storage unit?

Berger didn't remember telling anyone and that was the problem. When he combined booze with the pills, he was hard pressed to remember the last time he ate, much less what he said. He went over the possibilities, holding them in his mouth like marbles or whipped cream. The more he moved the ideas around the more he wanted to spit out, "Gallo."

Gallo had threatened him during their meeting at the docks. He'd said, "You do this for me, Detective, and I'll let you keep your retirement plan." At the time, Berger figured he was talking about the cop severance pay, and their *old* deal—the one where Berger quietly disappears to his house in the mountains with Gina. Now he was thinking that Gallo had a very different plan in mind, and it was just a hop across that mental terrain to conclude that it was Lou Gallo, who had taken his million in cash.

Deluca read the front page of the newspaper. *Insiders say Strike is Imminent-Two Sides at Odds Over Benefits.* A union strike, even a slowdown like the one they had planned would disrupt the regular scheduling of thousands of ships loading and offloading at The Port of Philadelphia. According to economists, it would cost a billion dollars a day with dire consequences for the entire North American economy.

Deluca dropped the paper.

It had taken Berger almost an hour to buy the supplies. By the time he pulled into the garage, he knew there was no way he was going to let Gallo, or anyone else, get the best of him. Whoever said revenge was sweet had gotten that fucking right. *I'm going to hit you where it hurts, Lou. Right in the wallet.*

Berger tossed the book in the fireplace and watched it burn. Part of the cover curled back; the seal of The United States Government was barely visible as the flames rose higher.

Berger talked to the flames, "Think you can get me to do your dirty work? What the hell am I protecting? The reputation of a dead man? Fuck it. My family? What family? That dumb bitch won't let me see my kid, and now that I've lost Gina, nothing matters. Nothing."

He moaned, swiping his arm across the coffee table and sending empty beer cans and plastic pill containers flying. Then Hiram Berger tipped his head back and howled.

Twenty minutes later, he steered the Impala toward the pier. Heavy duffle bags shifted in the trunk, something clunked against the tire well. Berger didn't blink.

Ray sat in the recreation room reading his book. Some men cheered for the transvestite on *The Jerry Springer Show*. Others played chess in the corner. A few hunched over pads of paper with stubs of pencils—drawing, writing, or just dreaming.

He opened his book.

"What you got there, Ray? *Life Behind Bars*?" The skinny black man laughed, his mouth a red cave with stumps of rotten teeth. He alternated between scratching at his arms and flapping them.

Ray scrunched his nose. "Shit, Amos. You stink. What the hell have you been doing?"

"Working in the kitchen. We're having French Onion Soup for dinner, Ray. And that be some good shit, too." A line of blood dripped from his arm. "They was talking about you. You and your boy, Stash."

"Who was talking?"

"Some of the regulars on the line. Seems like somebody got a problem with Stash Neely. You best tell him to fly low." Moses flapped his arms some more, then leaned closer to Ray. "You want some of Cook's hooch? I can get you a deal, brother."

Ray smiled. "You know I don't do that stuff any more, Amos. Here." Ray palmed him a few bills. "Go on and get some for yourself—and take care of that arm." Amos looked down, seeing the blood and doing nothing about it. He pocketed the bills and wandered off, looking to hit up somebody else. Ray made a note to steer clear of the soup and tried to go back to his book. But he kept thinking about Stash.

Sailor kicked off her running shoes and stepped out of her sweats. She tore her t-shirt pulling it over her head. "Damn it!" She wasn't used to the honking cars or the smell of exhaust or stopping at every street corner in Philadelphia. She missed the long winding trails of campus, the path around the tennis courts of the family estate, grass and dirt beneath her feet. That's how you should run. Not on a treadmill. Not on a dirty city sidewalk.

Thinking a long shower would make her feel better, she was headed to the bathroom when the house phone rang. She wrapped herself in a towel and flopped across the bed, reaching the extension on the nightstand.

"Hello?"

"It's me."

"Well, hello me. How are you?"

Sailor tugged the towel tighter and smiled into the receiver. The day was already looking up.

Ray passed by the yard on the way to the laundry room, where he hoped he'd find Stash. He stepped into the bright sunlight, instinctively shielding his eyes.

Ace and his white brothers were counting out the push-ups of an overweight newcomer.

"Six? That all you got?"

"Six? I think that was five, Ace. You ain't counting that first one, are you?"

The fat prisoner's arms began to shake. He looked up, pleading. Bad move. The metal toe of a highly polished boot cracked the fat man's lower teeth away from the jawbone in a swift shot.

"Stay out of the weight room, fat man!"

Another kick, another stream of blood and a high-pitched scream. The fat man rocked and moaned in the dirt, his hands clamped over his bloody mouth.

Ray almost offered to help the poor guy, but Ace was watching, and a second later, the CO was there to give the fat man an infirmary pass and a soft bed for the afternoon.

Ray changed course, taking the long way to the Laundry. No pass for him today, not with a white fat fish as a roommate.

He pushed through the double doors of the laundry area, smelled the bleach, felt the heat of the dryers. The place was usually busy, but he saw no one. A whining sound came from the back of the room. Ray walked past tables of laundry—stacks of neatly folded sheets, piles of stained jumpsuit, threadbare blankets. Where was everyone?

The closer he got to the machine, the louder the whining. Like a jammed gear. Like something that needed fixing.

Ray turned the corner, expecting to see five guys with tools and ideas, and a CO standing over them, pointing. Instead, he saw a pool of blood and Stash Neely's tattooed left arm dangling from the jaws of the Milnor press.

Sailor knocked on Reilly's door, then walked in.

"You ready?" she called.

Dressed and looking handsome in his pinstriped suit and blue shirt, with mismatched socks, he sat on the couch tying his shoes.

She said, "Hey, I was looking for you last night, at the office."

Reilly froze. "Really?' He didn't look up, just paused, then went back to tying and said, "Why, what's up?'

"I wanted to show you something. I found something interesting in Deluca's files."

Reilly stood and began stuffing gadgets in his pockets.

He barely looked at her as she spoke.

"I found some documents that had nothing to do with his prosecutions in the seventies, but a lot to do with Berger."

Reilly grabbed his briefcase. "Why would Deluca keep files on Berger?"

"I don't know. Maybe Berger was going to hire him at some point."

They left the apartment. Reilly locked the door and said, "But don't cops have private representation? And what was Berger accused of?"

"Besides being a crooked cop?"

"Yeah, besides that."

Reilly's cell phone rang with the tune of *La Cucaracha*. Sailor shook her head and pushed the elevator button as Reilly glanced at the incoming call display and smiled, putting the phone to his ear.

"What? Wait a minute, slow down." Reilly closed his eyes. "Where is she? You're sure she's breathing?'

Sailor knew that tone, having grown up in a doctor's house. She could hear the high-pitched voice on the other end.

Reilly said, "No, you're doing the right thing. Turn her head to the side, she's going to be okay. Just don't leave her. Do you understand?" The elevator doors opened. "I don't care, listen—I'm on my way."

Reilly looked at Sailor. "I need to borrow your car."

She said, "I'm coming with you."

"No."

Sailor touched his arm. "Reilly, I'm coming with you."

He looked in her eyes, saw a fight. "Okay. But, I'm driving."

They pulled up in front of a brick walk-up. Reilly ran through the small lobby and took the stairs two at a time with Sailor close behind. The hall carpet on the second floor was new. The smell of glue and synthetic fiber hung in the air. At number seventeen, Reilly didn't bother to knock. He went right in. Sailor followed.

A bushy-haired blonde in white leather knelt beside her friend passed out on the floor. Her face was streaked with tears. "What the fuck! Right, Reilly? I mean what the fuck is this? She was fine. She was fine!"

Reilly ignored the blonde and spoke to the girl on the floor. He placed his fingers on her carotid and put his face next to hers. "Shelly, come on now. Wake up." He lifted her eyelids, then her arms. "That's a good girl. Come on, now."

He looked at Sailor. "Get me a cold wet washcloth and see if there's a medical kit—smelling salts or ammonia."

Sailor hustled to the rear of the apartment. She looked in two rooms before she found the bathroom. The place was neat and nicely decorated. It would have been a nice place to visit under different circumstances. She pawed through the drawers of the bathroom vanity. In the last one she found a first-aid kit and raced back to the living room.

Sailor handed the smelling salts to Reilly. He broke a capsule open and waved it under Shelly's nose.

Shelly tossed her head, gagging, then scrunched up her face and opened her eyes. "What the fuck?" She pushed Reilly's hand away. "What are you doing here?" Shelly looked around, focusing on her friend, then Sailor. "Who the fuck are you?"

Shelly pushed Reilly away, rolled over and tried to sit up.

"I don't feel so good."

Reilly scooped her off the floor and carried her to the bathroom.

Sailor paced the living room, and when she heard the shower start up she wondered if she should leave. There wasn't anything else for her to do.

The blonde said, "I like your suit."

"Thanks."

Sailor sat next to the girl on the couch. "Were you here? When she? When it happened?"

"Yeah. I mean, I didn't see it or nothing. I was in the other room with a friend."

Sailor said, "Shelly's lucky you were here," and wondered where the friend was now.

"Yeah. I guess. She's going to be okay, right? I mean, it was just some bad blow, not like it could...you know." The girl looked away, still talking but not like she wanted to hear the truth.

Sailor knew how she felt. So she didn't say anything.

> *Mutual interests suffer consequences from known opposition, offer opportunity for sacrifice before defeat. Vitriolic confrontation avoidable. D.*

Sailor was sitting in Deluca's office reading his email, copying some to a personal document and hiding it under some layers of spam. She was trying not to think of the morning, how the whole thing had felt surreal, when her cell phone rang.

"It's Reilly, just wanted to thank you for this morning. I'm sorry about all that. You were great."

"Me? You're a regular Rescue Hero."

"Not quite." His voice softer, "I should've done more."

"It wasn't your fault."

"I should have been there."

"And what would you have done?"

Silence.

Sailor continued. "That's right, there's nothing you could have done. Not to stop her, not to change her, not anything. She—Oh God." Sailor closed her eyes and shook her head slowly.

"What? Sailor?"

Reilly barely heard her when she said, "It's just like my mother."

"Your mother? Wait a minute. She died of cancer."

"Yeah, my adoptive mother did. My real mother died of a heroin overdose when I was three months old."

"Your *real* mother?"

Sailor sighed, then decided to tell him everything. "The Beaumonts adopted me through a Philadelphia attorney. He knew the girl's—my Mom's family. My parents never told me anything, not until Mom got sick. She said she wanted me to know, in case I ever wanted to find my family."

"Did you?"

"No. *They* were my family. Besides, from what my dad said, my mother had been disowned. The family even refused to speak her name. What would they want with her daughter?"

"What about your father?"

"I never got the whole story. He abandoned my mother when she was pregnant with me. He married her, but it was all screwed-up from the start. Young black street punk meets upper-middle-class white girl. Add some drugs into the equation and you know the ending. I'm glad it was different for Shelly."

"Sailor, I'm sorry."

"Sorry for what?' Sailor wiped her eyes, sniffed. "You didn't know, Reilly. How could you have known? Look at me, I'm no better than those whores we saw at Graterford."

"Don't say that. You're amazing. You're smart and kind and beautiful and I bet you don't even own a trench coat."

Sailor laughed, loved that he could make her laugh when she felt like shit.

When Sailor hung up, she couldn't help thinking about her mother and wondering who had found *her* all those years ago, and where her father had been when her mother needed him most.

16
It's All in the Timing

TONY CIGARS and Billboard waved to the men in the tractor-trailer. Even from his vantage point on the hill, Berger heard the throaty rumble of the big engine, the shouts above it. Tony pointed to a stack of red-striped containers at the far end of the terminal yard. Berger peered through his binoculars and scanned the area around the pick-up point. Clean. Nothing gave him away. They'd never know what hit them.

A bearded man in a yellow T-shirt jumped from the truck's cab then jogged to a forklift and set it in motion. The driver went around to the back of the truck smoking a cigarette and laughing at something Tony Cigars said. As they swung the big doors open, Berger lost them for a minute. The metal door obscured their faces, but he saw their legs, their shuffling feet. If only they knew this would be their last tango, they might have made a better effort. Berger smiled, then pressed the button in his left pocket.

It was all over the morning news. A split screen interruption ran on all the local stations: *Dock Explosion. Several presumed dead. Ten wounded. Cause unknown. Investigators on the scene.*

Reporters rushed to the site to see first hand what had shaken the Parker Avenue Marine Terminal. Producers wondered if they could use this coverage to segue into the growing union concerns. Would they still strike? Did the union have anything to do with the destruction of the Chinese electronics shipment?

Hiram Berger listened to the breaking news on the radio as he drove his Impala through the automated carwash and vacuumed the empty trunk. At home he clicked on the TV in his bedroom and watched the people scurry. Huge shipping containers had been reduced to piles of ash and twisted metal. Tractor-trailer parts were strewn across the terminal yard. One of the heavy rear doors had landed on the roof of a four-story building a block away.

Berger whistled on the way to the shower and grinned as the phone rang.

Reilly looked up from his keyboard only to notice he had typed the last three paragraphs in capital letters. He cursed under his breath, wishing he'd paid more attention in typing class.

When Banning came around the corner, all conversation stopped. There were only two reasons a partner would be found slumming in the cubicles, and the way this guy was all business, it wasn't romance he was after.

Banning asked the first guy he came to, "Where's Sailor Beaumont?'

The young man thumbed over his shoulder. "Back there."

Banning found empty cubicles at the end of the row. Two were clearly abandoned, one neatly arranged and bearing the scent of violets. He stepped in and heard a familiar voice singing about large derrieres. He leaned over Sailor's cubicle wall and saw Reilly typing like an accompaniment to the song. The girl on the computer in the adjacent cubicle bobbed her head and sang the words with him. "...my anaconda don't want none, unless you—"

Banning said, "Reilly?"

Reilly looked up, fingers still on the keyboard. "Mr. Banning? What are you doing here?"

"I tried to call you—and Sailor."

Reilly's eyes went to his phone. The receiver was off the hook, half-buried under a stack of papers. He leaned over and fixed it, shrugged at Banning. The phone rang. Reilly didn't flinch.

Banning spoke over the ringing. "We got the okay from Montgomery, and I'll find out today if Judge Shanahan—Don't you think you should get that?' He tipped his chin toward the phone.

"What? Oh, sure." Reilly answered the phone, then handed it to Banning. "It's Sailor."

Banning told Reilly, "This is for your ears too," then spoke into the phone. "Okay. This is where we are. Montgomery wants to move forward on Bentley, and Shanahan's willing to meet with us. All we need is Neely. Preferably today. Hold on, I'll ask." Banning looked at Reilly. "Can you go to Graterford today?"

Reilly shook his head, "I'd *much* rather be in prison than typing." The head-bopping girl across the way chuckled. "But I promised Mr. Scott I'd have this to him by five. There's no way."

Banning spoke into the phone. "He's under the gun. Looks like it's you and me. Meet me in half an hour." He handed Reilly the receiver and started to walk away.

Reilly said, "What do you think his chances are?"

"Ray's?"

"Yeah."

"With *this* team on his side?' Banning grinned. "How could we lose?"

Reilly thought, *what team*

Lou Gallo lay on the chiropractor's table with his face

in a padded hole. A tall blonde woman pulled on his left leg, jingling the change in his pockets. The door inched open. Bobby 'White Shoes' Pizelli walked in.

"Woah! Lou. You okay there, big guy? Jesus Christ. Looks like she's going to tear your leg off! Easy, Sheena."

Gallo directed his muffled comments to the man's footwear. "Leave her alone, White Shoes. Unlike you, *she* is a professional."

"Unlike *me*? What are you saying, Lou? Huh?" Bobby squatted awkwardly by the table.

Gallo swung his arm. "Get out of here. What the fuck you doing here anyway?"

Gallo pulled his leg away from the chiropractor, rolled his beefy body over. There were creases on his cheeks from the paper-covered headrest.

Gallo was looking old. Lying on his back, his face was all sagging flesh and dark circles. His once tanned skin appeared sickly under the lights. Used to be Gallo could have his pick of broads wherever they went, NY, Vegas, Miami. Everyone wanted a piece of the powerful Lou G. He was fit, handsome, sexy, well endowed and rich. Now, he was mostly powerful, and rich. And sometimes angry.

"I thought you'd want to know about some recent transactions." Bobby lifted his brows, indicated with a tip of his head that these business transactions may not be fit for the ear of the lady chiropractor.

Gallo held up a hand. "Doc. Give me a minute here, will ya?"

She made a final adjustment to his lower leg, snapped the ankle with a quick downward motion then rotated it and set it gently on the table. Bobby cringed. Gallo sighed. As the door closed behind her, Gallo swung his legs over the edge of the table and sat up. He ran a hand through his graying hair, pushed it back in place. "This better be good, Bobby."

"Oh, it's good all right. Somebody blew up our container."

"What? Christ! Blew it up? What the hell happened?"

"We don't know. Tony and Billboard went down there to meet the truck and put a little pressure on that shrimp, Vince."

"Who was driving the truck?"

"What?"

"Who was driving the truck? Was it my nephew?"

"No, Lou. It wasn't your nephew. It was two guys from Jersey. They're dead, too. Cops found one of their shoes two blocks away, foot still in it." He shivered. "That fuckin' creeps me out."

"Dead *too*? What the fuck?"

"Whoever set this up knew what he was doing. He rigged the container so it'd blow when they tried to move it. Killed them all." Bobby crossed himself. "Tony Cigars, Big Ollie, the guys from Jersey, even some kid three blocks away. It's all over the news. Where you been anyway? This is the third place I been looking for you."

"Enough. All right? Enough all ready." Gallo stood, twisting his back and wincing. "Let's get out of here. I got some calls to make."

Paris Kendrick adjusted her camisole strap. "Ted, that's wonderful. Imagine the press." She zipped her skirt then leaned across the rumpled sheets to kiss him. "You'll be all over the news."

"Yes, well, that was what I was thinking," Ted said, suddenly interested in a ball of lint on the sheets. "I knew you'd understand."

"Understand?' Paris stopped buttoning her blouse. "What are you saying, Ted?"

He forced himself to look at her. "What I'm saying, is that with this much interest in our firm, nothing will be held sacred."

"And you can't afford to be seen slipping away for an afternoon with your mistress? Is that it?' She hated having this conversation, especially now with her bed-tangled hair and make-up kissed away. Paris Kendrick was not pretty when she was angry, but there was no going back now. "Are you going to try to play the loyal husband role, again?"

Ted Montgomery said nothing. He threw back the sheets and walked naked across the room to the valet, his back to Paris.

That was enough for her. "You bastard. After all these years! You never *really* planned to leave her." Paris threw her hairbrush. "Did you?"

Ted flinched as the brush hit the small of his back. He picked up his shoes and left the room with Paris right behind him.

"Don't do this," he said.

"What? Don't do what? Cause a scene? Overreact? What, Ted? What *should* I do?" She grabbed his sleeve.

"Let me go." Ted stood, one hand on the doorknob, avoiding Paris's eyes.

"You don't mean that."

Her voice was now oddly calm; her words spoken slowly like a line in a newly delivered script. Paris, auditioning for a part she didn't want. She opened her hand and felt the starched shirt fabric slide over her fingertips and out the door.

She stood in the foyer, fighting back sobs of self-pity. "You're making a big mistake, Theodore Montgomery! You'll...be...sorry."

The words escaped in pieces, as broken apart as her heart. Paris collapsed against the door then slid to the cold marble floor.

"Just you wait and see," she whispered.

Maria escorted the policemen to the entrance hall.

"We'll do all we can." The detective tapped the photograph of Stephan. "Thanks for this." He slid it into his breast pocket.

Maria nodded. She was afraid to speak, afraid she'd

start crying again. She hated how weak that made her look. She watched the cops drive away and stood on the porch for a moment with her face to the wind. She told herself, he's fine. They'll find him and bring him home. As if saying the words could convince her.

Sonja came to the porch door, phone in hand. "I'm sorry, Miss Chetta. The gentleman says, 'It's important.'"

Maria reached for the phone. Sonja hovered, hoping the news was about Stephan.

"Hello?"

"It's Lou. I need you to do something for me."

"Oh, hello." Maria waved Sonja away. She followed the wrap-around porch to the ocean side and lowered her voice. "What do you mean, Lou? Do something for you? I did what you asked in Philly. Just like twenty-four years ago. I'm done. Leave me alone."

Gallo laughed his fake laugh, the one reserved for jokes and circumstances that aren't funny. It raised goose bumps on Maria's arms.

"You ain't done till I say you're are done, babe. Boy, you sure are forgetting a few things about how life works. Your pretty boy chef was right about that."

"Stephan? Do you have him? Lou, I swear to God if you so much as harm a hair on his head."

"Maria. Maria. Just relax. The fag is fine. I think he even likes being tied up."

Maria heard someone laughing in the background.

Gallo said, "I'll give you an hour to rethink your decision." The line went dead.

Maria clicked off. She caught her reflection in the window and moved closer. She drew a hand down her face to the gold chains at her throat. She looked like a hundred other rich women. Women who had sold out their dreams and bought into the world. She yanked the chains from her neck and dropped them over the railing into the sea oats. The rings on her fingers were more resistant.

Banning eased the Jag through the bumpy prison parking lot. Sailor saw the purple sports car. A thin film of dust covered its hood.

Banning had been quiet most of the ride, lost in thought. At he gate he said, "I think we should talk to them together. I'll call Neely and put you down for Ray. Once the CO's deliver them, we can sit at the same table." Banning caught Sailor's eye. "Let me open the conversation. I don't want Neely to know how important his deposition is just yet."

"Isn't that why he came forward with the information, to help?"

"To help? To help himself is more like it. I don't think Neely wants Ray to step up to the plate before he has *his* chance."

By the time they reached the waiting room, Sailor was mentally exhausted. And they hadn't even started. She picked up a day-old paper and passed part of it to Banning.

It might have been a nice moment, one in which two people could have shared the daily crossword, or laughed over the funny pages. Instead, they read of a pending dockworker's strike, an economy in upheaval, unrest in the Middle East, local tragedy after tragedy—just the sort of news you expect when you're sitting in a maximum security prison waiting to meet with a convicted murderer.

RHU was nothing like the regular visiting room. In the Restricted Housing Unit, you only got one-hour visits, no contact and the guard was always there.

"He's dead?' Sailor asked Ray, again.

Banning touched her arm, patted it lightly.

She was still having a hard time understanding what had happened to Stash Neely. She felt like saying, Okay, so now what, but realized that would be neither professional nor appropriate.

She watched Ray walk his fingers over his bruised jaw and up his swollen cheek to his puffy right eye. He winced at a tender spot, then told then how he'd carried the bloody arm to the hospital ward. How the COs wouldn't let him in. How they just watched Stash die, and how he'd lost control and the COs took him down. Stash was dead and Ray was in the hole.

Sailor shifted uncomfortably on the hard chair. She glanced at the burly CO and wondered if he was the one with the happy fists.

Ray said in a soft, low voice, "I'll be okay. I don't mind the hole, it's really not so bad. At least it's quiet. And safe."

Sailor said, "Safe? What do you mean?"

Ray shifted on the hard chair in the metal cage. "I was thinking, you know about Stash? It doesn't add up. Stash was finally learning to keep his mouth shut and stay away from trouble. Only thing he was doing was talking to me. About Berger. He told me he knew something about Detective Berger that would be *real* interesting to his new attorney. I didn't pay much attention. He was always talking like that, like it was all about him."

Banning said, "Apparently, someone else found it interesting, too. Who else knew about his case?"

"Lots of guys. Stash wasn't exactly the shy type."

"And look where that got him. Listen," Banning said as he shifted his eyes to the guard, "until we can figure out who's behind this, and what they're after, RHU might be the best place for you."

Ray held his hand up to the mesh window, "Loud and clear."

"I'll put in a call to the Superintendent," Banning said. "I know Graterford has an EPA case pending, so they might want some legal advice."

Sailor thought she should say something positive, or do something. When she placed her hand against the mesh window, it matched perfectly with Ray's. She felt the heat from his palm, the strength of his fingertips gripping the mesh. He looked at her, meeting her eyes for the first time. And when he dropped his hand, she kept hers there, feeling the loss.

She whispered, "We can still do this."

"That's right," said Banning. "We have the earlier depositions and Stash's case file. I wasn't going to put him in front of the judge, anyway."

Sailor dropped her hand to her lap. "Maybe this could work in your favor, like a conspiracy theory, or to show how your rights have been—"

Banning cut her off before she could dig the hole any deeper. "Hang in there, Ray." He stood. "You need anything?"

Ray looked at Sailor, who had her eyes on her shoes, and shook his head.

"All right then."

The guard took his time letting them out.

For most cons, this was the hardest part: people leaving. It made an empty cell seem all the emptier, and a life sentence longer than life itself.

For the visitors, it was like going to see Grandpa in the hospital. You hated going, weren't sure how long you'd be there, and could only guess what condition he'd be in the next time you saw him.

Outside the prison, Sailor had mixed feelings. Pleasure at being back in the warm day, and guilt at taking for granted the freedom others could only dream of. She tried to remember Frost's poem about the wall, and got as far as the opening line, "Something there is that doesn't love a wall," before Banning said, "Quarter for your thoughts."

"I thought it was a penny."

"Inflation." He smiled and put his hand on her shoulder as they walked.

They drove from the concrete house in the country to brick in the city. Forced to take a detour, Banning negotiated through what might have been Ray's old neighborhood. They drove past corner stores where kids in baggy pants blared music from parked cars, the bass throbbing in Sailor's chest. Mothers sat on crumbling stoops smoking cigarettes while small, dark children splashed and squealed in plastic pools.

They drove their fancy car through the wrong part of town, Banning telling her how things were in the good old days of Philadelphia, before graffiti took over the walls, before unemployment and welfare, broken families, drugs, disease, and drive-by shootings. He went back in time, to days of telephone poles and hanging wires, one-lane roads and horse carriages, sturdy houses with yards and flower-filled gardens. When people strolled down the street visiting neighbors on warm summer nights and you could hear radio music drifting from stuffy sitting rooms, where young couples planned their futures holding hands on the settee.

Sailor liked that, and wondered if it still existed—somewhere.

Reilly checked the clock on his computer then pushed the heels of his hands into his eyes and rubbed, as if he could erase the last six hours of work. It was still quiet from Sailor's side of the wall. He looked at the phone then decided he needed a break.

Deluca's outer office was empty. Reilly knocked once and entered. Sailor looked up from Deluca's big desk and smiled, pleased to see him.

Reilly thought she was beautiful today, like yesterday, like every day. *"Bon soir, Mademoiselle."* He made exaggerated bowing and saluting gestures.

Sailor laughed.

Reilly sat on the corner of the desk. "So, how did it go? How's Ray holding up?"

Sailor's smile shrank. "He's in RHU. I tried to call you."

"What happened?"

She told him about Stash Neely and the accident and Ray. She said, "Banning's making some calls now." She turned the laptop toward Reilly, pointed to a message.

When Reilly leaned in, Sailor smelled rosemary and pine needles. She didn't know whether to dip him in red sauce or lie on top of him.

He said, "Sounds like the sender wants to avoid confrontation." He gestured to the keyboard. "May I?"

"Help yourself."

A few clicks later, a dictionary listing for 'vitriol' appeared. Reilly pointed to the word, 'caustic'. "See, not good. Who sent this?"

Sailor shrugged. "I don't know. It came from an anonymous account, routed from a public server."

"Wait a minute. This is Deluca's email?"

Sailor hesitated, then nodded.

Reilly smiled. "Nice job." He read it again. "Maybe the known opposition is another firm, it could have something to do with a current case." Reilly watched Sailor's thumb find her lower lip. He tore his eyes away and asked, "What's Fast Eddie working on?"

"That's just it." She dropped her hands onto her lap. "As far as I know, there's just this Witherspoon thing, and that's basically pled out. His load is light. He even said something yesterday about taking a vacation."

Reilly looked worried. "Fast Eddie doesn't vacation."

Sailor caught his eyes, held them with hers and forgot all about Deluca and the email and the office. She saw herself in Reilly's pupil and looked deeper.

Reilly felt something. Sure, she had pretty eyes; lots of girls did. And yeah, she smelled nice. But when Sailor looked at him like this, there was something else. He felt like a cliff diver, balanced high above an emerald pool with the desire to leap

.

17
To Understand Each Other

THE light was green but the silver minivan didn't budge. JR Pantaglioni felt like giving it a little shove in the 'My child is an honor student' bumper sticker. "Come on, lady, Jesus Christ."

His passenger, Frankie "Four Eyes" Germano said, "She can't go nowhere. There's a cop holding a stop sign."

"Holding a stop sign? The light's green; you're supposed to do what the light says, not what the sign says. And the light says, go."

"Don't you know anything? A cop overrules all the other signs and lights. If there's a cop holding a sign that says, 'Eat my shorts', then that's what you do."

"Yeah, that'll be the day."

"Hey, ain't that him? Over there, with the fat kid."

"Yeah, that's him all right. Berger."

Retired Detective Hiram Berger held a stop sign in his left hand and motioned to the crossing guard and her string of children. He watched them follow the crosswalk to another corner, look both ways and cross again. The guard made her way back to the school and Berger waved the buses out into the traffic. The sighs of the car drivers were audible. No one wanted to get stuck behind a noxious school bus on a hot afternoon in Philadelphia.

"There, that's the last of them buses."

"I can see that, Four Eyes. Get out here. I'll pull around."

The tall thin man wrenched himself from the Caprice and stepped to the curb as the line of cars edged forward impatiently.

Berger watched the buses pull away. He saw Four Eyes by the light post then heard the squeal of the Caprice's tires on the hot asphalt as JR swung in tight behind the Impala.

Berger walked to his car and tossed the hand sign through the open window, then pulled the reflective vest over his head.

JR came up behind him. "How's it going, pal? Get the kiddies across the street in one piece? I would hate for something to happen on your shift."

Berger spoke over his shoulder, "What the fuck are you doing here, Junior? You need someone to hold your dick, huh? Four Eyes can't find it?"

"Real funny, Berger. You ain't gonna be laughing after the Boss is through with you. Come on. We're going for a ride."

"I don't think so." Berger brushed JR's hand off his arm, reached for the Impala's handle. "I've got other plans."

JR smiled. Berger opened the car door and froze. Four Eyes sat in the passenger seat, one hand slung over the blue vinyl back, the other aiming a gun at Berger's crotch. "Your plans have changed."

"Get in and drive," JR said. "And no funny stuff. I'll be right behind you." He slammed the door, rattling the window in the frame.

Berger asked casually, too casually, "Where to?"

"I think you know. Gallo wants to ask you a few

questions." Four Eyes pushed up his thick glasses with his middle finger.

Berger pulled out, saw the Caprice follow. "You know, they make contacts now that anybody can wear."

"It ain't natural," Four Eyes replied, shoving the glasses up again. "I mean, whoever came up with the idea to put a piece of plastic in your eye. Jesus." He shuddered.

Berger glanced sideways. "Bet you'd see better."

"I see just fine. Had these glasses ten years now and still got twenty-twenty." Four Eyes lowered the muzzle of the gun slightly.

"Yeah, twenty-twenty? That's pretty good."

"Yeah."

"But what about your peripheral vision?"

"Per-what?"

"You know, how you see out of the sides of your eyes."

"What the fuck you talking about, the *sides* of my eyes?"

Berger gunned the Impala's big engine, swung out around the minivan in front of them and cut back in, just making it through the amber light and leaving JR in the Caprice sitting at the red light.

"Jesus, where'd you learn to drive?" Four Eyes glanced into the side mirror. "You lost him! "

Berger chopped his hand down hard on Four Eyes' wrist, then slammed on the brakes throwing his unbelted passenger into the windshield. The pick-up truck behind them swerved to avoid the crash, jumped the curb and ran head first into a pizza shop.

Berger reached for the gun that had slid from Four Eyes' hand and fallen to the floor. He raced through traffic, going deeper into the city as JR came up fast behind him. Berger pulled into the passing lane. Going nowhere. He cut back in, ignoring the shouts and honking horns. There—an opening. Berger gunned the engine and sent the Impala surging down a side street, smashing through pothole after pothole. Four Eyes' head banged into the starred windshield like a bobble-head toy. The last bounce jarred him awake. He turned his bloody face to Berger, thick lenses embedded in his pulpy forehead and squeezed the trigger.

"Fuck! You fucking shot me!" Berger grabbed his leg then pulled his hand away, bloody. "You son of a bitch!"

Four Eyes slumped against the dashboard, his gun dangling from his limp hand.

The car catapulted down the narrow street. No one behind him—yet. He jammed his left foot on the brake and squealed into a parking garage. He smashed through the wooden gate and made his way down to the lowest level, to a dark corner behind an industrial van.

Berger didn't have much time. He figured the cops would send two cars to deal with the casualties back there, one to chase him. He ripped the keys from the ignition and surveyed the damage.

"Goddammit!" Berger pulled a rag from under the driver's seat, tied it tightly around his leg. It looked like the bullet had gone straight through his calf. He pushed Four Eyes off the dashboard and reached into the glove box, grabbing his cell phone, his wallet and his ball cap. He slid the hat on his head and left the Impala, then limped to the elevator hitting re-dial on his phone as he hobbled along.

On the second ring, and answer: "Hello?"

"Gina." He struggled to slow his breathing. "I need your help."

"Hi?' She paused, knowing his tricks. "Listen, you agreed we needed some time apart, and I meant it, now if this is your idea of making up—"

"Gina, please. This isn't about us. I really need your help."

"Why? Are you off the meds again?"

"Gina, it's not that. I need you to meet me at the library. Please, it's important. And bring your first-aid kit."

"First-aid kit? Hi? What's going on?"

He hung up as the elevator doors opened. Five minutes later he drove a borrowed car to Philadelphia's Central

Library on 19th and Vine.

"Chuck? I've gotta go out for a little while!" Gina yelled as she ripped off her apron and tossed it over the coat rack. She scrambled through drawers in her office, throwing a first aid kit and green t-shirt into her silver backpack purse.

Chuck stood in the doorway, his hands on his hips. "Hey! Where are you going?"

"I've got to run an errand." Gina squeezed around him and jogged toward the front. "I'll be back. Listen, call that new girl. Tell her to come in early, and make sure she pulls her hair back today, okay?"

Chuck nodded. "Hey, Gina?"

She looked back at the cook, one foot already in the sunlight.

"Be careful."

Gina smiled grimly and was gone.

Deluca's desk phone rang. Reilly reeled backward, blinking rapidly. What the hell? He eased himself from the edge of the desk, away from her eyes. The phone continued to ring.

Sailor calmly raised the receiver. "Mr. Deluca's office." She listened then raised a brow at Reilly.

The man on the other end sounded sick, or really drunk. "I said. Put Eddie on."

"May I tell him who's calling?"

"No, you may not. Jesus Christ! Just put... him...on." The guy groaned.

"Sir?" Sailor switched the call to the speakerphone.

Reilly heard traffic noises.

Sailor said, "Are you all right?

"I'm fine. Get me Eddie." The man breathed heavily, his words paced upon the exhale.

"One moment, please." Sailor reached for the hold button, but Reilly grabbed her hand.

On the other end, the man kept talking. "Goddammit,

Gina. Did you have to pour that shit on there? That fucking kills."

They heard a woman's voice. "Shut up, Hi. I'm trying to help."

Reilly released Sailor's hand.

She pushed the hold button and a red light blinked. "Oh my God, it's Berger."

"And Gina." Reilly looked away.

"What should I say?"

"Tell him Deluca stepped out. And get his number."

Sailor hesitated, then punched the blinking light. "I'm sorry, Sir. Mr. Deluca is unavailable. May I have him call you?"

"You tell Eddie I need him to deliver a message to his pal."

"A message, sir?"

"Yeah. Tell him, I don't stop till I get back what belongs to me. You got that?"

"Yes. I'm writing it down." Sailor grabbed a pen. "Who should I say is calling? Sir?"

But Berger had hung up.

Sailor looked at Reilly. "What the hell was that? He wants Deluca to deliver a message to his *pal*?"

Reilly had some questions himself like, why was Gina with Berger when she said they were through?

There was a tap on the door and Mimi leaned her head into the office. "Thanks for covering for me, Sailor."

"No problem."

Mimi noticed Reilly and smiled. She smoothed her blouse and looked for something to say. Finding nothing, she started to close the door, then popped her head back inside.

"Pretty crazy what's happening on the docks, isn't it? My sister lives over there, says she can't even get home. All the streets are closed off."

Sailor and Reilly looked puzzled.

Mimi said, "The explosion... Wait, didn't you hear?

They're probably still talking about it." She nodded toward the TV, then pulled the door shut.

Reilly found the remote and the local channel's breaking news report.

The reporter, Taylor Dunne, a round-faced salon blond stood at an entrance to the Philadelphia Docks, a flurry of activity behind her.

"Officials have reason to believe an incendiary device was planted under the Chinese crate. There is still no confirmation on the origin of the tractor-trailer. Pier authorities are investigating—"

The anchor in the studio interrupted, "Is there any word on casualties, Taylor?"

"Yes. We have at least four fatalities, Stan."

"Do we know who they are, Taylor?"

"Not at this time, Stan. Authorities won't release that information until the victim's families have been notified."

Reilly hit the mute button. "Holy shit." His eyes went to the message from Berger.

"Wait. You don't think Berger did *that*, do you?" Sailor pointed to the scene. As firefighters held hoses on a black smoking mass, a crowd of dockworkers gathered around another reporter, some with cuts on their faces, others with tears in their eyes.

"One way to find out." Reilly pulled out his phone.

"Who are you calling?"

"Gina."

"Gina Chamblee? Berger's Gina? Lou Gallo's ex-wife?" Sailor said, "Hang on Reilly, Let's think this out. What would a retired detective be doing at the Philadelphia Pier?"

"Maybe he planted the bomb?"

"Or he was with the truck."

"Why would he be with the truck?" Reilly said. "He's not a dockworker."

"Who said the truck drivers were dock workers?"

"What are you saying, Sailor?"

She scribbled something on the message pad. "Did you see the door of the truck? The one they kept showing on the roof of that building?"

"Yeah?"

"How's your Italian?"

"Besides cannolli, spaghetti and Chianti, not so good."

"Look." Sailor turned her pad of paper around. She had written, 'apirs a vicen', the words as they appeared on the wrinkled truck panel and under that, 'capirsi a vicenda'.

Reilly ran a hand through his hair. "That sounds familiar."

"It should. It's one of Lou Gallo's favorite sayings. He said it at least four times during the trial. It means 'to understand each other'."

Reilly lowered his voice, "That was Gallo's truck?"

Sailor nodded.

"And we know Berger and Gallo have a past," Reilly said.

"Right. So now we—"

"Do nothing. Yet." Reilly looked at her. "Deliver the message to Deluca. He'll have to contact his *pal*, right?"

"Probably won't call him, not if it's someone involved in that." Sailor pointed to the TV screen and the smoldering remains of the semi.

"Okay, so he'll meet the pal in person, or–"

"E-mail him." Sailor picked up the phone, punched in three numbers.

"Who are you calling?"

Sailor spoke around the receiver. "Early. He's a computer genius. I wanted to talk to him about the disc, anyway. He'll help us. He likes me."

Reilly rolled his eyes. Didn't she know? All the guys liked her, some more than others.

Ten minutes later, Richard Early left his cramped corner in the firm's basement and made his way upstairs. He wondered what Sailor needed and why the air seemed better up here

18
I Know You Know
That He Knows What We Know

SO, that's it?' Sailor stepped back. She'd been leaning over Early's shoulder. She enjoyed watching his fingers fly over the keyboard, hitting all those F keys like he knew exactly what each one would do.

Early wanted to turn his head and sniff. Just one long, deep inhale. Sailor was close enough to lick. Not that he'd lick her. He was just trying to place the high points in her cologne. It was driving him insane. He got the floral undertones of peony and gardenia, but there was something else, something that reminded him of tabouli or baby powder. It was an intriguing mix. Usually commercial colognes were simple, but Early had been distracted by the programming, and by Sailor's breasts.

He'd been asked to do a few unusual things since he began with MDB&S, but it was usually by pudgy men who bore the aroma of bacon and Crest with a hint of desperation. Not like Sailor. Early had been able to follow the anonymous email back to the internet provider. Now he was hacking the customer base.

"You're amazing," Sailor said. "Where did you learn all this?"

Early grinned, his eyes on the screen. "I could tell you, but then I'd have to kill you."

Sailor's eyes went wide, until she realized he was joking. "Ha-ha. Very funny."

Early snorted, his laugh more of a choke and gurgle.

A flashing warning appeared on the screen.

Sailor said, "Uh-oh."

Early hit a few keys, watched the download figures. "Ten more seconds, come on." He typed faster, opening and closing windows.

The screen went blue. Then blank.

"Darn it." Early smacked his hands on the keyboard.

"What happened?"

"They slammed the door."

Early sunk back in the chair. "You know, it's probably not such a good idea to do this here." He looked around Deluca's office. "But, I could work on it at home." He looked at Sailor. "If you wanted to come over."

Sailor said, "Are you saying you'd be able to find out who sent the message and if there are any more?"

Early rocked rapidly in the chair. "No sweat. I'd be glad to help you."

Sailor wished he'd quit bouncing. She touched his arm. "So, something that's encrypted would be..."

Early stopped rocking. "As easy as finding a geek at a Star Trek Convention."

Sailor wrote on a notepad. "Here's my number." She handed it to him, then grabbed Deluca's computer disc from her purse and held it up. "I'd be interested to see what you can find on this."

She leaned close enough for him to feel her breath on his cheek. "Richard? This is just between us, right?' She nodded, waited for him to nod back. "Call me as soon as you know anything."

Richard Early slipped his first beautiful girl's phone number into his left front pocket next to the rabbit's foot and smiled.

Sailor walked him to the lobby, where Early got on an elevator and went back to the dark halls of taxes, with tabouli, baby powder and peony on his mind.

Paris Kendrick, jilted mistress, unhappy wife, keeper of secrets, watched from the reception desk. The call to Mrs. Theodore Wells Montgomery hadn't gone as planned. The old bag said she'd known all along, and that it would take a lot more than a two-bit floozey pumped up with silicone and Botox to get the best of her. What Paris hated most was how Alice said, "Dammit, now he'll expect *me* to sleep with him."

Here was Paris, actually missing her husband, Arnold, who was thousands of miles away and not due back for a week. She would have thought the idea of Ted and Alice going at it under the silk sheets would be enough to turn her off sex for the rest of her life, but oddly, she felt her blood rising.

It was a toss up. Her optometrist had a nicer ass—and a voice that said, I'm looking at more than your pupils when I blind you with my penlight. Paris was sure that brush against her thigh last week was not accidental. She sighed. Of course, there were plenty of opportunities right here at MDB&S, and don't forget Jerry, the delivery guy. There was something about that curly chest hair peeking out of his brown shirt that bugged her, but the guy had eyes the color of Yves St. Laurent's spring collection, and she knew she looked good in blue.

A girl's got to be choosy, or else she'd end up with something like the geek who was getting on the elevator. What did Sailor see in him? And what were they doing in Deluca's office?

Paris didn't like this girl. She was too beautiful, too

savvy. She made Paris feel old and resentful. Paris sipped her tea and was thinking of tanned cabana boys in Oaxaca when Deluca stepped off the elevator smelling like gin and trouble.

"Hello, beautiful."

"Eddie."

"So when are you going to leave that husband of yours and run away with me?"

"Who says I have to leave him?"

Deluca raised a brow. Paris winked. She'd invented this game. She leaned over her high desk, twisted her headset mic out of the way and lowered her voice, "You might want to keep a better eye on your intern."

He looked up from her cleavage.

"Leave a girl alone in your office, and you never know what she might find—or hear."

Deluca unlocked his door, saw tomorrow's calendar on top of the in-box, just where he'd told Mimi to leave it. Everything seemed in order. Sailor could poke around all she wanted. There was nothing for her to find here. He sat at his desk, loosened his tie and unbuttoned the top button of his shirt then pulled a glass and a bottle of Macallan from the bottom drawer. What a fucking mess. He poured himself a snoot and kicked off his shoes. On the third sip, he saw the message pad. He slid it over and read it, then downed his drink. Goddamn Berger.

Deluca tore the paper from the pad, balled it up and dropped it in the nearly empty wastebasket by his desk. It joined another pink paper. This one was neatly folded. Deluca fished it out and read Sailor's precise writing, "*Capirsi a vicenda.*"

It was late and all Reilly wanted was another cold beer and a soft bed. That wasn't true. What he really wanted was a line of coke the size of his middle finger, a girl who never said no and a week in a hot tropical climate where clothes were optional. But he was trying to be good. He knew things could get out of control. Hell, look at Shelly. It wasn't going to happen to him, he was too smart for that, and the way Sailor felt about drugs, he was seriously thinking about giving the whole thing up, just as soon as this caseload lightened.

He opened the door to his apartment, paged his dealer and grabbed a beer. While he waited for the call back, he flipped through TV channels, watched the end of a bad movie and finally settled on a shopping network where a gorgeous brunette sold jewels from her cleavage. He had his hand on the phone when it rang.

"Hi. It's Sailor. You busy?"

Reilly hit the TV mute button, saw the ticker across the bottom of the screen, '...last chance for the Executive Hotdog Rotisserie...'. He tore his eyes away. "It's late. What are you doing up?"

"I've got something you might want to see."

Yes, you do. Reilly thought.

Sailor said, "Can you come over?"

"Sure. Give me a minute." Reilly hung up the phone, saw the 'sold' banner flashing over the Executive Rotisserie and sighed.

Ace called a meeting in the prison weight room. The CO outside the door had been plied with money and favors. He was one of theirs and they treated him well.

"There better not be no miscommunication on this matter. You hear?' Ace looked around at the blank faces. "What I mean is I want this done right, and nothing comes back on me, understand?"

They nodded, four pale white heads bobbing.

"The Man says Bentley stuck his nose where it don't belong. He needs someone to teach him a lesson, show him where his black-ass nose do belong. Alright?"

The CO knocked to signal someone was coming.

Ace raised his fist in a powerful salute, and the others

raised their fists in kind.

Sailor answered on the first knock. If Reilly hadn't known better, he would have sworn she was wasted, the way she was smiling, the way her eyes glittered.

"Check this out."

Reilly followed her to the dining room. The blank spaces under the photos had been filled in and there were more lines connecting more people.

"The email?"

She pointed to a new card, "Shanahan."

"You're kidding."

She shook her head. "Early's positive. He's been sending me stuff from the encrypted disc. Emails about meetings and cases, and all of the files. I haven't even looked at these yet." She pulled a stack of papers from the printer and handed them to Reilly.

He scanned a few pages. "Mostly business documents. Here's one Deluca filed for Angelina Imports. He lists the owner and CEO as Maria Chetta, AKA Maria Rosarita Conchetta," Reilly looked at Sailor. "Ring any bells?"

"That's not the same girl who lied on the stand in Ray's case? Is it?"

"Let's run a search." Reilly sat at the computer and keyed in 'Chetta', then waited.

A list of files popped up. He opened the first one. It was a divorce decree between Maria Chetta and Louis Michael Gallo."

"Wait a minute. I thought *Gina* was married to Gallo."

Reilly said, "Don't look at me. Maybe he was married twice."

"Maybe."

"Or maybe he just marries people he does business with."

"What?"

Reilly passed her a paper. "Look at the stockholders."

Sailor ran her eyes down the list, Gina Chamblee, Maria Chetta, Edward Deluca, LMG Enterprises, Paris Kendrick,

Alice and Company. She looked at Reilly, her finger on LMG Enterprises. "That's a Gallo Family business, right?"

"Oh yeah."

"But, Deluca and Kendrick? And who's Alice and Company?"

"Might be something you'll want to ask Paris about in the morning." He checked the clock. "Or should I say later this morning? I've got a meeting with Harry in New York. So, you're on your own."

Sailor stared at the wall lost in thought, her thumb stroking her lip. Her voice was soft and dreamy when she said, "Ry, What does Angelina's import?"

Reilly read, "Celadon and carved jade...from China."

Sailor smiled. "Bingo."

"I think it was more like, Blam-o!"

Sailor's laptop dinged.

Reilly said, "You've got mail."

Sailor clicked on the new message. "Looks like Early's retrieval program worked."

Reilly leaned in as they read together, "quickE to LMG. Yellow Pages need recycling. Details at CC meet."

Reilly looked at Sailor. "What's Fast Eddie up to now?"

19

Just When You Think
You've Got It All Figured Out

THEY'D spent a sleepless night at Gina's. She'd wanted to bring Hi home after the library, had wanted to be done with this whole mess. But when she'd driven down his street, he'd freaked out about a big blue van and kept going on and on about 'them'.

Gina had patted him down like a teenager and found his meds. She was pissed when she found the bottles almost empty. She tossed them into her purse, then brought him back to her place and set him up on the couch and told him to stay there.

She wasn't sure how much of his story to believe. Gallo hiding drugs in Chinese shipments. A million bucks in cash gone missing. The dock explosion and some guy named Four Eyes taking him for a ride.

She knew he was in trouble when an early morning knock on the door was accompanied by a stranger's voice.

They scooted out the back way to the neighbors,

leaving Gina's car in plain view on the street. Right in front of the stranger's black sedan. Maybe Hi wasn't paranoid after all. If anyone knew what Lou could be like, and what both these men were capable of, it was Gina.

"Jesus, Hi, why didn't you tell me that you were low on meds?" She spoke over her shoulder.

Berger caught the look, like he smelled as bad as the back of the fucking car. He lay on the floor between the seats, wounded leg propped up on a few towels, pint of Jack Daniels in his hand. From here all he could see clearly was blue sky and a little tan air freshener someone had stuck to the underside of the driver's seat.

"Smells like shit back here." He snorted, "Who the hell still drives a station wagon, anyway?"

"Hi, you know what they say about beggars. My friend was nice enough to lend me her car, what was I going to say, 'No thank you, I'd prefer a Cadillac?'" She shook her head.

"I'm just saying, it smells back here, like a fucking farm."

"Must be the compost. She hauls it for the community garden. Stop distracting me. What about the meds, Hi?" This time she tweaked the rear view mirror so she could see him.

Berger said, "I'm fine, Gina. Really. I'll be fine. Besides, I've got you." He smiled at her reflection in the mirror, tears welling in his eyes.

It broke her heart. He could be such a softie at times. Not all the time, she reminded herself, and flicked her eyes back on the road, squinting against the glare.

Gina's family kept a hunting cabin in Dauphin County. It was a simple place in the woods and seldom used anymore, as there was no electricity or running water, which meant no Nintendo for the boys, no showers or flushing toilets for the girls and no football or pizza delivery for the men. It was time to either renovate the place and bring it into the current century or sell the land to the cult across the water and let them expand their organic mushroom gardens.

She hadn't been there in years. Gina hoped the road was still clear and the key still in the coffee can. And she hoped the bears had left the outhouse standing. Being stuck in the woods with her bi-polar boyfriend who'd started a one-man war with her ex-husband, Philly's favorite mobster, Lou Gallo, *and* having to pee in the bushes. Great.

Sailor left Reilly sleeping in her bed. Last night, they had discovered a few things and not all of them had to do with the case.

She showered, dressed, brewed coffee then peeked in on him, wondered what the hell she was doing and where she thought this was going. But things didn't always have to go somewhere, did they? She put her extra key on the counter with a note then locked the door behind her. She'd never been good at the morning-after talk and was glad Reilly had a meeting in New York and that she'd be at MDB&S.

Sailor needed to talk to Paris before the meeting with Banning and Judge Shanahan. Reilly said that if Shanahan was crooked with Deluca, he'd be crooked with Banning and that might be good for Ray. Sailor wasn't so sure. All she wanted was help getting to Berger and a few answers. Reilly told her, things don't work that way. This wasn't Connecticut.

She slid behind the wheel, all business until she remembered how Reilly had kissed her. That wasn't like Connecticut, either. It had felt like a magnet. She knew if she closed her eyes—was even half a room away, her lips would still find his without a bumped tooth or an embarrassing last minute tilt of the head. Reilly kissed her as if he had been doing it for years. She smiled and drove a little faster.

Sailor stepped off the elevator into the cold, empty foyer of MDB&S and headed straight for Paris on her pedestal. Nothing like stepping into the lion's den.

"Can I ask you a question?"

Paris looked at Sailor like she was a bug to be squashed. "What is it?"

"It's about Angelina Imports."

"I don't know anything about that. Perhaps you should ask Mr. Deluca."

"Oh, I intend to. I just thought you'd like to get a word in first, as a stockholder."

"I'm not a stockholder. Not anymore."

Sailor waited.

"Check your data. I sold my shares to new investors."

"Who are these new investors?"

Paris shrugged. "No one I know, I can assure you." Her eyes flitted away, then back. "The others had different plans for the business. Let's just say, I'm not like them."

Sailor let that go and asked, "How well do you know Maria Chetta?"

Paris sniffed. "Not well. I mean we're not friendly."

No. I don't imagine you are, thought Sailor. She waited.

Paris said, "She came here a lot in the beginning. When she was Maria *Con*chetta. The firm handled her inheritance."

Sailor looked lost. Paris explained. "We were smaller then, just Montgomery and Banning. Maria had made some sort of deal with King. Her name was on everything. And when King was murdered in 1977, she got it all. Houses, land, stocks, cash. Later, she made millions when the city bought the waterfront property. Ted, Mr. Montgomery, said they should have named the firm's yacht, *The Maria*." Paris met Sailor's eyes. "I don't know who she thought she was kidding when she changed her name and moved to the Cape. You know what they say, you can take the girl out of the projects, but you can't take the projects out of the girl." Paris laughed.

Sailor remembered what she'd read last night. "The girl from the projects seems to be doing pretty well for herself."

Paris looked like she wanted to say something else, but two lines buzzed and the elevator doors opened. The meeting was over.

Sailor walked away, putting the pieces together. A small puzzle of a man wrongly convicted now covered a large table, pieces strewn from end to end, and somewhere a bottle of glue that would hold even the mismatched pieces together forever.

Banning assured Sailor there was nothing to worry about. He'd handle it from here. They made plans to meet in his office after he'd spoken to the Judge and made some calls. Of course they'd need Berger's deposition and there were some questions for Deluca, but things had to be handled a certain way.

Sailor conceded. What choice did she have? Reilly was on his way out of town, her father was unavailable, and frankly she didn't think she should involve him anyway, and Jeremy, well, she hadn't talked to him lately and he did work for Deluca.

Banning closed the door to his office and placed the call to Maria Chetta. She sounded as if she'd been expecting him, though they hadn't said more than ten words to each other in twenty-some odd years. And when he asked her to come to Philadelphia, she agreed. He arranged for a suite at the Rittenhouse, no expenses spared.

The high hollow sounds of a Chinese pipa played on the small stereo. A fountain bubbled and trickled next to the chair where his clothes lay. The stub of incense still burned, coiling its exotic scent to the low ceiling.

"No, Mai, no happy ending today. Mr. Eddie has important meeting."

Deluca sat up and the sheet fell away from his lower body. The naked girl stood there like she was waiting for him to change his mind, or waiting for a bus. He had no idea. He didn't even know her name. He called them all Mai. Damn. She looks really sad, maybe I should let her give me the happy ending.

Then he glanced at the clock, his decision made for him. The people he was meeting wouldn't wait.

She dropped her head.

"But, I'll pay you for it anyway," he said and pulled on his boxers and pants.

Smiling broadly now, she came up behind him and held his shirt. They were so agreeable, thought Deluca. No wonder all those army boys brought home their overseas cooch. They'd never get an American broad to treat them this well. Got to have Mimi book me a vacation to Vietnam or Thailand this fall.

Deluca tossed two bills onto the table by the fountain. He watched the girl wrap her robe around her slight body, her eyes never leaving the money.

He exited the building through the back, found his car and opened the trunk to lay his suit coat out, and then saw the gym bag. He folded it so *Berger* was hidden then slipped it under the metal lip of the dumpster in the alley.

Deluca pulled into traffic. Of course there was traffic. He switched on the radio and waited for news, a report, anything that could tell him why he was sitting here in a line of cars going nowhere. He had just spent a hundred bucks getting rid of the knot in his lower back, and could feel it balling up again.

He reached for a CD, selected track four and started the slow, deep, yoga breathing he'd learned from Mariel.

In the first week of their courtship, she'd dragged him to yoga at the gym. The class wasn't so difficult that he couldn't enjoy it, or so easy that it didn't challenge him. The exercises were really pretty good, but it was the looks he got from the guys when they saw him come out of the candle-lit room. He tried to tell them he was only there for the babes. Hey, you haven't seen nothing till you've seen a roomful of beautiful women with their asses in the air doing Down Dog.

They joked about that for a while, until a few of the guys actually started going on a regular basis, quoting some bullshit about increased blood flow and rejuvenation which ruined it for him. Deluca didn't care about any of that. He'd never admit it, but he liked the feeling in that room, and the candles and the whispery breath and the sound of OM.

By the time DeLuca pulled through the iron gates of the Philadelphia Country Club he was calm and centered. The men waiting for him in the private room upstairs were neither.

Judge Shanahan half-rose from his chair and pointed a crooked finger across the table. His hand shook as he tried to curb his anger, "You little fuck! You shite!" Beads of sweat popped out on the man's forehead, and small blue veins pulsed at his temples. "We had a deal, we had a deal."

Ted Montgomery put a hand on his arm, "Come on Judge. Sit down. He's not worth it."

Shanahan looked down at the cool, reserved Montgomery. He felt his heart curiously close to the surface and for a moment forgot where he was. A quick glance around the room reminded him he was in a place where you didn't jump out of your chair or point your finger at a mobster and call him a little shite. Not if you ever wanted to see your lovely Kate again you didn't. He slumped back in his chair and mopped his forehead with a white linen napkin.

Jeremy Strom stood outside the door listening to every outburst. He placed a name to the voice and imagined where each body was around the table. He closed his eyes for a second, a mental snapshot of the room flashed. He'd been three steps inside five minutes ago and already knew two ways to get out of there quickly if something went down. And that there was enough room behind the oak bar in the southwest corner if he had to get Eddie to cover. He checked his watch. Where was Deluca, anyway?

Gallo continued. "As I was saying, we think it's best to hold off on the strike for two more days. There's a shipment coming in we can't afford to miss. Once they pull the cops off the site, we'll have our guys back in line and move the merchandise as planned. When the strike hits and the goods are tied up, we'll be the only source. And the price will be ours to set."

"Yeah, yeah." Shanahan turned to Montgomery. "Isn't that what they said last month? I did not drive all the way out here to have you numb nuts tell me what I already know."

Deluca walked in. "I hear you, Judge. What *I* want to know is, when do I get my money, and who's doing the holding before the split?

Reilly told himself a jog would do him good. He locked up with Sailor's key then went to his apartment to change. He'd left the TV on and the cell phone open. It was dead and the charger was at work. Reilly had almost forgotten the call to his dealer. Almost.

He went to his bedroom, strapped on a waist pack to hold money and keys and stretched on the way down in the elevator. By the time he reached the lobby his resolve had faded, but he figured he'd give it a go anyway. Three blocks later, he wished he'd stayed in bed.

He felt his firm, muscular legs straining and pumping beneath him and thought, *I'm in good shape, what the hell am I doing killing myself here?*

Had he gone one more block, he might have pushed through to the other side. He knew the place where pain feels good and endorphins pulse. That place where you're smiling on the inside. An addict knows that place. Reilly knew that place. He slowed to a walk, crossed the street, bought a paper and a coffee and walked back home to the condos, where a car from MDB&S was coming to pick him up for a meeting in New York City.

White Shoes wanted to crack the guy over the head and knock a little sense into him, shake him up and re-arrange the marbles. They argued the whole ride down, about not pausing at yield signs, merging too slowly onto the highway, failing to come to a complete stop. It was more than his driving. It was the way the bonehead thought. He swore he should have taken Junior out a long time ago. He glanced over. Son of a bitch was smiling.

"What's so funny, JR?"

"Nothing," JR said. "I'm just in a good mood."

"A good mood? What the fuck is that? Cause of you, Four Eyes is in the hospital, you said yourself, you ain't been laid in a week, and right back there," White Shoes jerked his thumb over his shoulder, "when you ran that stop sign, you said you hated this fucking city and couldn't wait to move to the shore. You call *that* a good mood?"

"Hey, White Shoes, settle down. I was just ranting back there. That don't affect my mood."

"Ranting?"

"Yeah, you know, getting shit off my chest. It's healthy."

"Might be healthy for you. But it ain't so healthy for those of us who gotta hear it. Know what I mean?"

JR started to whistle.

White Shoes shook his head. "Ke-rist." He read the street numbers, checked the paper in his hand. "Hey, Happy." He pointed to a building on the left. "There it is."

Swerving across three lanes of traffic, JR crossed the median and pulled up in front of Oakwood Condominiums with White Shoes firmly attached to the Jesus handle.

JR read, "'Luxury furnished Corporate apartments for temporary or long-term lease.' That sounds real nice."

White Shoes rolled his eyes. "Come on. Get the tools."

JR opened the back of the van, pulled out two metal toolboxes and three orange cones.

"What the fuck?"

"Makes us look official," JR said, setting the cones around the vehicle. "And this way, we won't get a ticket."

"I'm driving on the way back, you hear me?" White Shoes pulled his ball cap low over his forehead then lifted one of the toolboxes and started up the steps.

No one bothered them in the vestibule of mailboxes. No one looked twice as they jangled their way down the halls of the condominium complex. Everyone knew the sound of a service worker. The clomp of heavy-soled shoes, the rasping bark of a smoker's cough, the smack and rattle of a full metal toolbox. No one thought anything unusual about two men in blue coveralls entering Sailor's apartment.

"Nice." JR twisted his ball cap around so the bill shadowed his neck. "I could live in a place like this." He ran his hand over the couch, straightened a pillow on the side chair. "Except I'd want more leather, and maybe a lighter shade of yellow on the walls."

"What are you, a faggot? Get the fuck in here."

White Shoes stood in the dining room in front of the wall of photos from the retirement party.

JR pointed. "Hey look, that's you."

White Shoes squinted. Son of a bitch, it *was* he, at Berger's party, talking to that redhead with the rack.

"Who's she, White Shoes? Nice set." JR ran his finger over the breasts in the photograph.

"Yeah, yeah."

White Shoes pushed the guy's hand away and skimmed the other photos. There was Berger with the Judge, Berger with Deluca, and Berger with his cop buddies and some young red-haired Mick who was always smiling. How did they miss somebody with a camera that night? Gallo was right. This girl was in it deep. Who the fuck was the beat up black dude in the mug shot? And why were all the lines coming back to him?

"Look at these books. Think she read them all?" JR lifted two law books, hefting them like weights. "Man, they're heavy."

"Put those down. Lou said don't disturb nothing. Just find the computer, then start on the phones." White Shoes reached in his pocket, took out a CD, handed it to JR. "You sure you know what you're doing?"

"Sure. No problem."

Reilly reached into the waist pack for his apartment key and came up with Sailor's instead. He looked down the hall toward her place, smiled, then dug around some more and found his own key.

Inside, he dropped the paper in the kitchen and looked around. It was still early; too early to get dressed, too late to go back to bed. What was he supposed to do? He went to the bedroom and checked his stash drawer. Nothing. He went through pants pockets, jackets, even the trash can. Then he remembered the black binder, the one he'd used at Sailor's last night, the one with the little pocket in the back.

White Shoes said, "Did you hear that?'

"What?"

"Someone's coming."

JR's eyes widened as the key turned in the lock. He slipped into the dining room and hid behind a small palm tree. White Shoes ducked behind the couch. The guy walked in like he knew his way around. White Shoes wondered if maybe they had the wrong apartment. JR crawled under the table, pulled a chair in close behind him.

Reilly headed straight for the stacks of books and files in the dining room. JR watched the feet approach, recognized the shoes. His kid wanted the same kind.

The feet moved around the table. JR heard books

sliding, a pencil rolling across the table. He heard a zipper, pages being turned.

Reilly said, "Hello, beautiful," then sat with his knees inches from JR's face.

JR looked around. Who the fuck was he talking to?

Reilly reached into the waist pack, removing a credit card and a ten-dollar bill. On the table, he opened the tiny baggie from the binder pocket and dumped the contents on the table. He cut two fat lines with the card and looked at the coke, felt his mouth water, his insides tighten then loosen and told himself this was it, the last time. Just finish this shit and that would be it, he wouldn't buy anymore. He rolled up the ten, held it just inside his nostril and snorted the first line, then closed his eyes and pinched his nose, never noticing the man behind him with the gun.

White Shoes said, "Hey, Howdy-Doody."

Reilly jumped. "Whatthefuck!"

"Didn't anybody ever tell you, drugs are not your friend?' Reilly twisted round to look at the guy. "Who the hell are you?"

JR climbed out from under the table. "That's not the question, pal. The question is, who are *you*?"

Reilly sat there thinking the way these guys looked and talked could only mean one thing. He looked at the bill in his hand, the line on the table. "I guess you could say I'm somebody you need," he said. Then he bent forward, snorted the other line and smiled.

Gina checked on Hi in the backseat. He was still out. She saw a sign for gas and food and slowed down. The parking lot of the Convenience Mart was deserted, its sign hung askew, swinging in the breeze. For a minute she thought the store was closed, but she could see a faint light through the dirty windows, and when she pulled up to the pump, everything worked fine.

As she headed round the side of the building to find the restroom she got that creepy feeling, like someone was watching. She imagined this would be the moment she'd look back on and say, "If only..."

Gina felt stupid as she stood there thinking defeatist thoughts, so she shook it off and tugged on the sticky door of the bathroom. Nothing jumped out at her, there wasn't anything behind the door. The light worked fine. She was pleasantly surprised to find a full roll of toilet paper and a working flusher. She took a moment at the sink to rinse her face, apply some lipstick, and smooth her hair. She tried a thin smile, the one she used when she paid the clerk for the gas and coffee.

She had driven from city to town to village, and now, two miles down the road, the landscape changed again. Dense forest replaced houses and farms and streams. Gina turned up the air-conditioner and was fumbling with the radio reception when the deer stepped onto the road

.

20
Come Together

SOME people believe things just happen. They sit back like a baby in a tub balanced over a kitchen sink, trusting in the sturdiness of the molded plastic and someone else's hands. Jeremy Strom wasn't like that. The guys who worked out at Mick's Gym weren't like that. They knew you had to *make* things happen and you could only trust your own hands.

Mick's was open twenty-four hours. But that was just one of the reasons Jeremy loved the place. Mick's Gym had substance. It hadn't gone metro like the rest of them. There were gyms that called themselves health clubs——all slick and neon, with surgery-enhanced babes in spandex serving wheat grass and protein shakes to overpaid executives. Those same clubs had members who exercised only until they broke a sweat, then paid sixty bucks for a massage and drove back to the office to write the whole thing off.

No, Mick's was the real deal. Real sweat, real iron, real men. It was all about the body and what it could do today, right now. Nothing else mattered: not tomorrow, not next week, and definitely not wheat grass.

Jeremy pulled on his gloves and went to work. Escaping into his routine, he forgot about the job and Sailor and what Deluca wanted him to do.

The clerk made room for Deluca and the ledgers at her small square desk. She'd been reluctant to allow him to sit there, but he'd said, "Please. I won't be long," and looked at her in that Fast Eddie way. So what was she going to do?

She slid her picture frames to the edge of the desk and removed a potted plant. Deluca sat, feeling the heat in the seat of the chair. He glanced at the pictures of the clerk's family. They stood in a parking lot, the sticker of a rental agency on the Hyundai behind them. The husband, a thin, slack-jawed man, held the hand of a toddler in a stained t-shirt that read, 'Brat'. No one was smiling.

The clerk returned to her filing as Deluca flipped open the first ledger. He remembered Gina saying something a few months ago when they were talking about getting away from it all.

She'd said, "If I could go anywhere, I'd probably just go back."

"Go back where?" he'd asked.

"To Dauphin County. I have the *best* memories of that place. Maybe that's dumb. I mean, I'm sure nothing is the same as it used to be. But I can't help wondering..."

"What?"

"If it's still there." She'd begun clearing the plates and cups, walking away as she said, "My Grandfather's cabin."

Deluca wished he'd been paying more attention instead of trying to sneak a peek down her blouse. Gina still had the best tits. He opened another Dauphin County Real Estate register, ran his finger down the page of transactions and paused at Chamblee Acres. Gina was trying to protect Berger. That was her way, such a motherly sort, sweet in the hooker-with-a-heart way, but entirely unrealistic in the real world. What the fuck was she thinking?

"Find what you're looking for?" the clerk asked, waddling over.

"Yes." Deluca smoothed the page he'd been about to tear out. "You're such a sweetheart for letting me use your desk."

She blushed, waved him off.

"No really, I mean it." Deluca gave her the full wattage of his smile. "I know you're not supposed to, but could I have a copy of this?' The clerk's smile faded. She pursed her lips. Deluca pushed. "I won't tell a soul." He crossed two fingers over his heart then held them up, whatever that meant. He said, "Trust me."

Jeremy added two more plates to the squat rack and positioned himself under the bar. It was his last set of the pyramid, his quads were on fire. When the phone went off in his bag he almost ignored it, then remembered Deluca's face that afternoon. Something told him this might be important. He took a swig of water, shook out his legs and walked to the lobby.

"I need to use your office."

The neckless triangle behind the front desk shrugged and pointed to a closed door, "No problem."

Jeremy closed the door behind him, silencing the grunts and groans of the power lifters. He punched in Deluca's number and wasn't surprised when he picked up on the first ring.

"Shit!" Gina slammed on the brakes then remembered too late—you're supposed to pump them.

Steering was impossible. The car had become a sliver of soap on its way to the drain.

"Move!" she screamed.

But the three deer frozen on the middle line just looked

at her, an obstacle of muscle, bone and hair. She pulled hard to the left, felt the tires slide off the road, the steering wheel jerking under her grip. The station wagon slammed sideways into a fifty-year-old oak and came to a stop, facing the way from which they'd come. On the road bits of glass and chrome littered the blacktop.

"What the fuck!" Berger yelled from the back seat. "Goddamit, Gina! Oh, my fucking leg!"

Through the cracked windshield and the light of the one skewed headlamp, Gina saw them. The doe and her two fawns stepped lightly over a hubcap and bounded off into the woods, white tails raised like fat middle fingers.

"Shut up, Hi."

Gina dabbed at her bloody lip and released the taut seatbelt. She rubbed where the strap had cut into her shoulder and bruised her breast. "Just shut the fuck up."

She noticed how easily her door opened, thought that from this side you couldn't tell anything was wrong, except she might have parked too close to that tree.

Berger dragged himself out of the back seat, his bandaged leg held before him like a package of meat. He hobbled three steps and sat down on a limestone boulder. "Now what?'

Gina looked at him on the rock, rubbing his leg and scowling at her. She sighed, reached inside the busted window for the keys and her purse, hesitated a moment, then felt around the backseat for the bottle of JD.

"Now, we walk."

White Shoes had just finished with the transmitters in the bedroom and was cleaning up when his cell phone rang.

"Yeah?"

Gallo said, "I need you to go to Dauphin County. I just got word that Berger and Gina are running. You know that old place by the gorge? JR should remember, Big Pants used to take him fishing there. Convince Berger to come back, you understand? And White Shoes? No one gets hurt."

"Got it, Boss. Don't worry. I'm on it." Slipping the phone in his pocket, White Shoes grabbed his toolbox and called to JR, "Finish up. We're out of here."

In the dining room, JR wasn't ready. He sat at the table with the red-haired kid, his gun useless at his side.

"What the fuck, JR? C'mon. We have to go."

"Wait, wait." JR wiped his eyes, swallowed a chuckle. "The kid's funny, White Shoes." JR poked Reilly with the gun. "Tell him the one about the Italian and the firing squad."

White Shoes said, "I don't wanna hear no jokes. Get your shit, JR. We're leaving."

"What about—?" JR motioned in Reilly's direction.

"What?"

"You know." JR's head bobbed again.

White Shoes looked at the glassy-eyed kid, imagined him calling someone as soon as they left. "Yeah, you're right. C'mon kid, we're going for a drive."

Reilly tore open the plastic baggie, ran his finger around and rubbed the last of the coke over his gums. "Sure. Why not?"

On the way to the van, Reilly told White Shoes the joke about the Italian and the firing squad. White Shoes agreed. The kid was funny. He'd give him that much.

The harder Ray tried to clear his mind to go to sleep, the more he was bombarded with stuff he couldn't change. He had no idea when he'd find out about his case. He could do nothing from here and a tiny part of him wished he'd never even tried to re-open the whole mess. He hated to admit he was afraid of failure. Even more, he was afraid of success.

What if they did manage to convince the judge? Would there be a full-blown jury trial? Would all that stuff come up again? And what if by some miracle, some chance—no, some justice—he did gain his freedom? What would he do? No family, no job, no place to go.

In prison, he was told when to sleep, when to eat and when to work. There were too many choices in the free world, and Ray was afraid he'd make the wrong one, again. He rolled over onto his back, closed his eyes and saw his former life, what he'd lost. Tara.

He whispered to the chipped wall, "Tara, I'm sorry," and "I'll find her." His voice echoed back, sounding hollow and false. Lost in a canyon of doubt.

In Sailor's empty apartment, the answering machine went through its outgoing message and beep.

"Reilly? Are you there? I need you to pick up. Listen, if you get this message, we need you to delay the meeting with the Judge. We're driving to Dauphin County to bring back Berger. Jeremy says Gina's family has a camp at Clark's Creek. We think that's where they're headed. I'll try your cell again, and—"

There was a crackling sound, a few fragments of words, then just static.

Paris fingered the wrapped chocolates in the dish as she waited for the call to ring through.

"Hello?"

"She's in town."

"What?" Deluca pushed the girl off his lap.

"Maria's in Philly. She just checked into the Rittenhouse."

"You're kidding."

"No, I'm not."

"What do you want?"

"I think you know."

"Fuck. I'm in the middle of something."

"So finish and get over here. I'll be in the lobby bar, by the garden."

"Fine." He snapped the phone shut with his chin and then dragged the girl back into his lap, face first.

21
Well, Hello There

MARIA CHETTA fell asleep in the bathtub. It wasn't the first time. She dreamed: beach, garden, rose petals, a big white bed, gauzy curtains. Then it changed—a loud noise, a swirl of colors, a horrible car crash; five, maybe six cars. She was driving a truck, a big one. She looked down on a field of debris, huge tires rolling forward, crushing steel and smashing windshields, hubcaps, bumpers and twisted doors with their locks still depressed. There wasn't any blood just a shoeless leg in khakis on her left, half a man on her right. The man with one cheek pressed to the ground like he was listening for earthworms, or approaching horses. Long gray hair flowed over his collar, the wind tickling it over a cheek that couldn't feel on an armless man who couldn't brush it away.

Maria woke with a start, splashing bath water over the side of the tub, unsure for a moment where she was. The water had cooled, a chill from the dream seeped into the lavender bath. She opened the drain and felt the water swirl past her, gurgling and chugging down the hotel pipes.

By the time she'd wrapped herself in the white terry robe and padded over to the mini bar, the dream was just a bad taste in the back of her throat, easily disguised by the Glenlivet she poured over ice and drank in three swallows.

She stood by the window overlooking the Square, imagining James King saying, "You're just a dumb bitch who won't amount to nothing. I want you out of here, you and your fat Mama, always crying all the time. You got three days, hear me? And I don't want to see you around the store no more, either."

King was serious this time. He could even be in love with this one. Maria had to do something. She'd given up too much of herself to lose now, so she asked Lou for the gun. And called Chancy. No one had figured it out. Except Deluca. He was smart even back then. Determined.

Maria thought she'd done them a favor; the way she saw it, she'd done the whole damn city a favor, ridding them of a horrible man determined to ruin the lives of their children with drugs, bring their neighborhoods down, sap the strength of their community. But Deluca and the others, they missed the money.

Maria knew Banning was right. Twenty-four years is a long time to keep a secret. But that was just one of the reasons she was here.

Paris watched the waiter bend over the low table and place her martini precisely in the center of the napkin. She slipped him a few bills. "Thank you."

"Will there be anything else, Miss Kendrick?"

Paris ran her eyes over the young blond. "Maybe later. I have your number." She re-crossed her long legs, checked her watch and wondered how many sets of Kegels she could get through before her guest arrived.

Maria sipped her second scotch while perched on the window seat. She watched a fresh-faced brunette on the Square below. The girl held a red sign of protest or cheer, something about RENT or PETA. Maria wasn't sure. She was trying to read the small print when someone knocked.

"It's open." Maria didn't bother to turn around, absorbed in the protester's odd actions. She heard the door open and close. On the sidewalk below, the girl had wheeled a covered cage out of the shadows into the light of the street lamp. She whipped the red cover away to reveal a naked man squeezed into the tiny space.

Still staring, Maria said, "Everything's on the table, Len. I want to be there when you confront him."

People on the street gathered around the girl and the caged man.

"I want to see his face. I want him to know it was me who did this to him."

Someone handed the girl a megaphone, Maria could hear a few words, "*illegal, unfair, inhumane.*"

"But more than that, I want—"

Maria turned around and saw that it wasn't Len Banning and his associate she'd been talking to, it wasn't him bent over the loaded gun in the baggie and the piles of tapes. She barely spoke the word, "over."

Deluca smiled. "Hello, Maria."

Standing behind him, Paris reached into her jacket pocket. She fiddled with something then stepped back as Maria stormed across the room. "What the hell are you doing here?"

White Shoes had heard enough. No matter what the kid said, JR had done, seen or heard something better. "All right. Enough. Christ, the two of you are like my Aunt Rose and Uncle Vinnie. What the fuck are you doing back there, anyway?"

JR and Reilly had been messing around in the back of the van for the last half hour. The kid was funny, sure, but he couldn't sit still for a goddamn minute, and it was driving White Shoes nuts. He figured he'd pick up a few beers on the next stop, maybe get the kid to mellow out.

He hoped Howdy Doody didn't have any more coke on him, and he really hoped he wasn't joking when he said he could rig a pipe bomb.

The gas station had certainly seen better days. and the tinny music blaring from the blown speakers of the shithole bar next door assured White Shoes they'd left the city behind. Someone once said, Pennsylvania was Philadelphia and Pittsburgh, with Alabama in between. White Shoes slid down from the van seat, stretched and said to no one in particular, "Welcome to Alabama."

He opened the rear doors of the van and let JR and Reilly out.

"Fill it up. I gotta use the can."

JR looked at Reilly, motioned to the pump. Smiling, Reilly shrugged and sat down on the van's rear bumper.

JR cursed under his breath, then went round to work the pump. He was standing there a few minutes later, nozzle in hand, when White Shoes came back.

"Where's Howdy Doody?" he asked, looking around, fiddling with his fly.

"Back there." JR jerked his thumb to the rear of the van.

White Shoes said, "Did you pay?"

"No."

"What do you mean? You just been standing here all this time?"

"Hey, the fucking thing's broke. I have to hold it like this, and if I push it all the way, it cuts off, it's delicate."

"It's delicate? What the fuck? Give it to me. Now, go pay the guy. Ke-rist!"

JR shuffled off, shaking his head.

White Shoes grabbed the nozzle, squeezed. The pump cut off, and when he squeezed again, a spray of gasoline covered his hand and splattered his shoes.

JR laughed as he walked toward the store. "I told you," he said.

The kid behind the counter had rigged the store's

security monitor to a game player and was in the middle of a battle with three tough looking Ninjas, thumbs pounding furiously on the controller.

He didn't look up. "Whatcha got, Dude?"

"Twenty in gas, some chips and candy."

The kid swapped out his Warrior for a Japanese fighting girl in a slinky red dress. He glanced at the food on the counter then back to his game. "Twenty-seven fifty. You need change?"

JR pulled some bills from his wallet and a few coins from his pocket, slapped the money on the counter. He spoke to the kid's back. "Nah, I'm good."

The boy's fighting girl took on a giant panda. The kid jumped up, jerking his arms and legs as if the battle were real. He never saw JR swipe the six-pack and magazines on his way out. JR dumped his take into the van through the window. White Shoes rubbed furiously at a damp spot on his Bucs.

"You all right there, Shoes?"

"Yeah, yeah. Just get the kid and let's go."

JR walked to the back of the van. Reilly was gone. He checked inside. No kid. He closed the rear doors and looked toward the restrooms.

"Hey, White Shoes?"

"Yeah?"

"Did you say he was, uh, in the toilet?"

"No."

"Oh."

White Shoes threw down the paper towel and came around to the back of the van.

"He ain't here."

"I can see that. Where *is* he?"

JR shrugged. Across the gravel lot, someone had opened a window in the bar, and now it was even easier to hear Creedence singing about a bad moon on the rise.

"Are you shittin' me? C'mon."

The moment they opened the door they knew they

were fucked.

It wasn't the twinkling pink Christmas lights around the bar or even the rows of collectible Barbies neatly displayed on the back wall. It was the way the song ended abruptly when they stepped over the threshold. The way three bushy blond heads swiveled round from their places at the bar.

"Well, girls," The bigger blonde said. "This must be our day." She slid from the bar stool, heavy boots clomped on the wooden floor, and spoke around the cigarette in her mouth, swaying a bit.

She pointed at White Shoes. "One," then to JR, "two," then reached between her pals and produced Reilly, like a rabbit from a magician's hat. "Three."

The second blond popped up, tittering. "And look, there's three of us. "One. Two—"

The third blond grabbed her by the hair, shoved her. "No shit, Shirley. Sit down."

"What did you do that for, huh? And why'd you call me Shirley?"

"Have a drink." The tough one said, shoving a glass in her direction.

The big blond approached the men and circled them with her hands on her hips like a farmer appraising his prize-winning bull. She licked her lips. "Good idea. Let's all have a drink."

JR started backing up, "Thanks ladies, but we really should be going."

White Shoes put his hand on JR's back. "We'd love a drink. Ain't that right, buddy?" He pushed JR forward. "And then the *three* of us need to be hitting the road, ain't *that* right?' White Shoes stared at Reilly, who tipped his drink and saluted.

The big blonde stepped behind the bar and spoke to them over her shoulder. "Name's Barbie. That's Stacy." The flaky chick on the nearest stool wiggled her fingers. "And Kenita."

The tough broad jerked her head in their direction. "Ken."

Barbie held two chilled shot glasses. "Vodka, boys?"

JR and White Shoes snapped the shots back, then set the glasses on the pastel pink bar.

JR looked around. "Nice place. It's what you call...whimsical." White Shoes rolled his eyes.

Stacy's empty glass was re-filled by Barbie, sugar-rimmed and full of chilled vodka. Stacy took a sip then dipped her finger into the sugar and licked it off. She looked at JR. "Know which one's my favorite?"

He shook his head slowly, unsure what she meant but hoping it had something to do with that sugar-tipped finger. She slid from the barstool and sashayed across the room in a sexy dance to the music in her head. Stacy looked like a life-sized version of the dolls on the wall. She selected a Barbie on the lowest shelf then hid it behind her back and returned to the bar.

"Wanna see?"

JR swallowed. *Hell yeah.*

"It's Malibu Barbie." She held the doll out to JR. "Feel her hair." He petted the fake hair.

"And look." Stacy lifted the doll's skirt. When JR wasn't sure what he was seeing, she pulled at the velcro straps and revealed Malibu Barbie's bra and crotch-less panties. Not exactly the kind of outfit you'd find on the toy store shelf.

"Now, that's my kinda doll."

Reilly said, "One more for my friends."

Barbie filled the men's glasses, leaned way over when she gave the drink to White Shoes. "I love a man in Bucs, buck-naked." She winked, held up her glass to clink his. They downed the shot, eyes locked.

Reilly couldn't believe this. Here was out in the boonies with a couple of mobsters, both of them looking for the same guy, for what he figured were very different reasons.

He'd lucked out, sneaking in here to use the phone while the bozos were busy. Sailor hadn't believed him at first, then Ken got on the phone and there weren't any more questions, except, "How long can you stall them?'

The ladies were pretty sweet, once you got past the, I've-been-hurt-by-my-asshole-of-a-husband-and-the-world-in-general-so-don't-fuck-with-me facade. Yeah, after that, they were really pretty cool.

So when he told them that these guys had taken him on a trip he hadn't packed for, if you get my meaning. they understood completely and told him not to worry. They could handle these city boys.

Reilly had to admit he sort of liked the show they were putting on, and from the way JR was dancing with Stacy, he was enjoying it, too. It was the other guy, White Shoes, who worried him. Not the footwear so much, but what he had strapped to the ankle above the Bucs. And the guy had no patience. Bad combination.

But Reilly figured you have to work with what you got and these are the cards he was dealt. He was just hoping that Sailor had a few deuces up her sleeve. He threw back his shot of water and slurred, "Who's going to dance with me?

"Come on, Hi. We're almost there."

Gina figured there was no use in telling him the truth. They were so far from almost there, it wasn't funny. But she was hoping against all hope that somebody would drive down this forsaken road and save her from thinking about the alternatives. So she hitched up her grip on Berger and repeated, "Come on, Hi." Like it was a prayer

.

22

Ready or Not, Here I Come

SAILOR told Banning, "It's going to be fine. Jeremy's great. Really."

She wasn't sure who she was trying to convince. After receiving Reilly's rushed phone call from the bar, she called Banning. When he said they should go up there alone, no cops, it had been Sailor's idea to bring Jeremy in. But Banning knew him better and there was something he wasn't saying.

Banning slowed the Jag. "You sure you know where we're going?"

"With these directions," she waved a piece of paper, "I could find it in the dark."

"You're going to have to." He looked at the sky. "How about in the rain?"

Sailor had seen the approaching clouds and hoped they'd out-run the storm.

They pulled up in front of a dilapidated brick warehouse. A graffiti artist had spray-painted a large red tongue on the wall over the door with drops of saliva dripping toward the sidewalk. Jeremy appeared under the tongue dressed in camouflage. He looked like a renegade action figure.

When he tossed two heavy bags into the backseat of the car and slid in, Sailor didn't want to know what was in them, or what he had been doing in that ramshackle building. All she wanted to know was that he was on their side.

"Okay, enough." White Shoes pulled away from Barbie's grip and called to JR on the dance floor. "Don't get too involved Romeo, we're leaving."

Stacy whined over JR's shoulder, "You party pooper." She pressed herself into JR and ran her tongue into JR's ear.

White Shoes grimaced.

"Here." The tough blonde, Ken, held the vodka. "One for the road."

He hesitated. *What the fuck was he doing here? He was supposed to be finding Berger, not watching JR dry-hump some backwoods slut in a Barbie bar. Christ! He needed a new life. If he ever got this job done for Gallo, that would be it.*

"Hold it right there!"

"What the fuck?" White Shoes spun around.

A cop stood in the doorway. At least he thought it was a cop. The halogen lights had come on outside. They cast an orange shadowy halo around the guy who was short— midget short—and holding something really long. From the looks of it, it was pretty damn heavy.

Instinctively, everyone raised his hands, even the girls. White Shoes took a step.

"I said, hold it right there."

White Shoes stopped, patted the air in an easy-there-boy way, and put on his biggest smile.

Stacy pulled her head out of JR's armpit and squinted. "Duane? Is that you? What the hell are you doing?"

She crossed the room, rumpled and swaying. "Does Melinda know you've got that thing?" She snatched the long-barreled revolver from the tiny cop's hand then walked over to the bar and laid it next to the vodka.

Her lips were moving, but no sound came out as she made herself a drink, booze sloshing out of the glass and onto the gun. Reilly thought it looked too big to be real, like a prop for a Clint Eastwood movie.

Barbie put her hands down and said, "I've got to pee."

The men watched her departing ass and were caught looking when she turned around at the restroom door.

"Close the door, Duane," Stacy said. "You're letting the bugs in."

Duane stepped inside, closed the door behind him then glanced in the direction of the restroom, then back at his gun on the bar.

White Shoes returned to his stool, figured he'd play this one out. "Buy you a drink, Officer? A soda, or something?"

The cop shifted his weight from foot to foot, took another look toward the back, then said, "I need to talk to the owner of the white van."

When no one answered, he jerked his thumb over his shoulder, hitched his pants up and sniffed. "The white van, at the pump? There seems to have been some misunderstanding with the bill."

He flipped open his notebook and read, "I told the guy it was twenty-seven fifty. He gave me six dollars and fifteen cents." Duane looked at White Shoes. "Is that right?"

White Shoes shot JR a look. JR shoved his hands into his pockets and seemed real interested in Geisha Barbie and her sushi tray.

White Shoes shook his head. "Sorry about that, Officer. Here." He reached for his wallet. Let me fix that."

The cop held his hand up. "Easy there, just keep your hands where I can see them."

White Shoes chuckled, "What? How am I going to pay our bill, if I don't put my hand in my pocket?"

The cop squeezed up his face and went back to shifting his weight from foot to foot.

"Well..."

"Jesus-fucking-Christ, Duane." Ken stood up, reached into White Shoe's pockets and pulled out car keys and a wallet. She snatched a twenty and a one, slapped the keys and wallet on the bar then reached over and grabbed the gun with her other hand. She stomped toward the door where Duane stood.

The gun was slippery with vodka and when Ken tried to change her grip on the barrel to hand Duane the money she dropped the gun. It went off just as Barbie exited the bathroom drying her hands on a paper towel. The bullet caught her right above the pubic bone and exited clean under her rib cage, spraying blood on School Teacher Barbie and Surfer Ken.

JR spun round, suddenly sober. "What the *fuck*?' He looked down at Barbie, bleeding and moaning on the dance floor and said it again with an echo from Reilly at the bar, "What the fuck?"

Their ears were ringing as a cop burst through the back door, dropped to the floor and rolled, yelling and firing wild shots that sent everyone running.

Duane, crouched by the jukebox with a hand over his head yelled, "Marks! Cease firing! Cease firing!"

One of the stray bullets hit the jukebox making a selection and a volume adjustment. Metallica blared—all wailing guitars and angst.

Stacy screamed from behind the bar, "I don't wanna die! I don't wanna die!" over and over again.

JR yelled something in English about his Mama and that he was sorry, then switched to Italian and half-remembered prayers.

The shooting stopped. Stacy was still screaming. It was sweet music compared to the warped blare of Metallica. Reilly figured this was as good a time as any. He patted the bar top, found White Shoes' keys, made a run for the stockroom and the rear door that the gun-happy cop had crashed through.

Reilly was three miles down the road before anyone noticed he was missing, and three miles after that he saw Gina. He almost missed her, and would have too, if she hadn't been squatting by the road. It was the whiteness of her bare ass and the way she scrambled up so quickly to cover it that turned his head. He slowed down, pumping the cranky brakes.

Gina ran up the road now, waving her arms and shouting, "Stop! Please!"

Reilly leaned over to roll down the window as she ran up to the van.

She said, "It's you."

He smiled, a faint attempt to assure her.

"What are you doing out here?"

"Need some help?"

Gina said, "Uh, yeah, it's Hi. He's been shot, and he's... not well..."

Her voice trailed off as she turned toward the woods, her arm in front of her like a divining rod. "He's right here. At least he was. Hi?"

"Hang on."

Reilly pulled the van off the road, left the headlights on hoping they'd help a little. He climbed down, saw the shape of Gina in the woods ahead of him. His eyes hadn't yet adjusted to the dark. The woods were just charcoal shadows and ebony shapes.

He stepped off the road, took two steps and was feeling around where to place his foot next when he heard a low voice. "That's far enough, Soldier."

Reilly turned his head in the direction of the voice.

"Ah-ah-ah. No funny stuff. I've been watching you, and the others across the ridge. Think you're smart, do you? Going to waltz right in here and take my patrol? Well guess again, Soldier."

Reilly blinked, his eyes now better adjusted so that he

could see Berger, down and to his left. There was something odd about the way he sat with his leg stuck out in front of him. But more than that, Berger had a gun—another fucking gun—pointed at Reilly's face.

Berger mouthed, "Gotcha," then aimed the gun lower.

Soldier? Patrol? Yeah, the guy's not feeling well, all right. Before Reilly could figure out how to handle the wack-job under the tree, he heard Gina tromping through the undergrowth, cursing at the whipping branches.

"Hi? Where are you? I told you I didn't want to play hide and seek. C'mon. I got us a ride."

Berger followed her voice with his gun hand, then looked at Reilly and whispered, "That one of yours, Soldier?"

Reilly thought back to all those corny war movies he'd seen as a kid. There was always a Commander, wasn't there?

He took a breath, and then barked, "Soldier! I command you to holster your sidearm."

Berger's gaze faltered.

Reilly turned on him, leaning into his face with as cruel a grimace as he could muster. "Are you with me Soldier?" He poked Berger in the chest. "Do you know who I am?"

Berger's gun hand dropped to his side.

"I am your Commander, Soldier."

"Sir?' Berger's voice sounded tiny. "Is it you, Sir?"

Gina crashed through the bushes. "There you are."

Berger snapped his head around, whipped the gun up and pointed it at Gina, who kept coming.

Reilly yelled, "Gina! No! He's got a gun."

Gina held her hands out. "Hi? What's wrong, honey? Don't you want to go for a drive?' She took a step forward.

Berger moved his gun between Reilly and Gina, and finally stopped on Reilly. "You almost had me." He laughed. "I know you."

Reilly smiled lamely, playing along.

"Hi?" Gina said, coming closer.

Berger swung the gun to her and said, "It's you I don't know." He squeezed off two rounds, hitting her chest and belly.

Reilly saw Gina's body jerk, her neck snap back like someone had pulled her from behind. He stumbled backward as he heard the sickening thump of Gina's body hitting the ground. He scrambled behind a tree and held a hand over his pounding heart. He tried to control his breathing, tried to think.

He counted to ten then called, "Berger! It's Captain Steubing! We need you back at Base, Soldier. The General requests your presence. Where are you at, boy?"

Reilly waited.

"Over here, Sir."

Berger might have been talking to his dear mother in their sunny kitchen in Kansas, not a hint of the previous psycho-military routine. Reilly wondered how many people were in Berger's head, and prayed to God that Berger liked the Captain.

"I'm injured, Captain. Going to need a little help."

Reilly came around the tree, approached with a swagger.

Berger looked pleased to see him. "And I sure could use some grub, Sir."

Reilly reached for Berger and the gun. He stashed it in the back of his pants, then hefted Berger up.

With an arm over Reilly's shoulders, Berger hobbled through the woods and up the slope to the road.

At the van he started wailing, "I'm sorry, Daddy. I'm so sorry. I didn't mean it. I didn't mean to get hurt."

Reilly patted his back. "It's okay. Come on now, son. We're going home." He got him into the back, gave him a jacket for a pillow and Berger was out, murmuring and crying a bit in his fitful dreams.

Reilly fished around inside the toolboxes and crates and finally found a flashlight under the passenger seat. He followed its beam through the trampled-down brush to the place where Gina had fallen.

If he didn't look at the missing part of her, Reilly could almost convince himself she was resting. He ran the flashlight over Gina's hair and scratched face. Yeah, she's just taking a little nap in the woods. Except people don't sleep with their eyes wide open. Reilly turned away; something silver caught his eye. He shined the flashlight at the bushes where Gina had burst through and found her backpack purse dangling from a branch. He grabbed it and headed back to the road.

At the van, Berger was still out. Reilly hit the van's interior light and dumped Gina's purse on the seat. He pawed through keys, tampons, lipsticks, mints, found a few bottles of pills with Hiram Berger's name then he hit jackpot. Cell phone.

He powered up the phone. There was still a little juice in the battery. It beeped. Reilly looked around. No service.

He slipped the phone in his pocket, checked out the pill bottles and selected three Ativan. He opened a can of beer from the gas station, dumped the capsules in and grabbed a bag of chips. Berger woke, murmuring and moaning about his leg, as Reilly climbed to the back. "Hey there, pal. Look what I got. A nice cold beer and some chips."

Berger propped himself up on an elbow, winced when he tried to move his leg. "Give me that," he said, pointing to the beer.

Reilly handed it over and opened the bag of chips and set it by Berger then climbed back into the driver's seat and started the engine.

Berger downed the beer, belched and said, "How much longer?" As if they were on a family trip.

Reilly smiled into the rearview mirror. "We'll be there before you know it."

Berger mumbled something else and shoved a handful of potato chips in his mouth, spilling some on his shirt and pants.

Reilly started up the road, looking for a clearing. The van was all bump and rattle with the gusto of a tortoise, but it beat walking and he had a full tank.

Hope was dangerous. Ray knew what it could do to a man. For some, it pushed them to accomplish wondrous deeds, like a magical charm. For others, it caused despair and desperate measures. It was what the hope was based on, more than hope itself that made the difference.

Did a mother hope her sick child well, or did she hope for a doctor who knew the cure or the plant to yield the extract that would provide the remedy? Was hope specific, or was it better to generalize and cover all the bases?

Ray had been down this path before, a number of times, and knew there wasn't an easy answer. He advised his clients against stepping down the path of hope. Better to stay on the broad, well-lit road of *it is, what it is.*
Just this once, Ray allowed himself the pleasure and the promise of hope. Because this time the path was wider, better traveled. This time Sailor would be his lantern

.

23

Not Anymore

IT'S too late, Fast Eddie."

"They don't call me that anymore."

Maria laughed. "Yeah, well maybe not to your face. Isn't that right, Paris?' She looked at the woman frozen behind Deluca then turned away, grabbed the cigarettes off the nightstand and took her time selecting one. She tapped it on the back of her hand then lit it and inhaled deeply.

Deluca said, "Haven't you heard, Maria? Those things will kill you."

Maria laughed. "Only if I'm lucky." Smoke rode on her words. "How long do you think that would take, Eddie? Tell me, because I'll smoke all day if I have to. Maybe I could just hook myself up to a machine."

"What are you talking about?"

"I'm dying, Eddie." Maria snubbed out the cigarette in the ashtray then walked to the bed. "Doc says I have a few months, maybe a year, if I'm lucky." She lowered herself to the edge of the bed then leaned back on her elbows and crossed her legs. The robe fell open to her lap. "Think I'll be lucky, Eddie?"

"I think you'll make a deal with the devil. You'll outlive us all." He looked at his watch.

"Going somewhere?"

"Just waiting for someone."

"Really? Company? Perhaps I should get dressed."

Deluca shook his head. "That won't be necessary. Jeremy won't care. Actually, the less clothes the better, I'd think."

Maria arched her brow. "Why Eddie, if I didn't know better, I'd think you meant me harm. You aren't threatening me, are you?"

Deluca laughed, fanned his arm over the cassette tapes and papers on the table. "Who's threatening whom, Maria?"

"That's not a threat, Eddie. It's the truth."

Deluca stared at her, then smiled. "Oh, I get it now." He clapped his hands. "The Final Act. Dying broad sets the record straight, clears her name and her conscious and all that bullshit before she passes on to—to where, Maria? Think I don't know what you and Lou Gallo did back then? Think I didn't know you planted that gun for LeChance? Christ. I knew everything. King told me about the heroin, even offered me a piece of the action. It was all going so well."

Deluca spoke to Paris but kept his eyes on Maria. "Paris, why don't you call Jeremy and find out what's keeping him. Stay close."

Paris nodded to Maria and slipped something from her pocket onto the table of evidence before she crossed the suite to the bathroom and closed the door.

The mirror was still fogged, the air steamy with a touch of lavender. It might have been cozy until Paris remembered what was happening on the other side of the door. She rubbed her palm on the glass, cleared an oval for her face.

In the other room, Deluca stepped closer to Maria and stood over her. "We could have made things work."

Maria craned her neck to see his eyes.

He reached out to stroke her cheek and ran his thumb from her temple to her chin. "God, you were something back then, you know it? Really hot."

She blinked her large eyes at him.

"Yeah, you still got it, don't you? I remember the first night we were together. When you came to me. You stood there in my shit-box apartment wearing that black raincoat." He took a deep breath and closed his eyes. "That black raincoat, and nothing underneath. God, you were beautiful, so damned beautiful." He opened his eyes. "You asked me—you begged me—to help you. And I did, didn't I? I would have done anything for you back then, Maria. All you had to do was ask."

He stepped back and murmured, "It wasn't just about the sex."

Maria scoffed. "It's always about the *sex*, Eddie." She stood up, wrapped the robe tighter. "Why would God give me this?" She ran her hands over her body. "If I wasn't supposed to use it?"

She lit another cigarette, smiled at him. "I like to think of it as a barter. A kiss for a favor, dinner for a blowjob, a few minutes in the coat closet for a passing grade in science. A night of fun in a shit-box apartment on Franklin Street to keep me and my mother out of prison."

She walked away from him. "See, Eddie, everything has a price. And for most of my life, I could afford it. This time, the bill's too high. It's time for somebody else to pick up the tab."

Facing the window, Maria saw Deluca's confusion reflected in the glass, his mouth open like he wanted to say something, his eyes hurt, then angry. She shifted to block the reflection, and waved her cigarette to the dark room across the street.

There was a rustling sound behind her, then Deluca said, "You never really loved me, did you, Maria? Gallo was right. You're a cold-hearted bitch."

"Me?" Maria spun round, "What about you?"

Deluca held the Colt, the gun from the baggie. The same gun Chancy had used on King. The same gun Gallo had used on Moreno. He raised it and smiled.

"There's something ahead." Sailor pointed down the road.

Banning slowed down. "Local cops. Probably just a barroom brawl."

"Stop." Jeremy put his hand on Banning's shoulder and leaned his face over the seat back. "Might be worth a look."

Banning glanced at Sailor. She shrugged.

"Park over there." Jeremy directed Banning to a dark corner of the convenience store lot. He pushed the duffle bags to the floor.

Sailor stepped out, stretched and looked around. It would have been pretty here if someone had cared enough to keep it up. She was no stranger to the country. Her Dad still took her to the lake house every year where they fished and paddled into tiny coves and bought their groceries from small stores like this one. Although in Connecticut they parked their Mercedes next to Range Rovers and Corvette convertibles, not pick-up trucks and Oldsmobiles, and they finished their meals with cognac and Cubans not Camels and Budweiser.

Sailor and Banning followed Jeremy across the parking lot to the bar.

Jeremy stood at the open door, saw the jukebox had taken a few rounds. Someone had dragged it away from the wall and pulled the plug. Twinkling Christmas lights that used to hang neatly over the bar drooped and dangled in a heap on the glass-strewn floor, their pattern of light and dark sending out a mysterious Morse code. A big cop knelt on the dance floor, cradling a woman's head in his wide lap.

Another cop was head-to-head with a bloody, disheveled blonde at a corner table. The blonde cried and wiped her eyes and nose with a paper towel, smearing snot and blood and tears across her face.

Across the room a man lay dead on the dance floor. It was easy to see he was dead. He was the one no one tended to. The one no one looked at. The spotlight that used to illuminate Theater Date Barbie, in her exquisite emerald green satin suit with matching pillbox hat, now shined on the dead man. A man Jeremy recognized as JR Pantaglioni. Junior Pants. One of Gallo's boys. They were in the right place after all.

Jeremy whispered something to Sailor then said louder, "You might want to wait out here." He tipped his chin to Banning, motioning for him to go first.

Banning stepped over the landing.

"We're closed." The voice came from the blonde on the barstool.

She spoke to their fractured reflections in the broken mirror, and rolling a glass between her hands she added, "For repairs," then drained her drink and set the empty glass next to an empty bottle and heaved herself off the stool.

"I'll be outside, having a smoke," she said to no one in particular.

The cop with the bloody-faced blonde said, "Don't go far, Kenita. We'll need your statement too."

She raised her hand halfway, as if the rest of the gesture was too much effort, and kept walking.

Banning and Jeremy stepped out of the doorway and into the bar to allow her to pass. They looked around trying to appear thirsty, not curious.

"I'm going to have to ask you fellas to leave."

The guy was like a lizard blending into his surroundings. Small little guy like that. What was he, a midget? Jeremy hadn't even seen him there.

"Need to protect the crime scene," the cop said, waving his arm over the shot-up bar. "You understand, now."

Banning said, "Hey, is that a 1971 Live Action Ken?" He walked past Officer Tiny, past the overturned tables and over the broken glass. He glanced at the dead man, the fat cop and the wounded woman.

The small cop made noises with his mouth, then gave up and turned his attention to Jeremy. The other cops weren't sure what to do with this Ken-loving guy and his beefed-up pal.

"He was a birthday present from my Dad," Barbie said. She tried to sit up; the fat cop helped. "He said it would give Barbie someone to argue with." She laughed sharply then winced and grabbed the bandage on her side. "Go ahead, batteries should still be good."

Banning ran his finger over the fringes of the doll's suede vest and his molded plastic hair, then hit the switch that set the stand vibrating and made Ken dance.

The fat cop yelled, "Hey!"

Banning turned the switch off and looked over his shoulder.

But the cop was speaking to Barbie, not him. "I didn't know he could do that. How come you never showed me before?"

Barbie shrugged. "You never asked."

The cop was about to say something, then remembered he wasn't here for a history of collector dolls. He called to the tiny cop, "Duane, get these guys out of here, will you?"

"It's okay. We were just leaving," Banning said.

Duane stood in the doorway, hands on his hips, and watched Sailor, Banning and Jeremy drive away. Kenita tipped her chin at the low-slung car. "Hope he doesn't hit a deer in that thing. He won't stand a chance."

In the car, Banning looked from Jeremy to Sailor. "What are we looking for?"

Sailor glanced back at the bar. The small cop sat on the steps with Kenita. "She told me Reilly's in a white van. The guy went after him in a red pickup." Sailor looked at

Jeremy. "He's got a gun."

Jeremy smiled. "So do we." He told Banning, "Head north. That's where they'll be. Then all we have to do is listen." Banning looked confused.

Paris heard Maria's voice change from calm, cool and confident to something unfamiliar: hesitant; questioning.

She cracked open the door. Deluca had his back to the bathroom. Maria stood by the window, her face in shadows. There was a bright light on them from the building across the way. Paris checked her watch. Damn that Taylor Dunne. She was early. Paris was about to close the door and dial Taylor to give her an earful when Deluca shifted his position and she saw the gun.

"Shit," she whispered, easing the door shut. "Shit. Shit, shit." She stabbed the buttons on her cell phone and sucked in a big breath.

Taylor answered immediately. "Paris! Sweetie! Where are you? The light is fantastic! I'm getting the whole thing. This is going to go national! You know that, don't you? My God, you are brilliant. How did you know he'd go for the gun? This is my Pulitzer."

Paris tried to muffle the bubbly voice of Taylor Dunne by jamming the phone harder against her ear. She cupped her hand around her mouth and whispered, "I didn't."

Finally, silence. She steeled her jaw. "Taylor, listen to me. The gun is loaded. Do you understand? It's loaded and it's old. This is not fantastic, Taylor. Maria could get hurt. I could get hurt. This wasn't part of the plan."

"No. This is better! See, it's more than you exposing Deluca, more than you bringing down Montgomery. This is big, Paris. This is Mafia-big. "

Paris whispered, "Just get the cops up here, will you?" She hung up then looked at herself in the mirror. *What the hell are you doing?* She braced herself on the edge of the sink, took a deep breath and came up with Plan B.

Bursting from the bathroom, Paris said, "Damn cell

phones!" She kept her eyes on the phone's display. "I can't get a signal in there. I'll just step out in the hallway and make the call."

"Wait," Deluca said.

Paris kept walking. It was only the sound of the Colt's slide being drawn back that stopped her. She squeezed her face up, exhaled through her teeth then turned slowly.

She said, "What are you doing?" She walked toward him gesturing broadly with her arms, to both make her point to the armed attorney and send a message to Taylor and the room of TV cameras across the alley.

"Come on," she said. "You got what you came for, let's go. Don't do this."

Like all things unexpected, the miniature tape recorder chose that precise moment to click off. Deluca snapped his head toward the sound, dropping his bead on Paris.

Maria saw the opportunity and lunged for Deluca. They went down in a flurry of terrycloth robe and imported pinstripes. Maria lashing out with her long nails, Deluca bloody-cheeked and throwing slaps and wild punches with his free hand. They rolled around, with Maria getting in a good gouge to Deluca's eye. When he fell back, she went for the gun. He got to his feet, pulled his arm free and slapped her with the back of his hand and the gun barrel, cutting her lip and cheek. Then he switched hands and yanked her up with a fistful of hair.

"Still feisty as ever," he said, panting. Then he grinned. "But who has the gun now?"

She pulled against his grip. He released her suddenly, sending her stumbling backward and falling into the air conditioning unit beneath the window. She slid to the floor, her chest heaving. She touched her bloody lip, pushed the hair from her eyes then pulled herself upright. Her robe hung open exposing her large breasts and dark triangle of hair.

Deluca adjusted his grip on the gun. "I know how to use one, in case you were wondering. Working for Gallo teaches a man all kinds of things." He stepped toward Maria. "It could have been different. Jesus! It should have been. This—" He waved his empty hand, dropped it limply. "This isn't where I'm supposed to end up. Not here. Not like this."

Maria stood facing him, her back to the window.

Paris edged to the door as Deluca spoke. She reached behind her for the handle and started to push it down, only to have it yanked from her grasp as the door smashed open, pinning her between the wall and the painted wood.

"Freeze! Police!"

Deluca pulled the trigger

.

24
Humpty Dumpty

REILLY followed the winding road up the mountain, thinking that if he just got high enough, and found a spot that was clear enough, well maybe. The cell phone beeped. He reached across the seat for it, squinted at the display.

"What? What's the beeping for?" He pushed a button and held the phone to his ear. "Hello?" Nothing.

He pulled off the road onto the shoulder and hit the inside lights. Now he could see it perfectly. The beep was a battery warning, one blip away from dead. Great. He turned it off to save whatever energy was left, hit the light and pulled back onto the road and continued up the mountain.

Berger stirred in his dreams, the bumpy ride turning into an ocean voyage on a sailing ship of pirates. He smiled as his dream-self whistled a jaunty tune and spilled gold coins through his fingers onto the flat belly of a bare-breasted maiden.

Reilly wasn't so lucky. He turned the bend and found taller trees forming a canopy over the road—a road that seemed to be going back down. He pulled over, got out of the van and tried the phone while pacing across the pavement.

"C'mon. C'mon."

The phone blinked. "No Signal."

"Dammit!"

He jumped back into the van and gunned it down the road.

White Shoes hadn't driven a stick shift in almost thirty years and there was definitely something wrong with this one.

"*Maledetto*!" He jammed the skull-head handle of the stick shift into third and held it there so it wouldn't slip out again.

The pickup's dashboard rattled. The shocks squeaked and the brakes hissed when he felt the need to use them. He hoped the gas gauge wasn't broken, because the only thing worse than driving this piece of shit up this mountain would be walking alone in the dark with all those freaking animals.

White Shoes was a city boy. His idea of country was the patch of tomatoes in his Papa's backyard. He was old and tired and a little drunk and the last thing he wanted to do was run around in the dark looking for a crazy redheaded kid and a wacked-out, washed-up dick. He wanted to be home in a comfortable chair with a cold beer, listening to the sounds of his house in a well-lit room.

He stuck his head out the window, popped the truck into neutral and listened. There it was—the distinctive growl of the van's engine and the whine of the fan belt he told JR to fix last week.

"I hear you," he whispered, and popped the clutch.

Banning drove slower as the road turned to dirt. Hemlock branches scraped the Jag's roof, brushed against its sides. The curves came more frequently now, and Sailor felt the shoulder strap tug at her with every turn. She was getting a little nauseous, so she closed her eyes. She must have drifted off, because when she opened her eyes, Jeremy and Banning were murmuring and the car had slowed to a crawl.

Banning parked, turned off the ignition. It was quiet—too quiet. Even the night birds had stopped singing.

In the backseat, Jeremy looked toward the woods, thought about telling them everything. That Deluca had sent him to kill Berger, and bring Gina back. That Sailor and Banning were as good as dead if they dug any deeper. That they needed to let this go—Berger, Bentley, Deluca—all of it. For that matter, Jeremy could use this opportunity himself.

A pop each in the back of the head, then hunt down Berger, Reilly and White Shoes. Take them all out of the picture. Because that was what he did. That was who he'd become: a stone-cold killer. Hadn't he?

He looked at Sailor.

She smiled, looking brave.

A flash came through the trees, followed by a loud crack.

Instead of telling them anything, Jeremy reached into the duffle bag and pulled out a gun.

He checked the sight, aimed it at Banning. Then he spun it around, offering it handle-first to the startled attorney. "You okay with that?"

Banning swallowed hard, then nodded and took the gun.

Sailor watched Banning. The moonlight was enough to illuminate his high forehead and the drops of sweat at his temple. He returned her gaze, lifting a corner of his mouth in a half-smile of apology.

Jeremy said, "Turn off the interior light and get out fast."

They ran to the edge of the forest, reluctant to enter. Jeremy swung the duffle onto his back. "Stay behind me."

Sailor hefted the sack he'd given her, glanced back at

the nice, safe Jaguar, and then stepped into the underbrush.

Gallo was about to come when the phone rang. The girl riding him cried out, "Fuck me, Big Daddy!" and ground her hips in a circle. She leaned forward, tits flopping in his face. He almost didn't hear the second ring when one of them slapped against his ear. Jesus. When he pushed his thumbs into her hipbones, she shot upright, "Oh yeah!" She moved her hips faster.

The phone rang again. This time Gallo reached for it, the girl moaning and grinding above him as he said, "What?" into the receiver.

The guy on the other end heard the moans and looked at the phone. "Uh, Mr. Gallo?"

"What?"

"It's Cecil. You wanted me to call you if I heard something from our friend?"

"Yeah, get to the point."

"Sir, I think there may be complications. Maybe I shouldn't be telling you this on the phone, or maybe I should.."

"Just fucking tell me, Cecil. Tell me what is so goddamned important?"

"JR's dead."

"What?"

"I called his phone and some broad answered it. She said he was dead. Some cop shot him in a bar, and White Shoes—"

"Ho-ho-hold it. Jesus! What the fuck, Cecil? No names!" Gallo pushed the girl off him and sat up on the edge of the bed. He squeezed his temples with his thumb and middle finger.

"This is what you're gonna do. Hang up the phone and get your cousin. Meet me at my office. Got that?"

"Yeah."

When Berger woke up, Reilly didn't know which guy he'd get, so he prepared himself for all three.

He knew he couldn't do this by himself, and after a few minutes with the wack-job in the back of the truck he'd come to the conclusion that Berger was the right guy for the job. Reilly could be two good legs and he'd let Berger come up with the rest. One gun, a box of explosives and surprise—that might add up to half a chance, up here on the mountain under a sliver of moonlight.

Reilly knelt next to Berger in the back of the van, shook him a little. "Rise and shine."

"What?" Berger squinted into the dark. "Who are you?"

"Reilly. Gina sent me. Said Gallo's goons are after you and I should give you a hand. She also said you should take these." Reilly gave some pills to Berger. He hoped they'd help. He watched Berger swallow, saw recognition in his face and went on. "There's a guy coming in a red pick-up about a mile behind us. This is his van."

Berger looked past him out the van's rear door. "What are we doing sitting here?" He pulled himself upright, bumping the box of wires and Semtex that JR and Reilly had been assembling on the way down. He sniffed the air, then reached inside the box. When he withdrew his hand he held a marble-sized ball of explosive and a tail of wire.

He looked at Reilly. "Well, what do you know?"

Reilly shrugged. "It was *their* idea."

Berger smiled. "And not a bad one." He tipped his chin. "Pull the van over there, like you ran off the road. Let's give that asshole a taste of his own medicine."

Reilly drove off the shoulder and down a slight incline into the trees. When he came around back, Berger had a small penlight in his mouth, wire and Semtex in each hand.

He spoke around the penlight. "Help me out here."

Reilly reached in, grabbed the older man by his good leg and dragged him to the edge of the van.

Berger hated needing help. The wound didn't hurt as much, but the damn leg had stiffened up and there was no way around it. He lowered himself to the grass and made his way around to the driver's side as Reilly closed the back doors.

A few minutes later, they were hunkered down behind some limestone boulders, well hidden in the copse of trees just south of the road. Though the night was dark, Berger had rubbed dirt into his face and hands and insisted Reilly do the same. The whites of their eyes stood out against the dark, dirty skin. Reilly looked at Berger and started to giggle, the way you do when you're not supposed to laugh. He faked a cough to get rid of it, got a stern look from Berger. He was about to explain when he heard the approaching sounds of a truck and someone wrestling with a tight gearbox.

The small pickup came around the bend at about thirty miles an hour, then began to slow. Berger shut his eyes against the headlights to preserve his night vision. They guy would have seen the van in the woods. He counted to five and opened his eyes. Perfect. The pickup had stopped on the side of the road, facing the van.

Part of Reilly hoped White Shoes would go straight to the driver's door of the van. He'd told Berger the guy was a little looped and might not be thinking too straight. Berger had grinned when he wired the rear doors and the driver's side. "This'll have him thinking straight—all the way to Hell."

Berger rigged the explosives, while Reilly tramped down a few paths into the woods. He'd come back scratched and out of breath, a little from the running and a little from the fear of what lay beyond the paths he'd tramped. It was better up here by the road, the darkness and rustling behind them and the promise before them.

White Shoes left the truck in gear and turned the key off. He listened. Nothing. He drew his gun from the ankle holster, flicked off the safety and stepped out of the truck, leaving the headlights on. The hot engine tinged and ticked. Large insects smacked into the headlamps, drawn to the blackness beyond.

Everything was images and illusions; a tree branch looked like a waving arm, a bush was someone crouched down waiting to spring. White Shoes cursed under his breath and wiped the sweat from his eyes.

He looked at the van then back at the pickup. The lights of the truck showed a path into the woods—broken twigs, fallen leaves. Someone had gone this way. He followed the trail, his distorted shadow like a phantom projected on a spook house wall. A few steps in, he was faced with a choice. Two paths ran off the main one and the dim light from the truck's headlights didn't reach this far. He listened, thought he heard something off to the left. White Shoes leaned into the darkness and headed that way.

Reilly peeked over the boulder and watched White Shoes disappear into the woods.

"He's gone."

Berger said, "Which way did he go?"

"To the left."

Berger grinned. "Good." He waited for Reilly to slip back down behind the boulder and sit next to him then asked, "What are you doing messed up in this?"

"Uh, you know, drugs." And it was true, in a way. He pointed to Berger's leg, "What happened to you?"

"Slight disagreement." He grinned. "You should see the other guy. Now quit changing the subject."

"I'm trying to help a friend. A guy you put in jail a long time ago. Ray Bentley."

Berger's shoulders started to shake.

Reilly thought, oh Jesus, the guy's crying.

Then Berger looked up, laughing a silent laugh, his face squeezed with the effort of containing the sound. Tears ran down his cheeks. "You got yourself mixed up with Lou Gallo to save some loser from a life in prison? You *must* be on drugs!"

He wiped at his eyes with his dirty hand. "Go home

kid," he said. "Go home and get yourself clean. You hear me? If someone gave me a second chance, I'd take it—in a heartbeat." His eyes glazed. "I'd be living in a small town with a lake. Fishing every day, and Gina, she'd be..." Berger stared off, seeing things that weren't there, things that never would be.

Reilly noticed fresh blood on Berger's bandages and wondered how much blood a person could lose before things got worse. The meds had made him clearer, but he seemed to be drifting now.

Reilly tried to reel him in. "So you remember Ray?"

Berger kept staring.

Reilly tried again. "Ray Bentley? He was with Jefferson "Chancy" LeChance when he killed James King in 1977 at the variety store." Nothing. "The guy you beat with a phone book for twelve hours, then took his confession?"

Berger blinked. "Bentley. Yeah." His eyes re-focused. "Yeah, I remember. He had a white girlfriend—pregnant at the time. Real pretty. Wait." He squinted at Reilly. "You ain't -Nah. What am I thinking?" He looked away. "Now that would be something."

Reilly tried again. The guy was losing it. "We need you to tell your side of the story. Enough time has passed."

"Never enough time passed for them. They hold a grudge until you die, and sometimes after."

"It was a mistake. Never should have happened."

"What never should have happened?"

"He pissed me off, that's what happened. Bentley wanting out. Then stupid-ass Chancy. Shit, King was my meal ticket. Best money in town. We kept his heroin off the street, took our cut off the top. It was like a sideline business, you know? And I could respect that, then the lines got blurry, where as a cop I was doing this one thing, then off the job, I was somebody else. Like the book said this is what you have to do, and the street said this is what you *need* to do." Berger touched his leg and winced, sucked air through his teeth. "*This* is because I never know when to stop. You know how that is?"

Reilly nodded, gave him a small smile.

Berger said, "Gina and me, we were gonna go away, leave Philly and start new. We had plans. Then here comes Gallo, asking for shit, like he owns me. But I figure, okay, one more time. Like going out with a bang, you know?" He laughed and said "bang" again, then shook his head. "Anyway, Gallo took something of mine he had no right to take—something I'd earned. So, I fought back."

He paused for a long time, and then finally said, "Just like Daddy taught me."

"What about Bentley?"

Berger bobbed his head. "Yeah. Poor bastard. Deluca took him for a ride. Shit, Gallo owed big after that one."

"Gallo owed him? *Who*? Deluca?"

Reilly saw the flash before he heard the shots. He scrambled around the boulder. "Shit. Who's that?"

Berger said, "Stay here. I'll check it out."

Jeremy brought them through the woods, a rock-lined stream on their left, and low scraggly bushes on the right. At first the gurgling of the water was soothing and mildly hypnotic. As they trekked uphill, the water seemed to gain momentum and the gently sloping banks became hard ridges of slick limestone dropping away to a rough-hewn gorge.

Banning trudged along, his footing going from rock to moss to rock again. The gun bumped against his leg. He heard Sailor slapping mosquitoes and cursing softly behind him.

Jeremy stopped suddenly. They heard the crunch and snap of footsteps. Jeremy slipped the pack off and raised his gun toward the bushes, then turned with a finger to his lips. He crouched down, motioning for them to do the same.

When the fawn pushed her head through the leaves, she was as surprised to see them as they were to see her.

She froze, then blinked her large brown eyes and flared her nostrils. Sailor could have touched her wet nose.

The shot rang out, slapping thick night air like an angry hand. The fawn bolted, kicking up leaves and breaking branches, joining two other deer in a fearful retreat.

Sailor grabbed Banning's arm. Jeremy yelled, "Stay down!" then crashed through the bush, leaving his pack behind. Tree branches snapped at his chest, thorny bushes snagged his pants, and roots and rocks tripped him as he barreled headfirst toward the sound of a skirmish.

White Shoes had been standing on the path where it forked, trying not to think about the shape of his Bucs or how bad he had to piss, when he heard him—the bastard—crashing through the forest like a wild man and coming right for him. White Shoes didn't have time to aim, he just leveled his arm and fired. Whatever it was kept coming.

The frightened doe clipped White Shoes, knocking him into a tree.

"Fuck!"

He tried to catch his fall with the gun hand and heard his wrist snap before the pain shot up his arm like a bolt of lightning. His hand flopped uselessly at the end of his arm. Over his shoulder, the branches still juddered in the wake of the fleeing doe.

When the guy yelled, Jeremy stopped. He rolled behind a thick hemlock and took a look around. Recently broken branches and snapped twigs made a path to the moonlit road. The dim headlights of a small pickup shone on a white van.

Ten feet away, he saw a big guy on his hands and knees scrambling around and cursing. Jeremy recognized the footwear. Of course Gallo would send White Shoes. This was his kind of thing.

"Hello, White Shoes."

When the man raised his face, Jeremy adjusted his aim,

settling the red laser dot between the his eyes.

White Shoes recognized the voice but kept fumbling in the undergrowth looking for the gun. Trying to stall, he said, "Strom! What are you doing out here? Did you see that deer? Man, that was something." His fingers struck pay dirt and curled around the Glock.

"Stand up!"

White Shoes moved slowly, awkwardly.

Jeremy stepped from behind the tree.

White Shoes drew the Glock, swinging his good hand across his body.

Jeremy saw it and rushed White Shoes, taking the first bullet in his arm. But he kept coming, and tackled him to the ground. They wrestled in the leaves and ivy, scrambling for position. Jeremy got in two good punches, breaking White Shoes' nose and shattering his cheekbone before the guy could draw the Glock again. Jeremy took the second bullet in the throat. He jerked back then fell sideways. His lifeless body pinned White Shoes to the ground.

The smell of blood and urine mixed with pine and rotten leaves.

White Shoes said, "Fuckin' Strom."

He wiped the spray of blood from his face then tried to push Jeremy off his thighs but couldn't move him and had to wriggle out one leg at a time, losing a shoe. He stood up, cradling his bad hand.

Plink.

The bullet zipped past White Shoes, nicked a nearby tree and ricocheted, sending bark flying. White Shoes returned fire, shooting wildly as he ran to the tree line in a hail of bullets.

Berger cut him off. Out of ammo and choices, White Shoes ran for the van.

Reilly sat by the road with his back to the warm boulder, wishing he could crawl under it. He'd watched Berger disappear into the woods dragging his bad leg behind him, heard the gunshots, the yelling, then three deer shot from the shadows, one with bloody hindquarters. Reilly watched them bound onto the road and hesitate, their tails twitching. The doe looked at Reilly then dashed into the forest on the other side with her family close behind.

From the gorge, Banning and Sailor heard the shots and thought the worst. When the second volley started they looked at each other, thinking the same thing.

Banning turned to Sailor, "There's something I need to tell you. I mean if we don't make it out of here."

Sailor touched his arm then shook her head. She knew what he was going to say. But when Banning said, "Ray Bentley is your father," she realized they hadn't been thinking the same thing after all.

White Shoes opened the van door.

The explosion traveled through the woods and hit Sailor like a wall of heat. Thrown backward, she smacked her head on a stump. Banning fell hard beside her. Flames spread through the dry forest raising wild life from burrows and nesting spots, pushing them to the gorge in a noisy parade of survival.

Sailor looked at Banning. His lips were moving but she couldn't hear him. She hoped he was saying, "It's all a dream. Wake up now." But it looked like he wanted her to move toward the fire, toward the road. He grabbed her hand and pulled her up. She stumbled after him down a trampled path, running as if the path might take her to Connecticut.

25

Because You've Got To Hope,
or The Long Way Around

RAY left the law library with three books under his arm, and a file sandwiched between them. It had been a long day, his first back in the population. Voices were too loud, smells too sharp, as if his senses had been honed through deprivation. He walked slowly, tapping his fingers on his leg and thinking about tomorrow. If his case were reopened, as everyone expected, it would be big news. All eyes would be on Graterford. The warden understood the ramifications and had given Ray special permission to be in the law library at this hour.

CO Munsing hadn't been too happy to get baby-sitting detail and he'd let Ray know it. Ten minutes after they'd arrived at the library, Munchy said, "Got to take a whiz, be right back." He'd wagged a stubby finger at Ray. "And don't get no ideas."

It hadn't taken Ray long to find the books he needed, or the files. He sat at the table and waited for Munchy. When he awoke with his head on the cool laminate, he figured, *Fuck him. I'm going back to the block. Isn't like they don't know where to find me.*

There's something about the way your body works when it's tired. Like mind and body go on automatic pilot, a kind of sleepy-headed funk. Ray was in this kind of funk when he focused his eyes on the men at the end of the long corridor. "Shit."

He'd taken the day route. Mornings and afternoons these halls were busy with COs and volunteers, safely occupied and fully monitored. But after five, you'd be a fool to come down here alone. He should have gone the long way around. He would have if he'd been thinking straight. Now he'd come too far to go back.

The boys who ran this strip stood less than twenty-five feet away, watching him. They were dark, but not black enough to be part of the gang that ran the block. Their skin had a soft mocha hue, making them light enough to 'pass' in the free world, had they tried. They might have had a chance at a different kind of life had they sold out on their skin, looked deeper into their heritage. Instead they went the other way.

Ray knew their kind. He thought of several ways to play it—lost, confused, crazy, mad, belligerent, friendly, tough, subservient. It all depended on them. He checked the hall cameras, looked back at the men, three of them now. One pointed in his direction.

Ray kept walking, knowing it would be worse if he turned and ran, not even sure he had the energy to run.

Fifteen feet away, one of them called, "Law dawg!"

Ray knew Skunk. He bobbed his head in the guy's direction, moved the books and files across his chest.

"What you got for me, Brother?"

"Just some books, Skunk." Ray shrugged, "Mostly bullshit, you know?"

"Books?' Skunk elbowed his pudgy pal. "We like books, don't we?"

They looked like poorly drawn cartoon characters,

cardboard cutouts propped in the doorway and dressed in baggy Graterford browns. Skunk's hair was a closely trimmed Mohawk, painted white and powdered. It accented his round head and tiny ears. Ray thought the pudgy one was the kid they called Nester. He had a habit of squirreling things away in his cell, in his nose, in his ass. Nester's head was shaved in a crooked swirl of colors. They started behind his right ear and encircled his conical head, ending in a purple Kool-Aid-dyed circle on the crown. Ray got a faint whiff of grape when the kid approached.

"Let me see that, Law dawg." Nester held out a beefy hand, fingertips rainbow-stained.

"Can't do that, man." Ray adjusted his grip on the books and glanced over to see that the third con had slipped away. Noises came from the room behind Skunk, a string of commercials that meant nothing behind these walls: a guy talking about the pleasures of driving a luxury car, a child excited about learning to read, a woman confessing her allergies to an audience more interested in the size of her breasts.

Ray tipped his chin to Skunk, "How did that plea work out? You gonna get some time off?"

Skunk shook his head, his eyes on the floor. When he looked up, he seemed to be weighing something in his mind. He pushed off the wall, approached Ray and fixed his gaze just above Ray's head as if he were talking to someone behind him, someone tall. Skunk tapped the law books with a long dirty fingernail and accented each word, "You...lied...to...me."

Ray said, "What do you mean?"

The missing guy took him from behind, locked his arms in a vise-like grip. Books and files fell to the floor. Ray lunged forward trying to break the grasp. He felt something rip in his shoulder. Pain shot down his arm. Skunk stepped out of the range of Ray's flailing body and kicking legs and gave Nester the nod. Nester waited for the big guy to control Ray's legs and came in low, like a junkyard dog.

Ray screamed as the shank pierced his skin. Nester looked into his eyes as he drove the sharpened spoon under Ray's rib cage. The thrust forced Ray up on his toes. Nester twisted the crude weapon until it broke then pulled back, the dull, bent bowl of a soupspoon in his bloody fist.

Ray felt the pain behind his right eye, like a flashcube spinning and burning on an old camera. Pop. Sizzle.

Then it was over.

Ray didn't feel himself falling, but knew he was on the floor. He had nothing left but words—syllables that weren't strong enough and vowels that bled. He lay there, moaning in a language only pain understands.

A shout from the end of the hallway was like a switch that sent the three men scurrying. Ray saw rapidly approaching black shoes and heard someone say, "Dear Jesus," from very far away.

She fell, unafraid. Maria Rosarita Conchetta had made atonement, paid in full. She was dead before her robed body smashed onto the empty metal cage and crushed the sign that asked passers-by to free the innocent creatures and give from their heart.

In the hotel room fifteen floors above, glass tinkled out of the window frame, joining the fragments on the carpet below. Three cops stood over Deluca. One knelt, put two fingers to the jugular then shook his head, his lips in a tight line.

Paris pushed past the news camera and approached the body of Fast Eddie Deluca, Esquire.

"Is he dead?"

The kneeling cop stood. "Yes, Ma'am." He grabbed her elbow as she turned white, then called to another cop, "Porter!"

They sat her in a low suede chair facing the open bathroom door. A gust of wind from the broken window rustled a paper soap wrapper on the floor, pushing it up against the wall. She closed her eyes, felt this same breeze brush the back of her neck and shivered from the tickle of air and the siren screams of the approaching ambulance.

Halfway across the state, fire companies from Third Mountain, Peters Mountain and the Susquehanna Reserve Paramedic Squad answered the call. There were helicopters and Humvees, TV news vans and a scrappy group of Vegetarian Environmentalists from New Buffalo who passed a jug of carrot juice and chanted, "Woods and bombs don't mix, no! Woods and bombs don't mix!"

Though the night air was warm, Sailor took the blanket the EMT offered. She held it around her shoulders with one hand and rubbed her head with the other. The bump felt like a quail egg.

As her hearing came back, she watched Banning with the reporters and the cops. He looked good, younger somehow, confident again. He had protected Reilly and Sailor from the verbal barrage and acted as their attorney during the police questioning. Now he stood in front of three cameras giving a concise yet veiled statement. He would come out of this fine, better than before. If that were possible.

Sailor was beginning to think nothing was *impossible*, as if they were caught up in a Hollywood production. The director would call "Cut!" any minute and the backdrop of woods, trees and smoldering fires would be rolled away and stored in a warehouse in Lomita while a clean-up crew swept away the undergrowth to reveal a cracked concrete floor and a bunch of trick wires.

But when the uniformed men lifted black-bagged bodies into an ambulance without lights and flew Berger off the mountain in a helicopter, there was no denying it was real.

Reilly sat beside her. "I was just talking to the city reporters and there's something you should know. Deluca's dead."

Sailor wrapped the blanket tighter around as she fought back tears. "What happened?"

Reilly told her what he knew. How Banning had asked Maria to come to Philly and give testimony, tell the whole story of what happened twenty-four years ago. How Paris offered to help, wanting to bring down Montgomery. How Deluca sung like a canary before he shot Maria Chetta with a gun that backfired and killed him too. How it all took place in a swanky hotel room on live TV.

Then there was Gallo.

Sailor held up a hand and shook her head. "Wait." *How had something so simple gotten so out of hand? All she'd intended to do was free a wrongfully convicted man.* "Shit! The meeting with the judge. Did you get my message?"

But the way Reilly was looking at her said it all. He had no idea what she was talking about. "Doesn't matter," she whispered, "we'll never make it. I'm sorry, Ray."

Sailor stood, dropped the blanket and began walking, then stopped. She didn't know where to go.

She turned around and Reilly opened his arms. Sailor began crying and he came to her and held her, wrapping his arms around her and closing out the world.

After a while she said, "Reilly?"

"Hmm?"

"What the hell am I doing?"

"Shh."

"God, this is so messed up, you know?"

"I know." Reilly lifted Sailor's chin, stroked the tears from her cheeks with his thumb then kissed her tenderly. "It's supposed to be messed up. That's how real life is."

EPILOGUE
There's Got to be a
Morning After

RAY heard the squeak of a window opening, a door close and latch and a second later caught the light scent of fresh-mown grass worn like perfume on the laughing women passing below. He almost smiled then moved his swollen tongue in his mouth against the sharp edges of broken teeth, tasted coppery blood and opened his eyes to a room that was too bright, too large, too white. Not Graterford white, but the white of the free world.

There was a blur across his right eye—a strip of bandage hung loosely from his wrapped head. He wanted to reach up and brush it away. He wanted to sit up and order ham and eggs and sip a cup of hot black coffee. Or did he prefer tea? He wanted to look out the window and see a patch of grass that went on forever with no fences in sight. He wanted to say, "Thank you," to the sleeping girl, the beautiful girl who held his hand and rested her head on his hospital bed. The girl who had been talking to him in his dreams.

And he wanted to ask what day it was and why he was here and would there really be sweet potato pie on Sunday? Maybe he'd ask her all those things. Later. He exhaled deeply, his breath fluttering the stray strip of gauze, and then he closed his eyes.

Gallo threw the last suitcase in the trunk and rested his hand on the Caddy as the hydraulic lid lowered itself with a whisper. He jogged around to the driver's side and got one leg inside before the black car pulled up.

"Motherfucker."

They parked at an angle, blocking the Caddy. Three men took their time getting out, buttoning their suit jackets, smoothing them, grinning in Gallo's direction.

One said, "Where you going, Lou?" and waved a folded piece of paper in Gallo's direction.

Shazad argued with the tough day nurse. "I am telling you, Miss. He is my brother. Ray will say to you. He has been calling me."

"Sir, you aren't on the family list. I can't let just *anyone* into Mr. Bentley's room. He's still in critical condition, and I'm *sure* he didn't make any calls."

"I know this to be so." Shazad touched her arm and caught her eyes with his. "Miss, he requires me."

The nurse fought the brown eyes, felt the heat of the man's skin on her arm, soothing and warm. She pulled back, flustered, and glanced back at her empty station. Something melted inside her when she said, "Ten minutes," and walked away.

Shazad stepped into Ray's room. There was a vase of daisies on the bedside table. A slim black girl was reading a poem about trees and noise and reckless choices. Her head was bowed over the thick book, her fingers tucked under the page ready to turn. Shazad closed his eyes and felt the energy in the room. If he had been an artist, then he would have painted this canvas with a broad brush loaded with sunny yellows, vibrant blues and just a touch of red, a small circle off-center. When he opened his eyes, the girl was looking at him. She had Ray's eyes.

"Are you here to see Ray?"

Shazad smiled at her. "He is pleased you are here, to be reading to him."

Sailor closed the book, held it on her lap.

She looked harder at Shazad. "Do I know you?"

"Only when you dream."

"Wait, this is so bizarre. Are you sure we haven't met somewhere before?"

"Never on this plane, Miss."

"On a plane? Was that it?" Sailor set the book on the bed as she stood up.

"No, no." Shazad shook his head. "Never mind. You are hungry. Go and eat. I will be with Ray."

Sailor wondered how the guy knew she was hungry. Did she look hungry? And it was the weirdest thing, she felt like she knew him. And not from her dreams. Somehow, she trusted him. Besides, what harm could he do to a comatose man?

"Maybe I could use a little something. Thank you."

"I am Shazad."

"Sailor," she said, extending her hand.

He took her hand, held it gently between his and nodded.

His fingers were slim, his hands warm and smooth like the lining of a mink coat. She could have left her hand there forever and was disappointed when he let her go.

Flustered, she said, "How do you know Ray?"

"He was my cellmate."

"Oh." Sailor looked at her shoes. "Maybe I will, you know, just go grab a little something to eat." She started toward the door, thinking she wouldn't be long.

Shazad smiled. "Take as long as you will be needing. Everything will be okay."

Sailor raised a brow then glanced at Ray and left.

Shazad waited until the door shut then approached the bed. He skimmed his hands over Ray's body, his eyes unfocused.

"There is not much time." Shazad's hands made small circles over Ray's heart, moved to his face, fingers parting as his hands opened, palms up.

"Hello, Ray."

Ray opened his eyes and blinked twice.

Sailor tried to see through the plastic lids. Not much of a choice. A squashed tuna sandwich, a limp green salad, or a turkey club stacked with pink tomatoes. She slid her tray down the rails and paused at the soup. Minestrone. Her Mom used to make minestrone.

"Smells good." Reilly pushed an overloaded tray next to hers.

Sailor glanced at his choices; coffeecake, turkey club and lime Jello. "Look at you. Brave one, eh?"

"The breakfast of champions."

Sailor laughed.

"Thanks for coming, Reilly."

"Anytime."

They paid the cashier and sat at a small table near the entrance. They ate in silence, unsure of what to say. Reilly wanted to joke, but was afraid his words would come out wrong.

Sailor pushed the soup away and wiped her lips on a paper napkin. "I have to get back."

Reilly nodded, then held up a finger as he chewed a bit of sandwich and swallowed.

"I'll come with you. Just a sec." He started to pile his garbage on the tray.

"No. I mean, finish your Jello. I'll meet you up there. Ray's got a visitor, anyway."

"A visitor?"

"Yeah. A little guy named Shazad. He's a bit strange."

Reilly snorted, "Shazad's more than a little strange. The

cons I talked to at Graterford said he was magic."

"Magic?"

"What the hell does that mean?"

"Got me." Reilly shrugged. "I just like the dude's name. *Shazad.*"

"Sounds like a really fast sports car."

"Or a venereal disease."

They laughed.

Sailor was still chuckling when she left Reilly. She took the stairs back to Ray's room, preferring the smell of Lysol and cigarettes to the claustrophobic elevators stinking of sickness and despair.

It had been five days of watching and waiting. Not sure what she expected, she knew she had to be there.

The doctors weren't encouraging. Between the head trauma and the knife wound, complete recovery wasn't an option. The word rehabilitation never came up. Sailor asked her father to help. Dr. Beaumont's name went a long way, and the best doctors gave Ray the best treatment. Sailor wouldn't give up.

She'd talked to Ray while he lay there in his self-imposed prison. She'd read Tolstoy to him, and when that grew too grim, she'd switched to Faulkner, and when her throat closed around the long sentences and pieces of a past she'd never seen, she opened a volume of poetry and let the masters say the things she longed to say—clear, concise, condensed.

She'd have to go back to Connecticut soon. There were things to pack, decisions to be made. But for now, she was here.

Sailor left the stairwell and wandered down the white hallway. Someone had abandoned a stretcher in the corridor; drops of blood stained the white sheets. She rolled it against the wall and tried not to think about the blood and the deep indentation where a head had once lain. She paused outside his door, took a deep breath and went inside.

Berger lay propped up in the bed with his eyes closed, one hand on the TV remote. The picture was clear, the sound muted.

Taylor Dunne jostled for her shot in front of the Courthouse as people and reporters ran around behind her with cameras and microphones and steno pads.

Sailor watched the lines scroll at the bottom of the screen. *Philly mob going down...long-time insiders make deal...Don Louis Michael Gallo takes some of Philly's finest with him...Deluca funeral tomorrow...coverage at noon...*

It would be a while before it all died down.

Berger said, "I keep dreaming of deer."

Sailor turned around.

He hit the bed control button, raising himself as she turned her way. "Why do you suppose that is? They have these big eyes, and they're so quiet, you know, like they're watching me." He laughed. "Guess I'll have to ask the Doc about that."

"How's that going?" Sailor asked, approaching the bed and pulling up a chair.

"We're trying some new meds. With that and therapy and time." He shrugged. "We'll see." He slid his eyes to the TV screen and pointed.

Sailor saw Len Banning standing next to Taylor Dunne. Berger turned up the volume.

"...The Alliance. The people of Philadelphia deserve the truth. They deserved it in 1977 when their streets were being run by crooked cops, their courts ruled by greedy judges, and they deserve it today, when we see the rich and powerful use their influence to control and disrupt our daily lives. The whole country—no—the *world* will be watching what happens here, in *this* court." He jerked his thumb in the direction of the imposing building behind them. "When the good citizens finally get to hear the *truth*, the *whole* truth—"

Taylor Dunne's red glossy lips finished the line, "So help me God."

Berger clicked off the TV.

"What a circus." He lowered his bed a little, looked at Sailor. "What are you gonna do, kid?"

Sailor shook her head. "I'm not sure. My dad wants me to come home, but…"

"Did Banning ever tell you that you look like her? Your mother?"

"How do you know about my mother?"

"Reilly told me everything." Berger stared at Sailor. "Yeah, you look like Tara, but I can see Ray in you, too. You got his fire."

Sailor smiled. "I hope that's a good thing."

"Listen, I—" Berger cleared his throat, looked out the window. "You tell him I'm sorry, you know? I was a real asshole back then."

He turned back. "I ain't using this as an excuse or nothing, but the Doc says it's the disease—that maybe I didn't know, didn't have a choice."

His fingers worked at the blanket threads, plucking the cotton, worrying a hole into the weave. He stopped suddenly and sighed.

"Shit. I did know. I got off on the power, tripping on the badge. And Gina. Sweet Gina. Christ. I really fucked up." Softer then, "Who am I kidding? I'm still an asshole."

Sailor reached for his hand. "You can't change the past, Berger, but maybe you can pay off the future."

Shazad smiled at Ray, into eyes like dull pennies, then pulled the lids down.

"Good-bye, my friend. I will never forget you."

Reilly waited on a plastic chair, watched the nurses flirt with the interns. He imagined a new comedy skit, a gay nurse with a thick accent and a limp. He smiled, felt his pockets for paper and pen.

"You didn't have to stay."

Reilly looked up. Sailor stood over him.

"How's Ray?"

"He didn't make it."

"I'm sorry. Do you want to sit down?" He motioned to the seat beside him.

She hugged herself. "No. Actually, I'd rather go."

"Sure." Reilly stood, tucking the paper and pen in his pocket.

Sailor pulled a worn notebook from her purse. "Shazad gave me this." She handed it to Reilly. He opened it carefully. Tiny precise handwriting covered the page, every page.

"It was Ray's. It's his story."

Reilly closed the book, smoothed his hand down its length, handed it back.

"It's your story now."

Sailor hugged the notebook to her chest. Reilly put his arm around her, started toward the elevator. "Did I ever tell you the one about the American, the German and the French guys about to be executed?"

Sailor shook her head, smiling, and punched the down button.

Paris stormed into the office and slammed the door behind her. "You!"

Banning turned from the window where he'd been standing, arms crossed and staring.

She said, "You are *something* else."

Banning raised his brows. "Go on."

Paris sauntered across the room. "I always *knew* you had it in you."

Banning dropped his arms as she crushed herself against him, kissing him deeply, and lifting one Manolo-clad foot off the antique Persian rug in Ted Montgomery's old office.

ABOUT THE AUTHOR

Best known for her award-winning short stories, flash fiction and essays, Linda's latest novels include the Southern Gothic *Not Waving, Drowning* and the Noir-esque *3 Women Walk into a Bar.* Linda divides her writing time between the beaches of Florida's Gulf Coast and the suburbs of Atlanta where she lives with her husband, two kids, fast cars and furry things. Learn more at lindasands.com.